DEAR AMERICA

The Diary of
Abigail Jane Stewart

The Winter of
Red Snow

KRISTIANA GREGORY

SCHOLASTIC INC. • NEW YORK

The Library of Congress has cataloged the earlier
hardcover edition as follows:
Gregory, Kristiana.
The winter of red snow : the Revolutionary War diary of Abigail Jane Stewart,
Valley Forge, Pennsylvania, 1777–1778 / by Kristiana Gregory.
p. cm. — (Dear America ; 2)
Summary: Eleven-year-old Abigail presents a diary account of life
in Valley Forge from December 1777 to July 1778 as General
Washington prepares his troops to fight the British.
ISBN 0-590-22653-3
1. United States — History — Revolution, 1775–1783 — Juvenile fiction.
[1. Valley Forge (Pa.) — Fiction. 2. United States —
History — Revolution, 1775–1783 — Fiction. 3. Diaries — Fiction.]
I. Title. II. Series.
PZ7.G8619Wi 1996
[Fic] — dc20 95-44052
CIP AC

Trade Paper-Over-Board edition ISBN 978-0-545-23802-1
Reinforced Library edition ISBN 978-0-545-26234-7

10 9 8 7 6 5 4 3 2 1   10 11 12 13 14

The text type was set in ITC Legacy Serif.
The display type was set in Dear Sarah.
Book design by Kevin Callahan

Printed in the U.S.A.   23
This edition first printing, September 2010

For
Tim, Catherine,
and Matthew Walker

Valley Forge, Pennsylvania

1777

December 1, 1777, Monday

It is almost sunrise and we are still waiting for Papa to return. What is taking him so long? Little Sally keeps running out onto the cold step to see down the road, but there is only fog.

We have been up since half-past four this morning, and mine apron is dirty from trying to keep the fire going. Mama's cries are what woke us. Elisabeth and I threw back our quilt and hurried down the stairs so quickly I caught a splinter in my foot.

A tall candle lit the room where Mama lay. Her face was damp. I told her that Papa had taken the wagon and should be back soon with Mrs. Hewes.

"Abby," she said, "this baby shalt not wait for Mrs. Hewes." She squeezed my hand hard, took a deep breath, then let out another cry. I began to cry, too. Poor Mama! Elisabeth put a wet cloth on her forehead and told me to wait by the window with Sally. I do not like waiting.

Finally! We heard horses and Papa's wagon. Sally and I ran out the door waving our arms. "Hurry!" we yelled.

Mrs. Hewes smiled at us when she came into the kitchen. We hung her cloak by the hearth, then followed her like worried ducklings. She was just in time. Mama screamed again, then an instant later there came a sharp little cry.

"Ye have a son," said Mrs. Hewes. Laughing, Papa ran outside and threw his hat to the sky. I could hear his shout echo in the frosty air.

He is happy and wants all of Pennsylvania to know he has a son. But I saw Mama's eyes — she is as worried as I am.

December 3, 1777, Wednesday

The baby is sick. Elisabeth and I have stayed home from school to help.

When I tucked Sally into her trundle last night she threw her arms around my neck sobbing, "Shall this baby die like the others?"

Elisabeth kneeled to kiss Sally, but she, too, began to weep, then so did I.

Mama has birthed nine children: three girls — that's us — and now six boys. We have not had a brother live through his first winter.

After Sally had cried herself to sleep, Elisabeth and I lay in bed whispering. Soon she was quiet. I crept across the cold floor to look out the window. The creek looked like a silver ribbon winding its way among the trees toward the Schuylkill River and the house where Mrs. Hewes lives. Her upstairs window glowed with candlelight and I hoped she was awake, praying for our baby. I was.

December 6, 1777, Saturday

Mr. Walker the carpenter rode up with a new cradle he had made for us. When he asked our baby's name, Papa looked at Mama and she looked at him. Elisabeth and I looked at each other, then at Sally. Our baby was five days old, but we had not named him!

Papa put the cradle by the fire, not too close, but near the stone bench where it is warm. Mama held the baby in her arms for a minute before setting him down in the blankets. She said, "I doth like the name John."

Papa smiled at her. "Yes. John is a good name. John Edward."

So now Elisabeth and Sally and I have a brother. John Edward Stewart. He is so still and so small that when I glanced at the cradle after supper I thought for a moment it was Sally's doll inside.

It is cold at night, especially upstairs with the

door closed. We have moved our bed and trundle next to the chimney for warmth. The string from my nightcap itches my chin, but at least by morning the cap is still on my head and has kept the chill away.

Deer have been coming down from Mount Joy and Mount Misery. Our orchards are full of their droppings, for they come to eat apples left on the ground.

December 7, 1777, Sunday

On our way to church a cold rain began. I was sore pleased Mama stayed home with baby John because of the wind. It blew wet leaves into the wagon and across the muddy road. All trees at Valley Forge are bare except for the evergreens, and there is a crust of ice along the creekbed. Papa said he's happy we are prepared for winter. The barn is stacked high with hay and our animals have cozy beds. The cellar is full of potatoes, onions, carrots and turnips, salted beef, and barrels of cider. We have enough dried cranberries to sell at market.

After prayer meeting we stopped at the Fitzgeralds' to see if Mrs. Fitzgerald needed anything. Her latch string is always out so we shall feel welcome, but I know not why she wants visitors. Her kitchen is untidy. It smells bad and there are mice in her cupboard. I saw them.

Mr. Fitzgerald was taken prisoner at the Battle of Saratoga two months ago and no one knows what the Redcoats have done with him. I puzzle why her boys help her not. They are lazy and quarrelsome, all eight of them. They were throwing mud at each other as we were getting ready to leave, and that bully Tom threw some at my shoes. It splattered my hem. I was so annoyed I walked around the back of the wagon to kick him, but he ran off with his thumbs in his ears and his tongue sticking out. I hate him. He is 11 as I am, but he is just a child.

Reverend Currie and Mr. Walker arrived at our house in time for supper, soaking wet from the rain. Elisabeth draped their coats by the fire (such a stink!) while Sally and I dished out stewed pumpkin. Mama's face went white when they told us the bad news:

The British tried to capture Whitemarsh, but have retreated to Philadelphia, our capital city, and they plan to winter there. We are worried sick.

Auntie Hannie lives there and so do Papa's three brothers and our little cousins. I said we must go right away to rescue them, but Papa said 18 miles is too much mud for our small wagon.

December 10, 1777, Wednesday

Elisabeth stayed home with Mama, so Sally and I walked to school without her. The sky was gray and there was a cold mist. I was pleased to be back and see Molly and Ruth and Naomi again. Before lessons, we were close to the fire drying off when through the window we saw a horseman. The boys ran outside and shouted for news.

"The Redcoats started another skirmish!" came the voice. We all started talking at once and the younger children began to cry with worry. Miss Molly tapped her ruler on the table. She told us to take up our slates and be quiet.

"Quaker families concerneth themselves not with matters of war," she said. Sally was in the front row with the other first graders. She turned around to look at me so I smiled. We are Baptists. Papa will let us be concerned.

December 12, 1777, Friday

Sally's hem caught fire this morning. She was mad because it was my turn to hold Johnny, but she said it was her turn. She pulled on his sleeve and nearly pulled me out of the rocker with him, so I put my foot up against her (not hard) and she fell back. While she was yelling that I kicked her (I did not), her skirt spread out on the hearth and all of a sudden there were flames. I jumped up with Johnny in my arms and stomped fast on her hem. Our screams brought Papa. Now Sally's left leg and ankle are blistered and she's been crying all afternoon it hurts so. I am heartsore and worried. Elisabeth and I made her a cozy bed by Johnny's so she shant have to climb upstairs.

Mrs. Hewes came with her bag of herbs. She also brought corncakes wrapped in cloth, still warm. After she tended Sally's burn, she sat with us to supper. Being a widow lady (she's lost two husbands), her nephew always checks on her and brings news, the latest even more disturbing: General George Washington and his troops are camped just a few miles away at Gulph Mills. Within the week they will march *here*, to Valley Forge, to make winter quarters. This is to keep the British from capturing more of Pennsylvania.

When Mrs. Hewes explained that meant *thousands* of soldiers in our front yard for the whole winter, Mama excused herself from the table and went over to the window. She stared out at the bare fields.

"What shall the Army do for food?" she asked. "Where shall they sleep?"

Sally called from her bed, "They may stay with us, Mama!"

After supper when we were changing into our nightgowns, Beth whispered a secret and made me promise not to tell. She plans to sew a coat and, on the inside collar, embroider her name, *Elisabeth Ann Stewart*, so that the soldier who wears it will remember her and come see her. Many girls have become brides this way, she said.

But I want her not to think about marriage. Even though she's fifteen and pretty, I would miss her too greatly.

I am upstairs writing this at my bench under our window. The candle flickers from cold air coming in, for we lost the shutter in the last storm. Elisabeth is asleep. I can hear Mama's and Papa's voices downstairs. They are worried about the soldiers coming, and about Sally's burned leg. And they worry our tiny John Edward shant live through the winter.

December 14, 1777, Sunday

Johnny fussed all day. He cried so hard he had hiccups. None of us dared to fret aloud, but I saw Papa's face, and Mama's. She nursed him every two hours and this time Sally and I took turns rocking him without a quarrel. When Beth rocked him, she sang in her beautiful voice.

When he's not in someone's arms he is in his warm cradle, and I kneel over him to whisper, "Johnny, thou must live, please."

December 18, 1777, Thursday

I was up early to help Mama with the big kettle, for she is still weak from birthing and it weighs some forty pounds. We put in a salted beef from the cellar and eight onions, then bread on the hearth to bake. Elisabeth and I hurried to the well, but returned slowly so our buckets wouldn't spill. The air was cold and dark and smelled like snow coming.

And by ten in the morning it did come, wet snow

that froze on the fence, but made mud in the road. Our guests arrived by noon: Mrs. Hewes, Mr. and Mrs. Walker and their three little ones, and a neighbour who had lost his wife last month. At the table Papa welcomed everyone while Elisabeth and I helped Mama set the bowls on, then he folded his hands for prayer.

"This day is for Thanksgiving and Praise," he began, all heads bowed. I stood by his chair, one eye open to make sure Sally didn't pick at the pies. He prayed that our Army would be able to keep the British away and he prayed for our health — I knew he was thinking about Johnny but wanted not to say it out loud. "Amen!" came the voices, and quickly the plates were passed around. Congress has set this day — December 18 — as a new tradition for all patriots (that's us) to give thanks to God for the many blessings He hast given America.

December 19, 1777, Friday

I woke to sleet hitting the window and another sound I'd not heard before.

A drumbeat.

Papa came in from milking and said, "The soldiers are coming."

Elisabeth, Sally, and I hurriedly ate our porridge, then wrapped ourselves in our cloaks and scarves. Mama watched from the window as we ran into the road. There on the wind from the south came the drumbeat, several drums now and the high trilling of fifes.

"I want to go see the soldiers," Sally said. But Papa said we must stay by our fence.

"It's too cold," he said, as big flakes of snow began to fall. The fields were turning white and the road looked like frosting with chocolate showing through.

Twice we went inside to warm ourselves, for the wind cut through our clothes. Finally through the gray we saw them. Three officers on horseback led. We ran outside to cheer, but the men were quiet and thin. The sight of them took my breath away.

"They have no shoes," Elisabeth whispered.

We watched for several minutes as they passed by. We were unable to speak.

Their footprints left blood in the snow.

As I write this upstairs, my candle low and our room cold, I think I shall never again complain. For many hours we watched the soldiers march single file into our valley. Hundreds and hundreds were barefoot, the icy mud cutting their feet. Some had rags wrapped around their legs because they had no trousers . . . no trousers, imagine! Mama cried to see their misery. Without thinking, I ran up to a boy—he seemed to be Elisabeth's age—whose arms were bare. I threw my cloak over his shoulders and the look of relief in his eyes is something I shall never forget.

Sally gave her mittens, and Papa wrapped his scarf around the neck of one poor boy playing a fife. As the soldiers passed I saw other families had done the same—if the Quakers had, I know not—but I recognized Mrs. Potter's cloak, her blue one with red trim, and someone had draped a shawl over a small drummer boy. So many were coughing and had runny noses. Elisabeth said, "Can we not please bring some of them in to warm by our fire?"

When we saw the horseman riding back and forth among the men we knew him to be the Commander in Chief, George Washington. His cape fell below his saddle and his tricorn was white from snow. I shall remember him always. He called continually to his soldiers, words of encouragement, and he had a most dignified bearing.

Now as I look down from my window, I see their campfires among the trees, hundreds of tiny lights flickering through Valley Forge. The wind is howling and blowing snow. Those poor men, how shall they sleep in such cold with no shelter?

December 20, 1777, Saturday

It snowed last night.

· Sally and I ran and slipped back and forth from the house to the barn to make a path. The snow is almost to my knees. In the barn while Papa milked, I plaited Brownie's tail so it would not swish into Papa's face. I asked Papa why so many soldiers have no shoes and why their clothes are tattered.

"They've been marching for several months, Abigail," he said. "Until the Redcoats return to England our Army shall have no rest."

Since I no longer have my cloak, I wrap myself in a blanket to go outside. Papa took us in the wagon to look across the valley. Some tents were up and there were smoky fires where men huddled. Paths between the tents were streaked red.

Bath night for all, even Johnny. Mama dipped him in the warm water and he let out a wail.

December 21, 1777, Sunday

Church. Mama stayed home to keep Johnny warm. It was dark and snowy out. We passed General Washington's large tent — a marquee, Papa called it. It was pitched under the bare branches of a black gum tree. We were surprised to hear a wonderful chorus of men singing a hymn.

Late afternoon, two officers came to our door and handed Papa a note. It was dated yesterday and signed "G. Washington." Papa read it, folded the paper carefully, and put it in his vest pocket. "I shall do what I can, Lieutenant."

When the men climbed into their saddles, Papa closed the door against the cold and turned to us. "The Commander in Chief needs our help," he said. "He is telling those who live within seventy miles of his Headquarters to thresh one half of our grain by the first day of February and the other half by the first day of March."

Papa looked into the fire, his hand on the mantel. "If we shant obey, the Army quartermaster will seize what we have and pay us only the value of straw, not grain."

December 22, 1777, Monday

Johnny is three weeks old. He is still so tiny the leggings I knit him must be pinned to his shirt so they won't slip off.

Tom Fitzgerald and one of his younger brothers came over. Their mother is in bed with fever. While Mama prepared a basket of ham slices, bread, and cranberries, I gave Tom a hateful stare. His hands were dirty with soot and mud and he wiped his nose with his fingers.

I said to him, "Our cow and five pigs do smell better than thee." Mama turned to me.

"Abigail Stewart," was all she said.

She sent me upstairs for the afternoon, no candle. I held my ink jug to the chimney so the ink would melt and finally I am able to write. There is dim light coming through the window, and though there is snow blowing I can see blurred groups of soldiers. They are in the woods, cutting trees. They are chanting something, but their words are lost in the wind.

At the floor where I'm kneeling, I can see through a crack down to the kitchen. Mama is at the kettle with Johnny in her arm, and Papa is hanging his coat. "The soldiers are building huts," he said. "Their mules are sick so the men themselves are dragging the logs with harnesses."

"What is it they're saying over and over?" asked Mama.

Papa put a log on the fire. He said, "They are crying 'No meat, no meat.' Sarah, our soldiers are starving. Tomorrow, I shall take General Washington some of our grain — two sacks."

December 23, 1777, Tuesday

Mrs. Hewes' nephew brought her over after breakfast to check Sally's burn. "It is scabbing nicely," she said.

I love her visits because she bears such interesting news: General Washington himself came to see her! He wants to rent her house to use as headquarters, because it is close to the main crossroads and is at the junction of Valley Creek and the Schuylkill River. He will pay 100 pounds in Pennsylvania currency. Quite a sum!

So now Mrs. Hewes will move in with the family of her brother-in-law, Colonel William DeWees. "General Washington was extremely polite," she told Mama. "I said I needed a few extra days to pack, but he said he shant mind waiting a week if that's what I needed, being a widow and all. My, what a gentleman, and here we are in the middle of a war with England."

But the General gave her grim news as well: Nearly 3,000 soldiers are unfit for duty because they lack shoes and clothing. Papa explained that means one man in four. They are starving because all they have to eat is firecake, a soggy mess of flour and water; there is not even any salt to cheer them up.

Our poor Army!

December 24, 1777, Wednesday

Christmas Eve. Cold, snowing.

Elisabeth and I made the Egg Nog to set aside for tomorrow's dinner. Mama said it's about time someone in our family wrote down the recipe, so here it is:

One quart milk, one quart cream, one dozen eggs, 12 tablespoons sugar, one pint brandy, half-pint rye whiskey, quarter-pint rum, quarter-pint sherry. Mix. Store by cool window or in cellar.

Mama baked pies — three mince, four pumpkin,

four apple. I whipped cream and eggs for custard. When Mama wasn't looking I licked the spoon, and as I swallowed the delicious sweetness I remembered the soldiers. Were we bad to have so much food when they have so little?

Papa took the wagon to help Mrs. Hewes move her trunks to the DeWeeses' house. Elisabeth and I and the three Potter girls stayed behind to clean the stairs and floors and the brass kettle that hangs from a crane in the fireplace. While we trimmed candles for the lamps, a Negro arrived with a small leather trunk. He took off his tricorn, bowed, then introduced himself as Billy Lee, Mr. George Washington's personal servant. He said, "Thank yous so much, kind ladies."

By one o'clock the General and nine more servants had moved in. They shall be warmer now. It is a fine stone house with a view of the river and a large separate kitchen off the entry. Its root cellar is deep and well-stocked.

It's hard to believe, but already there are huts with smoke drifting out of chimneys. Billy Lee told us the General would not move into a house until his men were sheltered in either tents or cabins.

December 25, 1777, Thursday

Christmas Day.

We could not open the front door because wind had blown snow two feet high. Papa poked a stick out and gradually worked an opening wide enough for him to step out. We measured four new inches along the fence rail.

The Potter family arrived by sleigh, with Mr. and Mrs. Adams and their little boy, who is learning to walk. It was quite a crowd around our table, and loud. Mama roasted four fat geese and two ducks. I found myself with a stomachache from Egg Nog, and feeling sleepy. We opened gifts in front of the fire. When Sally saw the doll I'd made her, she hugged it tight and would not share with the other girls.

(I do not like the scarf Elisabeth knit me — it is brown and itches my neck.)

Johnny was very quiet in his cradle all day.

Reverend Currie was in time for Papa's fiddle and Mr. Adams's tin whistle. The children made so much noise with spoons-on-the-bench (I was serving up pie) that Mama laughed about her Christmas Headache. Before prayers Reverend Currie told us a Negro soldier died in his tent this morning. He was from Guilford, Connecticut, and belonged to one of the captains.

December 26, 1777, Friday

More snow.

Elisabeth spent the day sewing her Bounty Coat. I've decided to make a hunting shirt for one of the drummer boys, I know not who. It shall be safe to embroider my name because they are too young to marry and too young to care.

My thimble fell from my hand and rolled into the fireplace. Sally was quick with the long spoon and scooped it out of the ashes for me.

Papa came in with ice in his hair and beard, but smiling. He said the soldiers — there are at least 12,000 — were served a Christmas dinner yesterday of roast fowl, turnips, and cabbage, plus a swig of rum each. Because Papa is a cobbler, he rode to camp to offer his help. There are soldiers from all thirteen colonies, he said, and all of them need clothes and food; many, many have no shoes or socks.

December 28, 1777, Sunday

It was so cold in church I was grateful Papa brought the tin foot-stove to put under our blankets. I do wish it was proper to build fireplaces in a house of worship.

The snow was blowing so thick we could see our way home only from the dark fence posts.

Bread and sausage for dinner.

December 29, 1777, Monday

Papa took us to the edge of the encampment. Rows of huts make it look like a village. No children are allowed, but I saw some playing near the tents.

"There are nearly 300 women," Papa said. "Some are wives with children, some are sweethearts. But some just like the excitement. Those are women" — Papa could hardly say these words — "of poor reputation."

December 30, 1777, Tuesday

We cannot see out our windows for the ice. It was too windy to go out, so we stayed busy near the fire all day.

Papa is tanning a hide from a neighbour's cow, to make shoes, though he was criticized for helping the Army. Quakers call themselves the Religious Society of Friends, but they will not be friends with General Washington. I understand not why their religion won't let them have anything to do with war.

So far the only families we know who will share their grain with the soldiers are the Walkers, Potters, and Adamses. Mr. Smith will not share any of his wagons — he has eight! — because he does not want the wheels to wear out.

I miss the girls at school (not Miss Molly) and I wish I could talk to Ruth. She has a new baby brother, too, and her older sisters are sewing Bounty Coats, like Elisabeth.

December 31, 1777, Wednesday

The Schuylkill is frozen solid. Several of us slid across with snow up to our knees. We went on purpose to the bend near headquarters hoping to see some soldiers up close. In some places the river is as clear as a window and I looked down to see fish, slow and silent.

Elisabeth and I wandered into the woods to gather pinecones for kindling. As we were filling our aprons we heard a voice. We stopped to listen. Ahead, at the edge of a clearing, was a gray horse with a fine saddle on its back. There beside it was an officer kneeling in the snow, his head bowed, his hands folded in prayer. His breath made frost in the cold air.

Elisabeth whispered, "That doth look like General Washington."

"Yes," I said. It was the same man we'd seen on the road the day the soldiers marched into Valley Forge.

Not wanting to disturb him, we crept away. I felt safer knowing the Commander in Chief of our Army was a man of prayer.

We returned to the ice and to the noise of children playing. When the Fitzgerald boys showed up with slingshots, I took Sally and left with our pinecones. I am unable to be polite when I see them, Tom especially. He threw icicles like little spears at us as we ran. He is a wretched boy.

After supper Billy Lee came to the house. He stood by the door holding his hat, just long enough to tell us Mr. Washington needs to hire a laundress. He will pay forty shillings a month.

January 1, 1778, Thursday

Mama asked me to deliver her letter to Mr. Washington first thing this morning. It was a twenty-minute walk and by the time I arrived the tops of my shoes had filled with snow and I was shivering. While I waited inside by the kitchen step I felt grateful to Elisabeth because she let me wear her cloak. I've decided I like her scarf. I'm sorry I hated it at first and am relieved I didn't tell her so.

The parlour looks different with Mrs. Hewes' cozy things gone. Tables and chairs are arranged in odd places and there are several inkwells with pens (they look to be crow feathers). Green felt tablecloths reach to the bare floor. There is one plaited rug by the hearth where a cat was sleeping. I counted six men in uniform, officers it seemed by their buttons and such, and not one paid me any notice.

Billy Lee came down the stairs and nodded to me.

"Mr. Wash'ton accepts your mother's kind offer. Can you come by this afternoon before one o'clock?"

"Yes," I said.

Now it is past bedtime and I have never felt so tired. Elisabeth is asleep, so is Sally. At noon Papa took us in the little sleigh to pick up two canvas sacks of laundry. We hauled water until my knees bled from the bucket banging them. The big kettle boiled for hours. (We used potato juice for starch.) Mama, Elisabeth, Sally, and I dipped with poles, scrubbed, dipped, then wrung everything out. My hands are raw from lye.

Papa strung rope from pegs across the kitchen and main room, even along the stairway where the heat stays. There are so many shirts, stockings, trousers, and (I try to stare not) private underthings hanging overhead, it feels as if we are in a forest.

Fried beef, ham, and cold apple pie for supper. Tomorrow we shall be able to cook in our kettle again.

Monday is wash day, so we'll do everything over plus Johnny's nappies and our own family's laundry.

Am too tired and too cold to tell more.

January 2, 1778, Friday

At sunrise the mercury said six degrees above zero.

We walked the cold mile to school, but were turned away because it is now a hospital! I tried to peer in.

"Small pox, Miss," the soldier told me. "Now go home, all of ye."

The boys made a carnival out of snowballs and rocks, but the girls and I hurried with Sally to the road. Ruth is cross the army can take over our little schoolhouse whether we like it or not. (I like it, but did not say.) She stomped all the way home.

About yesterday, New Year's Day:

Ten teams of oxen arrived in camp to much noise and surprise. They had come from Philadelphia and were driven by *women*. The wagons were filled with supplies and 2,000 shirts that had been sewn by patriot ladies. Elisabeth said they were Bounty Shirts, but I know not.

The oxen were slaughtered and cooked — their stomach parts were boiled with pepper to make Pepperpot Soup. (Mama calls this tripe, but I call it nasty.) We saw soldiers standing over the fires, using their bayonets as roasting spits. The carcasses are at the edge of camp, and some of the wagons are being broken apart for firewood.

Sally asked Papa, "How shall the women drivers get back to Philadelphia without oxen and without wagons?"

Papa glanced at Mama, then he said, "I know not."

January 3, 1778, Saturday

At six o'clock this morning we were awakened by the sound of drums and fifes. Papa and I hurried out in the blowing snow to see if there was a battle. Other families met us in the road. We expected to see guns ready, but instead saw rows of soldiers, all at attention, at the edge of a snowfield. In front were officers on horseback with the drummer boys and fifers.

In the center one horse was being led out of camp. A man without a saddle was sitting backwards so that he faced the soldiers and General Washington. His coat was turned inside out, his hands were tied behind his back, and he hung his head in shame.

I leaned into Papa's arms for warmth. He told me, "That soldier is being drummed out of the Army."

At supper Mr. Walker stopped in and told us the man stole two hundred dollars from an officer and now his crime and punishment will be published in all the newspapers.

Baths. This week it was my turn to go first.

January 4, 1778, Sunday

A terrible day. On our way home from church we saw a bare oak tree where soldiers were gathered. A hanging had just taken place and the body of the poor man was swinging in the wind. The talk we heard along the road was that he had deserted and been caught running across the iced river. I hate the Army. I wish they'd go home. Sally cried and cried at the sight.

It snowed all day.

January 5, 1778, Monday

Snowed another six inches.

Papa was using the sleigh to haul a dead horse out of camp. (The hide will make some shoes.) This is why Elisabeth and I walked to Headquarters and carried back the laundry. It was so cold, not until we'd been by Mama's fire and kettle for nearly an hour did we finally warm up.

I still have not met General Washington, although I saw the heel of his boot as he rounded up the stairway.

January 6, 1778, Tuesday

Elisabeth and I returned the General's laundry this morning, pressed and folded. There was much busyness. Billy Lee noticed us finally and smiled, taking the bags into his arms and turning for the stairs.

As we were leaving, a soldier came in from the snow with a rush of icy air. He looked not at us, but snapped his heels and saluted to an officer standing by the fire.

"At ease," said the officer. "Spread word that small pox inoculations are to begin immediately, by order of our Commander in Chief."

He explained there soon would be fifty hospitals throughout camp and the countryside. They had started with our little schoolhouse and were going to be taking over some of the barns and meeting houses.

"Abby," said Elisabeth when we were on the path outside, "what if they taketh our church, what shall we do then?"

I know not. Every day there are more things to puzzle over.

January 7, 1778, Wednesday

I am feeling unwell. Papa came in with a hide that smelled so bad it made our eyes sting. He said General Washington has ordered his men to bury the dead horses instead of leaving them where they drop. (They are dying of starvation.) Papa shook his head. "The ground is frozen," he said. "How they shall do this, I wonder. It is difficult enough to dig their necessaries."

January 9, 1778, Friday

The past two days have been above freezing. Snow is melting into mud, making the roads a dreadful mess. Papa's front wheel broke when he tried to haul hay to Potter's. (Mr. Potter helped repair it.) When Papa was returning home he came across another deserter being hanged, a man from Virginia.

Colonel DeWees brought over a cloth full of gingerbread, baked by Mrs. Hewes. He sat down on our bench, to drink Mama's raspberry tea (not English tea) and to complain about the soldiers. He discovered three of them in his barn, stealing hay and lumber. "How shall I feed my horses or mend my roof?" he said, his face in his hands.

January 11, 1778, Sunday

Thankfully our church has not yet been turned into a hospital. It is snowing again.

Johnny is almost six weeks old and has not been out of our warm house. I rock him and kiss his tiny fingers every chance I get. "Please, thou must live, Johnny," I say.

Before dinner I was leaning into the hearth to pull out the corncakes when I looked over at him in his cradle. An amazing thing happened.

Johnny smiled at me.

January 12, 1778, Monday

Laundry. My hands are raw and peeling at the fingertips.

The last few times we've gone to Headquarters, General Washington has been sitting at a table writing letters. I've seen only the side of his face. He wears a pigtail with a black satin ribbon tied on the end. I do not think it's a wig, but his hair is powdered.

January 13, 1778, Tuesday

Today when we returned the laundry, I was astounded to see only General Washington in the parlour, no other officers. I know not where Billy Lee was. The General was sharpening his quill with his penknife. He looked up at us and smiled. His face would have been handsome, I think, if it were not so badly scarred from the Pox.

"Thank you, Abigail. Thank you, Elisabeth," he said. I curtsied, unable to speak. How did he know our names?

He looked at us with kind eyes — they're gray-blue — then he returned to his pen and paper. Mrs. Hewes says Mr. Washington writes at least fifteen letters a day, mostly to Congress. He is pleading for food, clothing, and other supplies, she told us.

January 17, 1778, Saturday

It has snowed for seven days with only wind in between, no stars at night, no moon. I abandoned my journal because I've been ill. I cough until my ribs ache and have been unable to eat much more than broth. Sally said my neck is as thin as a chicken's. I have not had a bath in two weeks.

Two of our pigs are missing. Papa said footprints in the snow were from soldiers. He knew this because of the blood.

January 19, 1778, Monday

Washday. I burned my hand on one of the irons. We keep two in the coals to heat, one in use. I was watching Sally sneak a lick from the molasses jug when I ran the iron off General Washington's collar right over my left hand. It hurts but is only red, not blistered.

January 20, 1778, Tuesday

Sally came screaming that someone ruined her doll. She'd been playing in the barn and left it in the hay overnight, in a safe little house she made. We went to the barn. Someone had slept there and not cleaned up after their necessary. This same person stepped on Sally's doll and tore the dress in half and one arm off.

I can sew it back on for her.

January 22, 1778, Thursday

My cough is better, though I feel weak. Stayed by the fire all day and made onion soup for supper. Mama has asked me to write down instructions — so here they are:

To the small pot I added four large onions (sliced), two quarts milk, two large scoops of butter, salt, and pepper. When it came to a boil I eased the pot to the side of the coals so it would cook slowly until the onions were soft. In my tea cup I beat one egg, spooned a bit of hot soup into it, beat it some more, then poured it back into the pot. Cooked it ten more minutes or so. This we ate with brown bread and baked apples.

Papa is worried soldiers will steal our hens, but the warmest place is in the barn, so we can do nothing to prevent them. He filled a crate with firewood ashes and carried it to the cellar. This is where we're to hide the eggs, small end downwards. To keep them fresh we're to turn them endways once a week.

January 23, 1778, Friday

Sally wanted to bake bread this morning, so I sat in the rocker with Johnny to watch. She tucked her skirt into her leggings to keep the hem from catching fire, then swept a clean spot on the hearth. She took the dough that had risen overnight, set it on the bricks, then covered it with an upside-down kettle, the small one. With the long spoon she scooped hot coals on top and all around.

The aroma for the next hour was wonderful. Sally was so pleased with herself when Mama served it with butter for afternoon tea, that she announced she's ready to get married. We teased about her size (she's just six).

Before bed I brushed her hair into two plaits. She sleeps between Beth and me now because her trundle is cold and lonesome. We are like three cats curled together.

January 24, 1778, Saturday

We woke up to a shock. Our entire north fence is gone, all the rails and posts, all of it. Marks in the snow showed where it had been dragged, piece by piece, toward the encampment.

Papa was so cross his jaw turned stiff. "I am trying to help the Army," he said, "but by God, they are turning my home into firewood." After breakfast he buttoned his coat and said to Mama, "I shall report this to General Washington."

Papa let me ride in the wagon with him (there is not enough snow in the road for sleighs). He took the long way to Headquarters, around the stand of pines, past Slab Tavern, then by Joseph Mann's cabin. Joseph is a freed Negro like Billy Lee. As he lives on Valley Creek near where it meets the Schuylkill River, there were sentries with rifles. They were warming themselves over a small fire.

Two of the soldiers stood in their hats to keep their bare feet off the snow.

At Headquarters we waited outside in the cold. Through one of the windows we could see General Washington and several officers. A prisoner stood in front of them, hands tied behind his back. Soon he was led outside by guards.

"Two hundred fifty lashes for you, mister, ain't enough," said one soldier to the man. "Selling beef to the Redcoats should've got you shot, not whipped, that's my opinion."

Before we could step into the hallway, another prisoner was led out. He was on his way to one hundred lashes for attempted desertion. There were other men inside, handcuffed.

Papa walked to the wagon. "Some other day, Abigail," he said. "These court-martials will take hours."

Mrs. Hewes visited with her youngest nephew, who played marbles by the fire while we had tea. She said that soldiers are deserting nearly every day.

She knows this because some of the court-martials (of those who are caught) take place in the drawing room at her temporary home, the DeWeeses'; also at David Stevens's house where General James Varnum is quartered. (I wonder if Mrs. Stevens does General Varnum's laundry.)

"It's the foreign-born mostly," Mrs. Hewes told us. "They have not the same loyalty as those of us born here on American soil."

January 25, 1778, Sunday

It is warmer, but still we leave Johnny inside. Sally and I stayed home with him so Mama could go to services. I finished mending Sally's doll's dress and sewed its arm back on.

Mr. and Mrs. Smith came to supper. We all have family in Philadelphia and are worried for their safety. Papa and Mr. Smith talked about taking a big wagon while the weather's fair, then returning with as many as will come.

"But Edward," Mama said. "Thee could be shot, mistaken for spies. Please don't go."

"We shall be all right," Papa told her. "Many do it already. You've seen the wives bringing food back and forth, yes? They've not been shot."

They were still talking when we girls took our candle upstairs to bed. I tried to listen, but was too sleepy.

January 26, 1778, Monday

Beefsteak pie for breakfast.

Papa and Mr. Smith have decided to leave in an hour. I am hurriedly writing this because they are choosing two of us to go with them, so that our little cousins will be at ease. I have just heard my name called, and Lucy's, Mr. Smith's daughter. She's fifteen. My dear sister said I may wear her cloak, her beautiful blue cloak. . . . I'm truly going!

January 30, 1778, Friday

Valley Forge. It is late and everyone sleeps. I'm still too stirred up from the past few days and must put it all down before I can rest. I do hope this candle will last — it's as short as my thumb, so I will hurry.

The road to Philadelphia was eighteen miles of mud and ruts that made us turn and bump where we wanted not to. Lucy and I shared a blanket and foot warmer because of the wind. Papa was right. There were many travelers to and from Valley Forge. At the outpost pickets the guards we saw were busy questioning and searching.

It is a crime to sell provisions to the enemy, but people do it anyway because the Redcoats pay in silver coin and gold. The Continental Army pays in paper. Mr. Smith said it is worthless paper, that's why so many civilians are willing to take the risk.

Philadelphia's streets are paved in the middle for carriages, with a footpath of hard brick on each side. Cobblestones are bumpy but much easier on our poor wagon. Everything seemed new and wondrous as I'd not been here since I was small, about Sally's age — Lucy and I stared with delight at houses with lace curtains and painted shutters, outdoor lamps to light the way, and tall carriages drawn by matching horses. There were ladies in fine dresses with velvet cloaks and bonnets.

An assortment of boys, tall and small, hurried along the streets and lanes, carrying boxes. Papa said they were wigmakers' apprentices delivering freshly curled and powdered wigs. "To the arrogant rich," he said, "Philadelphians who'd rather spend money on themselves, than to help our starving soldiers. There should be a law against such vanities in the time of war."

Lucy and I looked at each other. It hardly seemed we were in the middle of a war with enemies everywhere, such was the feeling of gaiety. Shops were open, bells on the doors tinkled when we entered. We purchased nothing, but only wanted to find our uncles (who are also cobblers, one is a silversmith). Auntie Hannie lives with her husband above their little bakery. How happy she was to see us, and she's expecting another baby—I could tell from her full apron.

But when Papa learned she sells bread to the British commander, he was silent. How could she! General William Howe is our enemy. He and his aides are quartered just across the street, down four houses and—Hannie asked us this—would we like to meet him, he's very nice. I thought Papa would collapse with anger.

Candle is going . . .

January 31, 1778, Saturday

It's late again. Busy all day helping Mama with extra laundry from a general whose name I forgot. There are so many shirts hanging—many of Irish linen—we must duck between the rafters.

More to say about Philadelphia: Papa allowed us to stay with Auntie Hannie. The next day, Tuesday I think, he went with Mr. Smith to call on their brothers, while Lucy and I stayed to help Hannie cook and tend her five little ones. But we each did a terrible thing. First, Lucy:

During the babies' naps we went into the tiny shop next door—it is just four feet wide and there is a wood sign above the door that says Wigmaker. While I was admiring ribbons in his front window, I heard the sound of scissors. Before I could say a word, Lucy had allowed this stranger to cut off her beautiful brown hair! For nine shillings! I could speak not. An English officer might be the next customer!

Lucy is so willful and headstrong she just tied on her bonnet and curtsied. In the street she said to me, "It shall be days before Papa finds out and by then he shall be so pleased to have silver coin it will matter not. Dost thou know that a countrywoman's hair is considered far superior than that of one from the city, Abigail?"

I knew not what to say. I promised not to tell, but I worry that Lucy's pride will get her in trouble some day.

Now, to confess my deed (I see no harm, truly): I delivered rum cakes and strudel to the British general. It was just for fun and to see an Englishman up close, but still I dare not tell Papa.

February 1, 1778, Sunday

Elisabeth finished her coat this morning and very prettily embroidered her name inside the left lapel. My hunting shirt needs repair because I sewed part of the front sleeve to the back sleeve so that no arm can get through.

To continue about last week:

Auntie Hannie gave me a clean starched apron and a basket to hang on my arm. Into it she put two plates of strudel with pecan icing and thirteen rum cakes each the size of my hand — this is her Baker's Dozen, she explained. Auntie Hannie pointed me to the tall brick house down the lane.

I hurried, and rapped the brass knocker three

times. A Negro opened the door and showed me to a parlour where a stout man stood in front of the fire, lighting his pipe. He wore a scarlet waistcoat with a white vest, black knickers, white silk stockings, and pumps with silver buckles. (His knickers were tied at the knee with double bows.) I curtsied, then held out the basket.

He said, "Mrs. Loring, wilt thou see what we have here?"

She was most beautiful with blond hair twisted grandly on her head. Her dress was of peach-colored satin. "It's for tea I'm sure, Billy, come sit." She smiled, then dismissed me with a nod. I backed out of the room as a man entered through another door. He was quite round also, with thick lips, and was addressed as Lord Something-or-Other. His eyes were so pop-eyed he looked as if he had just swallowed a snake.

There were two other men in red waistcoats. They sat in parlour chairs and crossed their legs. All attention was on the tea cart and basket of sweets; no one noticed I was lingering. One of the men — he was plumpest of all — picked up a cake and spread butter on it with his thumb.

Auntie later explained that "Billy" is General Sir

William Howe, England's commander. She blushed to tell me that Mrs. Loring is his mistress. She has disgraced the patriots because she's married to another man, an American officer.

Twice more I delivered cakes and bread to the brick house. The third day Sir Billy wasn't there. He was playing cards at the Indian Queen Cafe, where he often enjoys late suppers.

Now that I'm home again I've decided not to be so angry at our soldiers when they take things from us. Our enemies (20,000, Papa says) are sleeping in warm featherbeds, eating sweets, and playing cards, while General Washington holds his men together with threads.

I've also decided that when the English return to their fat king across the Atlantic I shall confess to Mama and Papa that I served the British commander, but not before. At the moment they are too upset. None of our relatives would leave Philadelphia and none felt ashamed about accepting gold coin from the enemy.

"Business is business," mine uncle said to Papa.

February 2, 1778, Monday

When Beth and I picked up Mr. Washington's laundry, Billy Lee drew us aside.

"Lady Wash'ton is coming from Mount Vernon," he said. "She should be here soon. And Mr. Wash'ton wonders if yous and your kind mother could help upstairs, to make the sitting room — what he says — more suitable. It do need a lady's touch, misses."

When we told this to Mama she sat down, wiping her red hands on her apron. "Whatever do we have to offer the General's Lady?" she said. "She hath culture, and is one of the most wealthiest women in the colonies. Daughters, I need to think. . . . Can ye serve us a nice hot pot of tea?"

February 3, 1778, Tuesday

It is sunny and warm! The path to Headquarters is mud, not snow, and I need not wear my blanket. There is clutter on the second floor, so we arranged the boxes and smaller trunks at one end of the hallway. In what is to be Lady Washington's sitting room (it has a cheerful view of the creek), we brought in a dressing table with a looking glass and Billy Lee showed us where to position the bed. Its four posters at one time had curtains to draw across for warmth, but they're gone now. Mama wants to sew some herself, but our last cloth went for Elisabeth's Bounty Coat and my hunting shirt, which I still have not repaired (and have no desire to).

February 4, 1778, Wednesday

General Washington sent Colonel Meade below Wilmington to meet Mrs. Washington's coach. He worries she's been delayed.

Papa drove Elisabeth to the outer camp to deliver her coat. She told me a soldier on guard duty grabbed it and quickly slipped his thin arms into the sleeves. When he thanked her, she saw he was missing his top teeth and spoke with a coarse accent.

After we climbed the stairs for bed she burst into sobs.

"Oh Abby, I'm so ashamed of myself," she wept, "but I wanted a *handsome* soldier, truly."

I held her hand until she fell asleep. I wanted to comfort her but my thought was that two good things had happened: A cold soldier was made warm. And he thanked her.

February 5, 1778, Thursday

Again woke to drums and fifes. I worry not so much now about the British since I've seen how plump and lazy their officers are, so we took our time eating our morning potato (hot with fried bacon on top).

How shocked we were to see who was being drummed out of the army: a woman! She sat backwards, her legs (thankfully hidden by wide skirts) draped over the horse's flanks. "Who?" we asked among the people gathering at the edge of camp. "Why?"

This is what Reverend Currie told us, for he visited with the poor woman yesterday: Mary Johnson is her name — she was caught trying to tempt our soldiers to ride with her into Philadelphia where they'd have warm beds and plenty of food, courtesy of "Sir Billy." Her sentence: one hundred lashes and drummed out of the Army! I put my hands over my ears because I could bear to hear no more. One hundred lashes on a woman's back . . .

At supper I had no appetite. Papa told us that the women who've been passing freely through the lines of each army now will be stopped. Only generals themselves will issue permits.

"Who knows what damage hath been done, by woman or man?" Papa said. He glanced at me. "Or by child?" I kept my eyes down. Did he know about Lucy's hair, or that I curtsied to the British general?

February 6, 1778, Friday

Still sunny. On the warm side of our house is a patch of dry dirt. I spread a quilt and lay Johnny on his back. He squinted at the sunlight and kicked his legs. I was so happy to see him smile again until Mama came out. "Abigail! He shalt catch cold, he's just a baby . . ." I ran upstairs crying. I only wanted him to feel fresh air on his cheeks.

February 7, 1778, Saturday

Rain all day, winds are high.

Elisabeth and I brought six pumpkins up from the cellar and spent the day slicing them into strips that we hung on string from the rafters to dry (since there are no shirts today). It makes the house look cheerful and there is a sweet scent. The seeds filled the large iron skillet where we roasted them with salt until crisp.

Papa finished four pairs of shoes and took them to camp. He said a lieutenant delivered them to four soldiers who were married yesterday. It seems that some of the women drivers from Philadelphia have found themselves husbands.

Papa also told us another spy was caught. Her name is Ann McIntire.

February 8, 1778, Sunday

Lucy sat in front of me at church and I could not help but stare at the back of her neck. If I hadn't seen with my own eyes the wigmaker's scissors cut off her beautiful hair, I would have known not. Wisps curled from under her bonnet just as before. After the final hymn she turned around, leaned toward me, and whispered so softly I almost didn't hear, "Mama and Papa know naught."

Poor Lucy, carrying such a secret night and day, brushing her hair when no one will see, then quickly tying on her nightcap. She looks sad.

Outside I said to her, "Have you not been eating, Lucy? Your face is so thin."

She glanced at her parents who were over by their wagon then said, "Oh, Abby, the nine shillings are gone." Her eyes filled with tears. "I hid them in the barn under one of the nests. The other morning two hens were missing and all the eggs. And my shillings."

"Are you sure? Have you looked everywhere?"

"Yes . . . yes. Mama's waiting, I must go. Hast thou told anyone, Abby?"

"Not a soul," said I.

February 9, 1778, Monday

It snowed last night and all morning. Mama and I were wringing out the bedclothes to hang when a rumble of horses passed on the road. We ran to the window and scratched off the ice in time to see a sleigh round the bend toward Headquarters.

"That must be Lady Washington," cried Elisabeth, "all the way from Mount Vernon."

"May we go, may we go?" Sally asked.

Mama looked at her hands, red and rough from being in hot water all day. "My goodness, no," she said. "The dear lady shalt need rest from her long journey, not visitors." Mama looked at the hearth, where a fresh round of rye 'n' injun bread was almost done. She smiled. "But mayhaps we should extend our hospitality —" We interrupted her by hurrying into bonnets and cloaks, shoes and wool stockings.

(Elisabeth pinned my blanket over my shoulders.)

The snow was almost to our knees in the field so instead of taking the shortcut, we stayed on the road — a 45-minute walk.

Mrs. Washington's sleigh was by the stone stable, not as grand as we thought it might be and there were icicles hanging from its frame. Suddenly I felt most shy.

Billy Lee opened the door and bade us come in. From the kitchen came several female voices and an excited gasp when we were noticed.

"Who are these dear children?" said one of the women coming over to greet us. She was about my height, extremely plump, and had a friendly, smiling face, though I must admit she was not at all pretty. (I did not like her wide nostrils nor the mole on her cheek.)

"Ma'am," said Billy Lee, "these here are Missus Stewart's girls, those that keeps your husband's shirts, ma'am."

This was Lady Washington!

Sally found her voice first. "Mama says we're to welcome thee to Valley Forge. She hopes the inns you stayed at didn't have bedbugs like The King of Prussia Inn down the road here."

Mrs. Washington laughed. "Sweet child, thank your mother for me. Since you asked, I'll tell. I saw no bugs, but the beds were lumpy and damp for lack of a warm fire. There was quite a lot of noise downstairs in the taverns, but, child, I had nothing but kindness shown me the entire journey, thirteen nights I believe. Roads were rough, of course. We had to leave my coach with the innkeeper near Brandywine Creek because of snow. It is his sleigh outside."

She lifted the cloth to peek at our bread. "Oh, my, can you girls stay for tea? I'm deathly weary, but do need a hot cup, not English tea of course."

We no-thanked her politely and began to back out of the room, but her hand flew up. "Forgive my poor manners. I want to introduce my friends here — their husbands are officers and they've been staying with other families here in Valley Forge. Also . . . Oney, could you come here please?"

Mrs. Washington gestured to a Negro lady unloading food from a large traveling basket. My mouth began to water at the sight of hams and wheels of cheese, dried fruits, jars of preserves, salted fish, walnuts, and almonds.

"How do, Misses?" Oney said, dipping her head slightly.

I noticed General Washington standing in the doorway. (He is so very much taller than his wife, some say six-foot-two.) With hands behind his back he appeared the most relaxed I'd ever seen him. He smiled at us. As Mrs. Washington moved busily around the kitchen, his eyes followed her with tenderness.

February 10, 1778, Tuesday

Laundry done and dried, the bags are too heavy to carry, so Papa put them in the wagon. Elisabeth and I rode on the seat with him to Headquarters. After lifting the sacks down to us, Papa drove off and said for us to walk home within the hour.

Such busy-ness in the front room! General Washington was standing at one of the tables surrounded by an assortment of officers and two of his generals.

Oney was in the kitchen with the cook and two other women. There were eight loaves of round bread on the table — their fresh-baked aroma was wonderful. I peeked in to see a long narrow table against the wall where a soldier-in-apron was chopping turnips and onions. Hanging from an iron hook in the ceiling was a chunk of beef covered with peppercorns. It seemed a fine meal was being prepared to welcome Lady Washington. Oney pointed upstairs, but I heard not what she said because of so many voices talking at once.

Elisabeth and I together carried one laundry sack up the narrow stairway then returned for the other. At least four times we had to step aside to let officers and servants up or down. What a crowded house!

The door to Mrs. Washington's sitting room was ajar. The first time we knocked there came no response. Louder the second time. A woman opened it for us to enter. She, too, was my height and so very plump she had to step back and to the side for us to pass her skirts.

From across the room came Mrs. Washington's voice. She sat by the window to catch the light for her knitting. "Oh, girls, do join us. Let me introduce Lucy Knox" — the smiling one who opened the door — "and these other ladies are friends from Chester County. Come ye in, please."

I again was struck with shyness, but Elisabeth spoke for both of us. "Thank you, ma'am, but Papa says we're to deliver your husband's shirts then return home."

How I wanted to stay! I longed to hear more of their laughter and conversation. The room seemed tiny now with so many women sitting at needlework. Their skirts touched one another's, making it look as if one large quilt were spread over their laps.

"Well, then," said Mrs. Washington, "come again when ye can stay. We could use your help. These poor soldiers are in dreadful need of socks and shirts, so do come back with your needles. Thy Mother is invited as well."

After supper I began the repairs to my hunting shirt, feeling ugly with myself for being so lazy.

February 11, 1778, Wednesday

Finished the shirt. I embroidered my name, not as prettily as Elisabeth's, but it's there: *Abigail Jane Stewart*.

A thaw has made so much mud we did not take the wagon out. Papa told us to stay in, but Sally disobeyed. She ran out into the road and immediately sunk down several inches.

Elisabeth and I stood on a plank to help her. When she lifted her feet out, her shoes were gone.

They are lost in the mud and now she is just like the soldiers.

Papa looked at her muddy legs and said, "Thou shalt stay inside for the rest of the winter, young lady."

Sally cried all morning and would not be comforted by any of us.

"Why can Papa not make me shoes *right now*?" she wailed.

I said, "Sally. You have a warm house and a nice rug under thy feet. The soldiers have none."

February 12, 1778, Thursday

General Washington passed out handbills to all of us in Valley Forge. Too many farmers have been riding into Philadelphia to sell meat, eggs, dried vegetables, and fruits. The General cannot whip them all, says Papa, so he is setting up markets in his encampment—three sites, each open twice a week. This will help feed the Army, though we shall still be paid in paper not silver, and it may stop helping those big-bellied Englishmen.

Papa drove us to the southern edge of camp and pointed out one of the sutlers. This was a small tent with a cooking fire by its door. A man in a fur coat was warming his hands and looking toward camp.

"He's looking for customers," Papa said. "Sutlers follow the Army. They sell liquor, tobacco, and food stuffs to the soldiers, but their prices are high — imagine, two shillings per pound for hard soap. Generals dislike them."

We took cranberries and dried apples to sell at the Stone Chimney Picket. Tomorrow there shall be a market at the Schuylkill River, on the north side of Sullivan's Bridge. Saturday, near the adjutant general's quarters, but I know not where that is.

Coming home, we passed the Fitzgerald house. Six of the brothers were out in the mud playing. There was just a tiny bit of smoke coming from the chimney so we stopped.

Mrs. Fitzgerald sat in her rocker by the hearth, a shawl around her shoulders and two of the biggest cats I've ever seen on her lap. There again in the cupboard I heard scratchings of mice. Even her cats help her not!

Papa split wood, carried in five arms-full, and stoked up her fire. We gave her a sack of dried cranberries, a small ham, and the corncake we'd brought along for our lunch. Mrs. Fitzgerald started to cry when we asked about her husband. There's been no word as to what the Redcoats have done with him.

As I climbed to the wagon seat I looked for Tom to scold him, but he kept a safe distance. We were halfway down their road and he still was making faces at me. If only his papa were here to whip him!

February 13, 1778, Friday

There were many of us down by Sullivan's Bridge to enjoy Market Day and to look at the soldiers. The Schuylkill is still frozen solid and the snow on top is criss-crossed from all the children who slide and stomp across.

Lucy was there with her mother, looking thin and withdrawn. Suddenly there appeared four of the Fitzgerald boys, yelling and banging sticks just to make noise and scare the old people.

Tom ran up to Lucy, reached under her chin, pulled her bonnet string, then ran off hooting and waving it in the air like a kite. Poor Lucy!

The shock on her face — on her *mother's* face —

I cannot put in words. There she stood with her shorn hair for all to see. I hurried to her side untying my own cap, then put it on her head. Tears ran down her cheeks and wet my hand as I tied the string.

"It shall be all right, Lucy," I said.

February 14, 1778, Saturday

Baths. Tonight I washed my hair. As Mama poured cups of warm water over my head, I cried. I'm heartsore for Lucy and know not what her parents will do to her.

February 16, 1778, Monday

As weeks pass, the laundry is looking grayish from our ash soap. Mrs. Washington asked if we could please use bleach.

Mama brought out an old bucket that has been patched many times. She instructed Elisabeth and me to carefully (she would not let Sally do this) bring downstairs our chamber pot, then also the one under hers and Papa's bed.

We poured urine into the bucket, then began

soaking some of the dingiest items, which we later rinsed in fresh water. It is an unpleasant chore, but must be done.

All day it was cold out and overcast. I let Sally wear my shoes for ten minutes so she could step outside. There is a stray cat she wants to pet.

February 17, 1778, Tuesday

Mama came with me and Elisabeth to return the laundry and visit Mrs. Washington. Every day except Sunday officers' wives and ladies from Valley Forge are there in her sitting room or in the kitchen. There's much knitting of socks and mending of shirts and such.

I was so jealous and cross when Mrs. Washington asked Elisabeth to accompany her into camp, to deliver food and comfort to sick soldiers. Why did she not ask me? I wanted to go and think I deserve to go as much as anyone else.

Miss Molly was coming up the path when Mama and I were leaving. She spoke kindly to me, asked about my studies and so forth, but I could not take my eyes off the road — there went Mrs. Washington's wagon with my sister sitting next to her, chatting like old friends! Why am I not as pretty as Elisabeth? I'm greatly upset today.

February 18, 1778, Wednesday

When Elisabeth returned from her day with Mrs. Washington she took straight to bed. Her face was pale and she said she could not think of eating. She rolled onto her side.

"What ails you, Beth?" I asked.

For the longest time she spoke naught. Finally she began to cry. Through sobs all I could understand were the words "those poor soldiers."

February 19, 1778, Thursday

I brought my hunting shirt to Mrs. Washington. "It's quite nice, Abby," she said. "And I know just the boy. Will you come with me tomorrow?"

Will I! I wore Elisabeth's cloak, two pairs of woolen socks, leggings, and my wool skirt. Sally's cap is too small for my head, so Mama gave me hers.

It was windy and gray. A lieutenant drove us past Mount Joy toward the main encampment, past rows of huts, the largest ones belonging to some of the officers. We stopped at the 2nd Pennsylvania Brigade, commanded by General Wayne, and stepped down into mud. There was a stench coming from between huts and I knew why the instant I saw yellow snow and human waste. (Such a filthy habit!)

If Mrs. Washington noticed, she said naught. I followed her into the hut. We both bent over to avoid hitting our heads. It was dark therein, and so smoky my eyes immediately began to sting. The fireplace had a small iron kettle sitting on stones, but the wood was either wet or green so it gave off no warmth. In a corner lay a pile of beef bones from an earlier meal.

Each side of the small cabin had narrow bunks, stacked three high. On a lower one lay a soldier with no blanket, just bits of hay sprinkled over him for warmth. His bare feet stuck out at the end of his bed. His toes were black, the soles of his feet dark green, and there was a smell of rotten meat coming from them. I pressed my hand to my mouth.

A young girl sat next to him on her little travel bag, weeping.

"Mrs. Kern?" said Mrs. Washington. "May I offer you prayer? The surgeon will take thine husband shortly."

"Yes, ma'am, please." The girl could not control her weeping and I found myself crying, too. Following Mrs. Washington's example I knelt in the cold dirt. The poor soldier was shivering as she took his hand in hers.

"Dear Lord," she began, "please comfort this good man and his wife, be with them . . ."

She embraced Mrs. Kern (a girl near Elisabeth's age). Just then we saw a shadow of men outside and a stretcher.

My candle is hissing . . .

February 20, 1778, Friday

Again gray and cold. To finish about yesterday:

Mrs. Washington and I visited eight huts. Each time, she talked with the soldier, asked about his family, then knelt in prayer for him. If she was tired (or as cold as I was) she uttered not one complaint.

Near two o'clock in the afternoon we came to a tent at the edge of camp. Outside a woman bent over a kettle of wash. Rags were wrapped around her feet. Mrs. Washington smiled at her.

"Good day, madam," she said. "I'd like to

introduce Miss Abigail Stewart. She's made a shirt I think will fit your boy nicely."

"He's yonder, m'lady. Can y'hear the fifes and drums over the next hill? Such a racket all day long. But I will give him thy shirt, Miss," she said to me, "soon as he returns. God bless ye."

As we rode back toward Headquarters I stared at the outer tents, small and shabby most of them. There were laundry kettles, and clotheslines were strung between branches. Mrs. Washington said drummer boys are paid seven and one-third dollars per month, and some are so young their mothers camp nearby to care for them. She pulled her cloak up to her chin and turned stiffly to smile at me.

"The women offer much help to the brigades," she said. "But once the Army is on the march again, going toward battle or from it, my husband says camp followers are a nuisance."

The wind was cutting through my clothes when we neared the schoolhouse which, of course, was now a hospital. I was beginning to shiver after so many hours outdoors. My stomach felt hollow with hunger, for I'd eaten just two biscuits for breakfast and Mrs. Washington's food basket was now empty.

Several dogs were slinking about, trying to get near a trough that was below the window. A soldier jabbed at them with his bayonet, but as he had no shoes he remained standing on his hat and gave no chase. One dog lunged for the trough and ran off with what looked like a piece of wood in its mouth. Another did the same.

Our wagon driver pulled the reins to stop, but we did not get down. A man's scream from inside the schoolhouse was so horrible, so full of begging and pain, I looked at Mrs. Washington with tears in my eyes.

"What's happening?" I asked.

She, too, could not hold back tears. "I'm afraid, my dear, the surgeon is at work."

I then realized the trough was overflowing, not with firewood, but with human hands and feet.

February 21, 1778, Saturday

I have felt heartsore all day. When I told Mama about the soldiers, I buried my head in her lap and cried. Elisabeth also came to the hearth.

"They're dying from the Pox," she told us, trying to hold back tears, "and the Putrid Fevers. Mama . . .

I watched a surgeon saw off a man's leg, right before mine eyes." Elisabeth now could not stop weeping. Mama stroked her hair.

Finally Elisabeth dried her face with her apron. "The poor soldier had a bullet clenched between his teeth to keep from screaming, but so great was his pain . . . oh, Mama . . . when he did open his mouth to cry out, the bullet dropped back into his throat. While he was choking the surgeon kept sawing . . . and he died right there."

"Dear . . . dear . . ." said Mama.

Sally sat next to us, nervously rocking Johnny's cradle. "Why must his leg be cut off?" she asked.

Papa's voice came from the doorway. "Because the soldiers have no shoes, the snow freezes their feet."

We waited for him to say more.

"Is it like the frost that kills Mama's roses?" asked Sally.

"Yes," Papa said. "But a soldier whose hand or foot freezes must have it removed if it turns black, otherwise the black turns to green. Green means infection."

Papa took his coat off the peg and looked at us for a moment. His voice was soft.

"The only way to get rid of such an infection is

to cut it off. I'm sorry, daughters, that ye had to see such suffering."

It is late now. Mama is downstairs rocking Johnny, and I can hear Papa's snoring. Just before our noon meal, Oney knocked on our door, asking if we'd help her find some eggs.

"How many do you need, Oney?" Mama asked.

"Forty, ma'am."

"Forty?"

"Yes, ma'am. Lady Washington is baking a cake for her husband as tomorrow is his birthday, his forty-sixth birthday. Her recipe calls for forty eggs."

Elisabeth and I spent the afternoon calling on neighbours while Papa waited in the wagon with our crate of wood ashes. We had thirteen eggs ourselves, though small ones from our pullets. Mrs. Smith gave seven, and as we left I glanced up at the window by their chimney. There was Lucy, looking out, but she moved away from the glass so quickly I had trouble believing what I'd seen: her head was shaved.

By three o'clock we delivered 42 eggs to Mrs. Washington's kitchen. She herself did not receive us, because she, the General, and several officers and their wives had just begun their evening meal. Oney said this way they'll finish eating before they need to use candlelight.

February 22, 1778, Sunday

Windy and dark all day. Worship seemed longer than usual. I saw Lucy's two sisters and their parents in the front pew, but no Lucy. They've punished her by shaving her head and, to shame her, will not let her wear a bonnet. How I grieve for her, poor Lucy.

Though the ride home was bitter cold, I was cheered by the distant sound of singing among the brigades. Papa said General Washington encourages his troops to attend divine services every Sunday and to pray daily. He also said this:

"To the distinguished character of soldier and patriot, it should be our highest glory to add the more distinguished character of Christian."

It was most comforting to hear choruses of hymns on such a bleak day.

After sundown, the festive music from a band brought us, with shawls quickly wrapped over shoulders, from our hearth out onto our step. The air was icy and the road dark, but we could see torches of neighbours coming on foot to Headquarters. Papa let us girls hurry along the road with him—I was out of breath and my cheeks were numb when we arrived.

An artillery band was serenading General Washington!

Mrs. Washington stepped outside, clapping her hands with pleasure. "Thank you, thank you!" she called to the cold men. "How I love the sound of fifes and drums, such a fine way to honour his birthday. The General and I thank ye." She took fifteen shillings out of a tiny silk purse tied to her waist and paid the bandleader.

When she invited the musicians in, those of us watching turned for home. How they all fit in that snug house, I know not, because soon there was dancing. Through the window I saw the General with his hands on his hips and his pigtail bouncing—he was doing a jig!

February 23, 1778, Monday
When Elisabeth and I picked up the laundry at Headquarters, Mrs. Washington invited us into the

warm kitchen. There on a pewter plate were two slivers of cake.

"I saved these for you, girls, some of the Old Man's birthday cake. Here ye go."

It had been many weeks since either of us had eaten anything so delicious. I tried to be polite, but forgot my mouth was full when I asked for her recipe, and crumbs spit out over my apron. Elisabeth scolded me with her eyes, but if Mrs. Washington noticed my bad manners she said naught.

From her husband's desk she took up a fresh piece of paper, dipped his quill in ink, and wrote down the recipe (which I shall keep between pages of this journal instead of copying it all down). I remember the ingredients, but not how it's put together:

40 eggs
4 pounds butter
4 pounds sugar powdered
5 pounds flour
5 pounds fruit
mace & nutmeg
wine & some fresh brandy

Mama hugged us and laughed. "It's good ye were

able to taste such a fine cake," she said, "because the day we have forty eggs and four pounds of sugar to spare will be the day I grow wings."

The wind beat against the house all day so that we felt it blow in through cracks and under the door. Only the fire and hot kettle of wash kept us warm.

A great noise of horses and wagons passed by on the way to Headquarters, but we were unable to see out the steamy windows. Sally demanded I let her wear my shoes outside so she could watch the visitors, but when I refused she smacked our long spoon against the stones until it splintered in half. She stuck her jaw out and was not at all sorry for her temper. I was sore pleased when Mama put her in the corner with a swat.

Johnny is looking a bit more rosy in the cheeks. We lay him on the plaited rug, on his stomach, and after several minutes of wiggling he rolled over onto his back with a thump. He was so surprised he let out a howl and would not stop until I picked him up.

Sally sulked all day!

February 24, 1778, Tuesday

Elisabeth and I saw the new person standing by
General Washington's fireplace. His name is Baron
von Steuben and he is as stout and ugly as a nose.

At his side was a dog, a greyhound, with a thin
blue collar. His name is Azor and a more well-
mannered dog I've never seen, because when
General Washington offered him a cracker he
politely lifted his paw, put it on the General's knee,
then daintily took a bite. Azor holds his head high,
as if posing for a portrait. I should like to play fetch
with him.

As we carried the laundry downstairs Billy Lee
told us that when Benjamin Franklin was in Paris he
met von Steuben and asked him to sail to America
to help train our soldiers. He is an Army officer
from Prussia and speaks no English, but brought
an interpreter with him, a young Frenchman.

"There . . . see that boy by the window?" pointed
Billy Lee. "His name is Pierre —"

We heard no more because I, and especially
Elisabeth, could not take our eyes off the boy. He
was perhaps seventeen years of age, and was striking
in his looks, dark hair swept back into a queue with
a ribbon that matched his red waistcoat. His white

pants were tucked into tall black riding boots, and he was trim.

He was speaking in French to one of the aides, Mr. Alexander Hamilton. They both laughed, then continued a lively exchange.

"Misses?" Billy Lee said to us, gently trying to usher us to the door. I did not want to leave, nor did Elisabeth, but leave we did.

A wagon outside was being prepared to take the Baron and his charming interpreter to their quarters, Slab Tavern. With them would go their private chef and valet. And, of course, Azor.

This is what Elisabeth said on our way home: "I think I shall begin sewing right away."

"What shall you sew?" I asked.

"Pierre needs a good American coat," she answered.

I knew Elisabeth. She did not get what she wanted with her first Bounty Coat so she was going to try again. But she must have forgotten one thing: We have no cloth.

February 25, 1778, Wednesday

Elisabeth had not forgotten we have no cloth.

Without asking Mama or saying anything to me,

she went upstairs and took apart her cloak seam-by-seam (this I found out later). Now neither of us has anything warm to wear over our dresses — I hate her! She cares not for anyone but herself.

Worst of all is she did this secretly, pretending the reason she wanted not to go outside was because she didn't feel well. When I asked if I could wear her cloak, she said no, that she had snagged it on the fence and was mending the sleeve. She lied. And I believed her.

So when we went to Slab Tavern with only shawls to warm us, I thought nothing of it. We had a basket of corncakes Mama baked for the Baron, and for some reason I did not question Elisabeth about the package in her arms wrapped with string.

Slab Tavern is called such because of the large stone slab below the door. A wood sign above shows a horseman at full gallop. From here it is a short walk to Headquarters, but first you must cross the creek and pass Joseph Mann's cabin.

Inside were smoke and loud voices. Azor lay by the hearth lapping up a bowl of toddy. Von Steuben sat nearby with his pipe. His valet stood behind him, plaiting his pigtail. They looked not at us until we stood inches in front of them.

We curtsied and held out the corncakes. The Baron said something we understood not, then turned to his assistant. "Vogel," he called. Then Vogel said to us, "Little ladies, Lieutenant General Baron Friedrich Wilhelm Ludoff Gerhard Augustin von Steuben says thank ye. Now good-bye."

Elisabeth curtsied again and quickly held out her package.

"This is a gift for Pierre," she said, "from an American admirer. My name is inside on the collar, sir, please tell him." She backed away, tugging at my arm for I stood speechless, finally understanding what she'd done with her beautiful blue cloak.

February 26, 1778, Thursday

I have not spoken to Elisabeth since yesterday morning. I am too cross even to tell Mama what she has done.

Sleet and wind all day. We stayed in. For dessert after supper we roasted hickory nuts in Mama's long pan.

February 27, 1778, Friday

A great miracle has happened in Valley Forge.

We heard shouts early this morning and saw many neighbours running and driving their wagons toward the Schuylkill. Two miles above Headquarters at Pawling's Ford we saw nearly 100 cavalrymen riding into the icy water.

"The shad are running!" came the cry.

"Shad?" Papa said in amazement. "This time of year?"

We stood near Perkiomen Creek, where it flowed toward the Schuylkill, and watched. The soldiers formed a line across the river, wading their horses upstream while beating the surface with branches.

How cold their fingers must be! thought I.

Those standing in the shallows threw nets and pulled in shad by the thousands. These men were shaking with cold and their hands and lips were blue, but they kept working.

Finally an officer started a victory chant and soon all were out of the river and drying off with blankets brought by some of us. Along the banks many soldiers dropped to their knees in exhaustion, I thought, but soon I realized they were praying.

"Why?" I asked Papa.

He looked down at me and drew me into his warm arms. "Why? The famine is over, Abigail. Their prayers and mine have been answered. A river overflowing with fish in the middle of winter? It has not happened in thy lifetime, nor mine. Only Almighty God could arrange such a miracle, my daughter, and these good men are thanking Him."

A horseman caught up with us on the road back from the river and tossed a wet sack of fish into the back of our wagon.

"For thy family, Mr. Stewart," he called, and was off.

Papa waved his mittened hand and took up the reins. His beard was covered with frost, but still I saw his smile.

Mama baked the shad in vinegar then rolled up each piece. Sisters and I helped her tuck them into jars. Into each we poured vinegar and onions to pickle, then held dripping candles over them to seal. Our house stinks, but the pantry is full again.

February 28, 1778, Saturday

Sally lost her two top teeth, one early this morning when she bit into a biscuit, the other after she wiggled it for several hours. She kept sticking out her tongue through the space and making baby sounds, so I gave her my shoes to wear. Now she is in the barn playing with her doll and not bothering me any more.

Any time of day or night we hear drummers and fifers practicing. Papa calls it a "confusing noise" that disrupts the peace of our valley. Myself, it is the shots of muskets and cannons I most dislike.

March 1, 1778, Sunday

Johnny is three months old today. He is chubby! We made pretzels as big as Papa's hand by rolling dough into strips, then bending each one as if they were arms crossed onto shoulders. We pressed salt on top then baked them on the bricks. When they were done, Johnny held one in his little hand and chewed on it with his gums, for he has no teeth.

It snowed heavy all day. We could not see out the windows, so made do with firelight until bed. No church.

March 2, 1778, Monday

Still snowing.

I made up with Elisabeth. It is very near impossible to stay mad at someone you must look at hour after hour. Besides we had to make our way together through the storm to Headquarters. We took the little sleigh by ourselves, our old mare Buttercup pulling.

General Washington was sitting by the fire in a ladder-back chair. Nearby, trying to use light from the snowy window, sat an artist at his easel. He was sketching with charcoal a portrait of the General.

Mrs. Washington slipped us each a small square of gingerbread when we passed the kitchen. "That's Charles Willson Peale," she told us. "He painted the General a few years ago after the French and Indian War, and he plans to do the other generals here. He's a captain with the Pennsylvania brigade."

I knew he was a soldier because his toes were sticking out of his shoes.

March 3, 1778, Tuesday

Snowed all night. At seven this morning the wind stopped. We looked out to see a pink sunrise, but in the north were black clouds moving swiftly our way. Papa said to hurry, return the laundry to Headquarters before the storm arrived.

Billy Lee waved at us from the kitchen where he was pouring boiling water into teapots. Several officers in the front room talked in low voices as I hurried upstairs to knock on Mrs. Washington's door.

Thinking I heard an answer, I turned the knob and stepped in. A small fire blazed in the grate. She looked up from her desk under the window. A pair of spectacles was on her nose, and opened in front of her was a Bible.

"Ma'am, I'm sorry," said I, realizing she wished to be left alone.

"Quite all right, dear," she said, then turned back to her desk. At that moment Oney rushed in with apologies to her mistress and a hand on my elbow to usher me out.

"Shame!" she scolded me. "Lady Wash'ton is not to be disturbed at this hour. She has devotions every morning from eight 'til nine."

"I'm sorry, Oney."

"Hush, chile, don't cry. Billy Lee say he gots gingersnaps for you and sister, so come on now."

I felt miserable. To be scolded in front of Mrs.

Washington was something I'd not intended and though I managed not to bawl, my eyes filled with tears. Elisabeth and I stood in the kitchen to warm up and eat a cookie before the ride home. I heard boots in the hallway and men's voices, so I tried quickly to wipe my cheeks dry.

Someone came beside me, offering a laced handkerchief. I looked up into the blue eyes of Pierre. He spoke in French, then when I didn't respond, he said with a heavy accent, "Are you sad, pretty one?"

I said naught, only stared at him, wanting to hear more of his speech, so dear was his accent. Behind him stood Elisabeth. When I saw her mad face, I curtsied and immediately helped her carry the last bag to our sleigh.

We said nothing to each other the way home. I unhitched Buttercup and led her into the barn while Elisabeth dragged the sacks to our door. It was beginning to snow. When she looked at me I realized her chin was quivering.

"Abby," she said, struggling not to cry, "Pierre wasn't wearing my coat."

March 4, 1778, Wednesday

I have been trying hard to be nice to Elisabeth, for she breaks into tears every time I mention Pierre.

Mama isn't cross about the cloak, but she was most upset that Beth told so many lies.

"Elisabeth Ann," she said, "no matter how good thy deed may be, if thou art dishonest along the way that good deed will always be tainted."

Elisabeth was silent when we went to bed. She stared at the ceiling until Sally fell asleep then looked over at me by the window. I have a new candle so there's no worry of it going out tonight.

"Pierre is handsome and clever, yes, Abby?"

Yes, I nod. I'm trying to write.

"Suppose he stays in America after the war," she says. "He shalt need a bride, will he not? What dost thou think he's done with my coat? Answer me, Abigail."

"Well," say I, "mayhaps Pierre gave thy coat to a soldier who did not have one—that's possible. And about being a bride, thou art nice enough and pretty enough to marry anyone you please, Beth."

She is still awake *and* talking so I shall write this quickly before she asks me another question. Today Mr. Walker came by the barn while Papa was repairing one of the pens. I heard him say that a friend who lives west of Valley Creek was caught sneaking information to the British and he's going to be hanged tomorrow. Hanged! — one of our own neighbours! His poor family.

The other thing I learned is that a soldier I visited, the one who had his feet amputated, has died from fever. His wife, Mrs. Kern, would not leave his side and had to be carried away in a faint. She has no family now, no place to go. The Army says if she does not find another soldier to marry within three weeks she must leave the encampment.

I'm so sad for her. Tomorrow I shall ask if she can stay with us.

March 5, 1778, Thursday

It is very cold and windy. Mercury: 12 degrees.

Sally likes to help Papa with the milking. He carries her from the house to the hay so she shant get her stockings wet. When I saw her plaiting Brownie's tail, I laughed out loud. It reminded me of Vogel plaiting Baron von Steuben's pigtail, though I shall admit the Baron is a sight more handsome than Brownie's rump.

We spent the afternoon riding the edge of the encampment, asking for Mrs. Kern and asking the Army chaplains if there had been any weddings. Two, but none with Mrs. Kern.

Finally Papa drove south by Trout Creek. Here the tents were low and shabby. A woman came out to stare. She wore a cape over a ragged dress and her feet were muddy. She pointed down the row.

Papa drove on, calling for Mrs. Kern. The last tent had a small fire in front where a woman warmed her hands. Papa stepped down and told us to wait. He ducked into the tent and a moment later carried out in his arms a limp Mrs. Kern. We helped her settle into hay in the back of our wagon, Elisabeth and I on either side to warm her.

It's late now. We have made a cot by our bed upstairs for our new guest. She told us her name is Helen and that she is sixteen years of age. She fell instantly asleep and when Beth and I covered her with our quilt we noticed that Helen is soon to have a baby.

March 6, 1778, Friday

Sally and I had such a quarrel this morning that Mama put us in separate corners. I was most miserable and mad and embarrassed that our guest heard me crying.

When Ruth and Naomi came to call and invited me to slide on the river, I was bitterly angry to have to stay inside. It was a pretty day, no clouds.

But just before noon, when Mama was setting bread on the table, Reverend Currie and two men knocked hard on our door, calling for Papa.

"Hurry!" they cried, and Papa was off. Upon hearing their news Mama slumped at the table and lay her head in her arms.

"What, what?" we asked. Finally, the terrible words: "Some children have fallen through the ice."

I ran outside without my shawl. I ran to Headquarters and past. There in the ice, like a broken window, was a large hole. A crowd waited on the banks in the cold shade. Two soldiers stood wet and shivering, others shouted to one another. When I saw Naomi and Ruth huddled together I ran to them. They were dripping.

"Abby," they cried, "the boys are gone."

"What boys?"

"The Fitzgeralds, five of them, gone. They were chasing us and we heard a shot. We knew not until too late that it was ice cracking. It was shallow where we fell through, but, oh . . ." They embraced each other, weeping loudly.

It is half-past nine o'clock and my candle is short. Mama went with Mrs. Potter, Mrs. Adams, and the other ladies to comfort Mrs. Fitzgerald. I shall never see Tom again. I am sorry I hated him so.

March 8, 1778, Sunday

It rained all day. The air is warmer.

Some soldiers from the Vermont brigade were patrolling the lower end of the river. They found the bodies of Tom, Nate, Phillip, Howard, and Sammy near a beaver dam. I am so very sad for their mother and their three littlest brothers.

Helen Kern has brought much help to our chores of laundry and ironing. She made friends with Sally by sewing a tiny lace shawl for her doll. Helen is cheerful, but at night when the house is quiet I hear her crying under her pillow.

March 14, 1778, Saturday

The dark woods look green! There are buds in the orchard, on our apple trees.

Sisters, Helen, and I ran into the road without shoes. We ran across the fields. Our feet were cold, but it felt wonderful to have soft dirt in our toes. We ran to the crest of the hill and looked down into the valley below Mr. Stevens's house, where General Varnum is quartered.

There in rows and rows were soldiers drilling, marching, saluting, and loading muskets. Many were barefoot like us, but there were many in new uniforms, snappy blue jackets with buttons, white pants, tricorns. It was a sight!

We hurried as close as we could without being seen, and hid under some dogwood bushes still bare. Baron von Steuben paced in front of the men, shouting orders in several different languages — not one of them did we understand. There were three men with him interpreting. One listened to the Baron's commands, turned to Pierre, translated them into German, then Pierre turned to Alexander Hamilton with French words, which Mr. Hamilton then shouted into English. Only then did the soldiers respond to the "Left drill!" "Right drill!" or whichever it was.

Several times we heard Mr. Hamilton shout curse words, then shrug with embarrassment because that was what had been translated to him.

Thursday, Friday, and today we hid in the dogwoods to watch the soldiers. Elisabeth's eye was on Pierre, though he has not yet shown up wearing the coat she made him. Baron von Steuben, for all his arm-waving and swearing, is proving to be a good instructor and he's now learned enough English to curse directly at the men. His black coat comes to the top of his boots and flares out like a dress with his long strides.

Azor comes to the field, too, but often disappears after rabbits. I so want him to find us and play.

March 16, 1778, Monday

It has been a sunny week, no clouds, and the hills are greener each day. We can hear frogs at the creek and I am certain I saw a robin.

Yesterday we hung General Washington's shirts and such along our eastern fence to dry. I minded not so much the ironing and folding because the scent of fresh air has now filled our house.

Helen has taken up all Mama's mending and this morning baked a chocolate cake. She let Sally stir and lick.

Mrs. Washington sent Oney to ask our help. Tomorrow is a celebration for Saint Patrick's Day and she has many pies to bake. I'm glad she needs no eggs.

March 17, 1778, Tuesday

Sunny, breezy cool. We stood on the hill to watch the soldiers, our shawls wrapped tight. All afternoon there were blasts from muskets and cannons, mixed with rising puffs of smoke. The trill of fifes and steady rat-a-tat of drums made for a most festive mood. I hoped to see a drummer boy wearing the shirt I made.

After drills, the soldiers began a game called "Long Bullet," where they piled cannon balls in a heap, then stood back. With another ball they took turns seeing who could roll the longest and hardest and knock down the most.

We went in to help Mama with chores, then just before sundown returned to our hiding spot. There was the Commander in Chief George Washington playing catch with his officers! This turned into a game of wickets, using bent twigs poked into the ground for tiny gates. The ball they batted about was probably like the one we made Johnny out of deer hide.

I wondered if we were still at war, such was the sound of men's laughter and music. (This is Saint Patrick's Day, but who *is* Saint Patrick?)

March 18, 1778, Wednesday

When we woke again to drums and fifes I thought the soldiers were still celebrating. But on coming downstairs and hurrying through our breakfast, we realized the drumbeat was slower. I wanted not to go outside. If another woman was being drummed out of the army I would feel worse than if it were a man — I know not why, but I would.

Later Papa reported it had been an officer! — for perjury and other offenses.

March 20, 1778, Friday

Sunshine all yesterday and today. More buds on the trees, but not quite blossoms. We hiked to the creek — Elisabeth, Helen, Sally, and I — and found our secret pool. It is shallow with a sandy bottom, and as it's in the sun most of the day, it was not as icy as the running river.

Shrieking with cold we stripped down to our bare skin, jumped in heads under, then in an instant jumped out to dry ourselves with our skirts. We sat on the bank to let the sun dry our hair. Helen is smiling more. She knows not when her baby will be born, but the size of her belly seems to say "soon."

March 21, 1778, Saturday

Such a dark storm moved in this morning, so swiftly. Sally and I heard thunder while milking and quickly finished. We ran from the barn to the house in a blowing downpour, spilling much from our bucket. It rained hard all day. What we can see of the road from our window is a river of mud. In the distance was the sound of drums and fifes.

"Why are the men drilling even in the rain?" I asked Papa.

He said, "Von Steuben promised General Washington that he would turn our soldiers into an army and that is precisely what he is doing, Abby."

March 23, 1778, Monday

Still dark and rainy. We had to go to Headquarters as Monday is always Washday, rain or not. Such mud for our poor wagon. Helen came with me as Elisabeth is feverish and coughing.

Mrs. Washington and Mrs. Knox were in the kitchen — Mrs. Knox is so round I think she, too, is expecting a baby. They insisted we dry off before returning outside (to become soaked yet again!). I was sitting on a little stool by the kettle, my face and hands to the fire, when I felt something wet poke my side. I turned to see Azor, his nose now on my lap, and wagging his tail.

"Hullo, boy." I petted behind his ears and hugged his neck. When my hand felt the cloth on his back I could not believe mine eyes. Azor was wearing Elisabeth's coat!

The sleeves had been pulled up over his front paws and as it was a short waistcoat, it buttoned under his belly. Elisabeth's coat fit Azor!

It is late, the laundry is hanging through the house, still damp, and we girls are upstairs in our nightgowns. Elisabeth is shivering with fever — I have not the heart to tell her about Azor's new clothes.

March 24, 1778, Tuesday

As it is still raining, we are late returning the General's laundry. All morning we used hot irons with the hopes of drying things faster. It was almost suppertime before we drove to Headquarters. Papa covered the top of the wagon with planks of wood from the barn to keep the clothes dry underneath.

There in the parlour with Mr. Washington was von Steuben and Pierre and Alexander Hamilton, all speaking in a cheerful mixture of English and French. And there by the fire was Azor, having himself a nap, snug in his handsome blue coat.

What am I to tell Elisabeth?

March 27, 1778, Friday

Finally the storm broke. It has been sunny with just a few clouds in the afternoons bringing light rain, thus the roads are still muddy.

I was in the barn loft, playing dolls with Sally, when Papa came in the small door with a neighbour. When they began speaking in low voices I put my finger to Sally's lips, then mine, for they knew not we were directly above them.

"Why did you kill him?" Papa asked.

Sally and I looked at each other, wide-eyed, not daring to breathe.

"General Wayne told me to."

"A general told you to kill one of his men? Come now, this makes no sense."

"'Tis true. Every morning this same soldier has been coming into my barn and stealing a chicken. Every morning for a week, Edward. I reported it to General Wayne. He was sitting at a table writing a letter and would not look up at me. Finally I asked the General, I said, 'What shall I do?' General Wayne dipped his pen in the inkwell, kept writing, and without looking at me he said, 'Oh, just shoot him.'"

I could see through the crack in the floor that Papa's shoulders sagged and he was shaking his head. In a soft voice he said, "So thou shot the poor fellow?"

There were several moments of silence. "Yes," said the man. "He's buried by my south fence. No one knows but thee."

The rest of the day Papa was quiet. Sally and I spoke not about what we had heard.

March 28, 1778, Saturday

Baths after supper. (Papa always goes into the barn to brush Buttercup, so we shall have privacy.) We set the tub by the fire, but Helen is too broad to fit. She bent over to dip her head therein so I could wash her hair. She is very dear to us and this afternoon mentioned her dead husband for the first time.

"Today is my anniversary—we would have been married one year," was all she said.

Mama hung the lantern outside the door so Papa would know we were dressed and he could come dump out the bathwater. Before bed we popped corn and ate spice cake, sitting on the rug in front of the hearth. Color has returned to Elisabeth's cheeks, but she is still coughing. She sat in the rocker with Johnny, Mama's quilt tucked around them both.

"Abby," she said. "Hast thou seen Pierre? Is he wearing my coat, hast he mentioned my name?"

Helen glanced at me, because I had told her the story. How I wished I could spare Elisabeth shame and heartbreak, but too soon she would be well enough to visit Headquarters and one of these days Azor would be there, too. Maybe I should tell the truth.

I looked her in the eye and said, "I have seen Pierre, but he was not wearing thy coat."

April 1, 1778, Wednesday

Rain.

April 2, 1778, Thursday

Windy and cold.

April 3, 1778, Friday

Lucy came to visit! During tea she untied her bonnet, took it off, and handed it to me.

"Mama says I'm to return it, Abby."

We all were quiet. I was shocked by her appearance. Whoever had shaved her head had hacked away so that her hair was growing in uneven patches. She kept her eyes down. I tried to imagine what punishment her parents had threatened her with, that would have forced Lucy — willful, headstrong Lucy — to go out among people with a shaved head, no bonnet. I wanted to cry, she looked so drawn.

Mama gave one of her laced scarves to Lucy and showed her how to wrap it over her head. "Thou art pretty, dear," Mama told her.

Lucy said softly, "Thank you, Mrs. Stewart."

We crowded at the door to watch her walk away, up the road, and around the bend to her home.

April 4, 1778, Saturday

Mrs. Hewes brought news that a dancing master from New York is lodging at the DeWees house, down the hall from her room.

"He is small and limber," she told us, "yet old enough to be a grandfather. He plans to teach the officers and their wives how to dance."

When she said his name is Mr. John Trotter, I laughed so loud Mama and Papa stared at me. I know it was not polite, but his name makes me think of a dancing horse.

April 5, 1778, Sunday

A great commotion along the road met us on our way back from church.

Major General Charles Lee was finally freed by the Redcoats after more than a year in prison. I saw him on horseback as he rode up to Headquarters with drums and fifes escorting him. A grand dinner was given in his honour. Papa presented him with a new pair of shoes before the candles were lit, but when Papa came home, he was furious.

"He talks without listening, that man, and he has the foulest mouth I've ever heard use English. He was rude to Mrs. Washington, rude to the servants, and rude to me. Do ye think he was thankful that someone gave him new shoes when many men are still without?"

Papa slammed his fist on the table. "No. This is what he said, in front of the Commander in Chief and the other generals: 'I prefer pumps with a buckle. Must I wear garden slippers made for peasants?'"

April 6, 1778, Monday

Elisabeth and I learned something else about Major General Charles Lee and it wasn't nice.

When we arrived at Headquarters to pick up the wash, the long table was set for breakfast, but the officers and General Washington were only drinking tea, not eating.

Billy Lee whispered to us, "They's all waiting on Mr. Charles Lee to get out of bed."

We tiptoed upstairs to avoid the creaks. Just

past Mrs. Washington's closed door was another small bedroom and from behind its door we heard loud snoring. Elisabeth and I collected the laundry from the hallway, and hurried downstairs.

Oney was in the kitchen with Billy Lee and both were upset, whispering.

"Shame," she said, her hand on her hip. "That man don't deserve to be in the company of Mr. and Mrs. Wash'ton. He got stone drunk lass night and vomitted on the missus' finest tablecloth, then had to be carried to bed and now he's making everyone wait for breakfast. Shame, for shame. And yesterday bein' the Lord's Day."

Billy Lee shook his head. When we stepped down into the kitchen he handed us a small sack of kitchen cloths that needed to be washed, and he was still shaking his head when we left.

In the wagon we wrapped our shawls over our hair to keep the wind off. Elisabeth said, "Art thou going to tell Papa about General Lee?"

"No," said I. "It shall just give him a fit. He's likely to march over and take back his shoes and that might start another war."

April 7, 1778, Tuesday

Four other soldiers have been freed by the British and as they were being escorted to Headquarters we ran into the road, hoping one of them would be Mr. Fitzgerald, but no.

A young general arrived and is quartered with the Havard family. He has a fancy name — Marquis de Lafayette — and when he and Pierre speak to each other in French, they sound like two birds singing.

Mrs. Washington let Elisabeth and me serve tea to them. Lafayette has reddish hair, a narrow face, and a long pointed nose, which looks pinched on the end — he's not at all attractive, but he is quite cheerful. He holds his tea cup with his little finger in the air and laughs high and loud. I liked him, but Elisabeth said he needs to bathe.

"Also," she said, "the fellow should pick his teeth, for there's meat between them from last night's dinner."

This is the ninth day of high winds and cold.

April 9, 1778, Thursday

Johnny burned his little hand this morning and it's all my fault. I'm just sick, he cries so.

I was lifting the kettle lid, to pour in more oats, but from outside there came a loud boom of cannons. I was so startled I dropped the lid. Though heavy, it rolled like a shilling toward the rug where Johnny was and tipped over onto his hand. Poor Johnny! His eyes went wide then he began to howl.

I am upset at myself, but mostly cross — again — at the Army. I wish they would leave! Cannons are the worst — they're loud and wind carries the noise to our front step.

Mrs. Hewes brought ointment. Johnny lay in her arms staring up at her face while she rocked him. Finally he slept.

She said that she and Mr. Trotter are becoming acquainted. He plays the fiddle and has tried to teach her a minuet.

"I know not why the man thought he could start a dancing school at Valley Forge," she said after laying Johnny in his cradle. "The officers are busy and their wives are knitting night and day. Thank goodness the ladies think socks for the soldiers are more important than learning a jig."

April 10, 1778, Friday

Loud knocking on our door after all were in bed. Voices downstairs. A candle was lit. I could see it through the floor cracks, but I was so sleepy I pulled the quilt over my head. Soon there was the sound of boots coming upstairs.

"Abigail, Elisabeth." It was Papa. "Mr. Smith is here. Have ye seen Lucy?"

No, I shook my head. Helen stirred on her cot. Elisabeth buried her shoulders under the quilt with Sally. We were embarrassed to have Mr. Smith see us in our nightgowns.

"Do ye know where she is?" he asked.

"No, sir."

Mr. Smith held his lantern high, filling our room with light. He looked under our beds and in the wardrobe. Shadows on his face made him look sad.

"Forgive me, Edward, for waking thee," he said. "Lucy stepped out before supper to bring an egg from the barn. She never returned. We thought she might be with thy daughters. Lord in Heaven, what will I tell her mother?" He turned for the hall, his light sweeping across our beds and chimney, then down the shadowy stairs.

When we were alone again we began whispering.

"Where has Lucy gone?"

"Did she run off with a soldier?"

"Poor Lucy."

It was Helen who took our hands in the dark and said, "Let's pray for Lucy. Let's pray she shant harm herself."

April 12, 1778, Sunday

Lucy's family was in church, but they sat in back. I avoided looking at Mrs. Smith, but outside by the corral she caught my arm. Her eyes were wet and full of sorrow. The wind blew our skirts against our legs.

"Abby," she said, "if thou dost see Lucy, tell her to come home, please. All is forgiven, tell her."

"Yes, ma'am."

April 13, 1778, Monday

Washday, again bleached shirts and such. It takes all of us all day, from sunrise to supper—Mama, Sisters, Helen, and I—to wash, bleach, starch, rinse, wring out, hang up, iron, and fold. Papa keeps the fire hot and he has built a tiny pen by the hearth for Johnny so he shant crawl into the coals.

It was too windy to hang bed sheets on the fence. I shall be pleased when the Army leaves so our chores won't be so many.

April 14, 1778, Tuesday

After delivering the laundry to Headquarters, we took the long way home. As we came to Joseph Mann's cabin we saw several horses out front and one of the generals pulling himself up into his saddle. He commands the troops from North Carolina and Georgia, and is quartered here. He gave a friendly salute to Joseph, who was carrying firewood inside. Though Joseph is a freed Negro and a good honest man, two of the officers spit at his feet before galloping away. I was so provoked I wanted to throw a stone at the men, but the wagon seat was too high off the ground to reach one.

We crossed Valley Creek and soon came to Slab Tavern. Mrs. Washington had a note for us to give the innkeeper.

The tavern was crowded but we noticed Pierre.

He was sitting at a large side table and unlike the other men and officers with him, he smiled at us. Elisabeth and I curtsied. Pierre stood, then began making his way among the tables toward us.

"Dear ladies," he said, bowing slightly. He took Elisabeth's hand, kissed the ends of her fingers, then did the same with mine. We both were lost for words, but I knew from the color rising in Elisabeth's cheeks that she was well-pleased with his manners.

We were interrupted by the innkeeper, a gruff man, who took Mrs. Washington's note, broke the wax seal, read the message, then crumpled it in his large hand.

"Tell Her Highness that I have no plates to spare, nor cups, nor soap, nor whatever she might think of next." He pulled open the door and pointed us out.

That's when we saw Baron von Steuben coming up the path with Azor.

April 15, 1778, Wednesday

About yesterday:

At first Elisabeth did not realize Azor was wearing her blue coat, because he now also had a red sash draped over his back like a little soldier. We walked quickly past and not until we were in the wagon did she turn to study him. With her mouth open she looked at me with astonishment, pointed to Azor, and said, "Abby?"

That's all she said for the rest of the day.

Everyone is in bed now, except Mama is downstairs rocking Johnny. While we were fastening our nightcaps, Elisabeth stood with me at the window for a few minutes, looking out at the stars. Finally she whispered, "Please do not tell Mama who's wearing my coat, dost thou promise, Abby?"

I promised.

April 16, 1778, Thursday

The wind continues.

I woke in the night to the scratching of branches against the house. Sally woke up crying. She said she saw a man climb up the trellis by our window and he was waving his arm back and forth. I looked out, then tucked her in again.

"It's just our big old apple tree, Sally. Go back to sleep."

April 17, 1778, Friday

Mrs. Hewes invited us for afternoon tea. The wind was rough and as it was nearly an hour's walk, we dressed in wool and Mama carried Johnny inside her cloak.

Colonel DeWees has a fine stone house with many chimneys. The basement has become quarters for the army baker, a German named Christopher Ludwig. He uses several ovens to turn out all the bread needed, about sixty loaves an hour.

We sat in a parlour by a blazing hearth. The next room also had a fireplace and a broad plank floor where there was the sound of feet tapping.

"That's Mr. Trotter," she explained, "practicing. Sugar?" She cut off the end of the sugar cone and dropped it in Mama's cup, then one in mine, and all around, even Sally's.

"He has no students yet," she continued, "but last Wednesday evening that room saw a splendid theatrical performance."

"Dost thou mean a play?" I asked.

"Why, yes, dear. General Washington himself was in attendance, including several officers. There are plans for a production next month of the drama *Cato*. I hadn't realized how the General loves theater — he's quite a devotee."

Our visit was shortened because Johnny began to fuss and would not quiet down.

April 20, 1778, Monday

It is nine o'clock at night with a furious wind blowing. It is most frightening to look outside because the sky is red from fires burning on Mount Joy. Papa says mayhaps a spark from someone's chimney was carried by the wind. It has been six hours and still we see a glow from our window. I have just blown out my candle and my pen can see its way across the paper...

April 21, 1778, Tuesday

A messenger came this morning with a letter for me. I was alone in the house with Johnny because Papa had taken everyone in the wagon to look at Mount Joy.

The letter was from Lucy, telling me where she was.

After reading it I threw it into the fire.

"Tell not a soul," were the words below her signature.

And so I cannot even write about it.

April 26, 1778, Sunday

We woke this morning to silence. The wind has stopped! It blew hard for twenty-four days straight and we lost many branches in the orchards. The sun this morning feels warm like Spring. We girls ran out to feel grass under our feet.

The dogwoods are in bloom. Such beauty. Their branches look like they're wearing thick cotton leggings.

The fires on Mount Joy burned themselves out. Only steam rises from the hillsides.

April 29, 1778, Wednesday

Mama and I visited Mrs. Hewes to invite her to a wedding tomorrow. While water boiled for tea she led us through the various public rooms, showing us paintings on the walls, lovely scenics and portraits.

On entering the taproom we heard loud voices arguing at a corner table. Wanting not to interrupt, we quickly went through another door to the library, but we did hear this much: Colonel DeWees was complaining to three generals that soldiers had once again raided one of his buildings.

"Lumber and stones are missing!" he thundered. "How shalt I ever reconstruct the previous damage if the Army keeps stealing from the very people it's supposed to protect?"

We returned to the main hearth and over tea wondered in whispers how much longer we must bear with these soldiers.

Papa has stopped telling Mama how many tools and eggs have disappeared from our own barn. I'm thankful Brownie has not been stolen, else we shant have butter or cream.

April 30, 1778, Thursday

The wedding was held in perfect sunshine on the wide lawn in front of Headquarters. The bride is our friend Ann Pritchard from Chester County, and Papa has made her family's shoes for fifteen years. Her dress was white linen with lace along the sleeves and hem.

There were many tears among the older women watching, and some of the younger ones. Helen cried because the wedding reminded her she is a wife no more, but why Elisabeth wept I know not. Mayhaps because her Bounty Coat is being worn by a dog.

The groom we had not met before today. He is a cavalryman from Virginia. How handsome he looked in uniform. His tall riding boots were polished to match his scabbard. When the chaplain pronounced them man and wife, the groom threw his tricorn in the air and swept Ann into his arms. There were cheers and huzzahs as he lifted her into a carriage.

They are staying now at the Potters' in the small upstairs room above the kitchen.

After the wedding, Mrs. Smith came over to us. One glance at her sad eyes and I had to look away. Oh, I wish to God Lucy had not begged me to keep silent.

May 1, 1778, Friday

We were awakened at dawn by drumming and fifes. It was a jaunty tune. We hurried out to see soldiers parading and singing at the tops of their voices.

"What is it, Papa?" we asked.

He laughed. "Of course, how couldst I have forgotten? It's May Day."

Such celebrations all day. The soldiers had put up May Poles last night in each brigade, with streamers hanging down. They marched and sang in formation, their tricorns adorned with white blossoms from the dogwoods.

We watched from the hill while men played wickets and catch and Long Bullet. We could smell meat roasting from a huge pit barbeque by Headquarters, on the Schuylkill's south bank.

Papa took off his hat and waved it at the soldiers. "By God," he said to us, "it's about time those good men enjoy themselves."

May 2, 1778, Saturday

We have thrown open the doors front and back, and the small window in the kitchen. How good the warm spring air smells. All day we cleaned: scrubbed soot off the walls, raked the coals, Sally and I swept the floor with wet sand to gather up all the dust. Elisabeth and Mama moved beds and cupboards and wardrobes to mop. Helen carried the feather quilts out to hang over what is left of our fence — about fifty feet along the lane in front of our house is all!

General Washington made a new rule. Drummers and fifers may practice just twice a day, not whenever they please. From four to five o'clock in the afternoon and from five to six o'clock in the morning.

Mama is furious.

The noise wakes up Johnny and she does not want him fussing that early. He is now five months old and crawling everywhere. He crawled up six steps but knew not how to crawl down. He turned to look for us and when he did he lost his balance, tumbled headfirst, and raised such a wail we could not console him.

He has a bump above his right eye that is purple, but do you think he learned his lesson? No. He crawls for the stairs and one of us must watch him at all times. We are sore relieved when he finally goes to sleep at night.

This is why Mama is mad about drums and whistles — she calls them — playing at five o'clock in the morning.

May 3, 1778, Sunday

A clatter of many horses and two coaches interrupted our evening prayers. Papa got up from the table to look out.

Lights were blazing at Headquarters and there was the faint sound of singing.

"It seems someone has brought the General good news," Papa said to us when he returned from the window.

May 4, 1778, Monday

This morning while getting the laundry we heard much excited talk in the kitchen and front room of Headquarters.

Mrs. Washington wore an apron over her cotton dress and was overseeing the baking of pies and gingerbread. A roast pig turned on the spit, its juice filling the drip pan. General Greene's wife and several other ladies were helping. Their skirts filled the room with color and rustling.

I glanced in the other room. General Washington stood by the hearth, his arm on the mantel. He was smiling and listening to his officers.

"What hast happened?" I whispered to Billy Lee.

"Oh, Miss, the best news ever," he said. He nodded toward Pierre and Lafayette, who were surrounded by officers clapping them on their backs and shaking their hands.

Mrs. Washington leaned over to smile at us. Her sleeves were pushed up to her elbows and there was flour on her chin. "It's an alliance with France, Abby. They are coming to help us fight the British, praise God. We might be back in our own beds sooner than we think."

That explained why Pierre and Lafayette were having affection lavished on them. They were no longer just aides-de-camp, they were now our allies.

As Elisabeth and I carried the sacks down the hallway, we saw Mrs. Greene move gracefully into the parlour, also to shake Pierre's hand, then Lafayette's. She spoke perfect French! By the time we were going out the door, which stood open for the breeze, she was in a cheerful conversation with the two Frenchmen, Alexander Hamilton, and another aide named John Laurens.

How I wish I could speak that pretty language, too.

May 5, 1778, Tuesday

Ten straight days of sunshine!

Helen is so large with child she has trouble lying down at nights. Papa brought her cot down by the fire and raised the back so she can sleep sitting up. She complains not, but I know she is glad she doesn't have to climb the stairs.

Lucy's parents are sick with worry. They have come over twice this week. What am I to do? If I tell, Lucy shall feel betrayed, but if I keep her secret . . .

Is it proper to let her family suffer so?

May 6, 1778, Wednesday

What a grand day! It is late now, and I will try to put it all down before my candle goes.

At dawn we woke to the call of a fife and a single drummer. Such a beautiful morning, cool with sunshine, birds have returned to the trees, making nests and song. Finally there are flowers! The slopes of Mount Joy and Mount Misery are purple and red with azaleas; even the shade is bright with yellow from blooming laurel.

From 9:00 until 10:30 a hush fell over the valley. Everywhere soldiers with their officers knelt together in their brigades. Papa rode the outskirts of camp and said the chaplains were leading the men in prayer and thanksgiving; everyone is so humbly grateful for the French Alliance. We could hear voices rise with the singing of hymns, like an echo rolling across the valley. It was a most joyful sound and though I could hear no words, it filled me with peace.

When the singing stopped we climbed the hill to look down toward Varnum's quarters. There in perfectly straight rows the soldiers stood at attention. General Washington was on his gray horse, most dignified, flanked by his generals, all in sharp uniform. Papa explained this was "inspection."

We watched Baron von Steuben give orders. Each brigade responded in perfect form: turning, marching, and kneeling to load their muskets. (Azor, wearing his coat and sash, appeared nervous from the horses and guns; he ran off into the brush.)

Neighbours gathered to watch and there were excited cries of children when 13 cannons — six pounders — were rolled up to the rear of Conway's Brigade. General Washington gave a signal with a smooth wave of his hat and from the hill cannons began firing, one after another, a "13-gun salute."

It was so loud Johnny screwed up his face and would not stop crying. Sally held her hands over her ears. Papa raised his arm and cheered. I found myself with tears. I know not why, but there was beauty about the soldiers lined up so proud and clean, the cannons firing for joy, not war.

When the last echo from the last boom faded away, there began what Papa called a *feu de joie*. Now, one by one, muskets began to fire along the front rank from right to left, then down the second rank from left to right. The shots rippled back and forth, raising smoke like dozens of chimneys. The whole effect filled every one of us with excitement and hope — this was our army! No longer weak or frightened or cold. This *feu de joie* truly was a "fire of joy."

When the soldiers and officers — hundreds and hundreds of them — burst into cheer shouting "Huzzah! Long live the King of France!" Mama covered her face with her apron and wept with happiness.

My candle! Too short . . .

May 7, 1778, Thursday

To finish about yesterday:

When the ranks of muskets had quieted, there began another 13-gun salute from the hill, followed by another *feu de joie*, then the men again cheered. This time they shouted, "Long live the friendly European powers!"

Then once more the 13 cannons blasted, one after another, and once more the musket shots rippled through the ranks. Such smoke rose and filled the valley. By now every neighbour, child, and soldier was cheering and we heard the words, "Long live the American states!"

Johnny finally stopped crying, but he had hiccups and an unhappy face. Helen carried him into the house so he could settle down.

Papa stood behind Mama with his arms around her as we watched the soldiers file out. General Washington rode toward Headquarters on his beautiful horse, his arm waving his tricorn. We could not see his face, but we did hear him shout "Huzzah!" again and again.

Papa said, "Darling, if ever our Army was ready to stand up to the British, I believe it is now." We have just finished supper. The days are getting longer so I am writing by the last bits of sunlight.

I can see Headquarters. Our door downstairs is open for the cool night air, and we can hear laughter and singing. All afternoon officers and their ladies rode up to attend Washington's celebration. I wonder if Mrs. Washington baked enough pies!

Papa said that being allied with the French might help us shoo the Redcoats out of America for good.

May 8, 1778, Friday

Helen has been uncomfortable all day and unable to eat. Mama said this means her baby is ready to be born.

Now it is late, nearly half-past ten o'clock. Papa and Sally are sleeping, but Mama is downstairs with Helen. Every few minutes she cries out, then apologizes for crying.

"It's all right, Helen, dear," Mama tells her. "Thou mayest cry as loud as y'want."

May 9, 1778, Saturday

Before breakfast Papa left with the wagon to get Mrs. Hewes. Poor Helen. She is exhausted.

2 P.M. — Johnny and Sally are both having naps on the rug. There is sunshine on them from the side window. How they sleep through all our voices is a mystery.

Mrs. Hewes soothes Helen with a wet cloth. Now she and Mama are making Helen get up and walk around. She is so tired she cries without tears. "Thou must not die," I whisper to myself.

5 P.M. — Papa took Sally and Johnny to the Potters' where they shall stay the night.

May 10, 1778, Sunday

Am nearly too tired to write this, but Mama says there must be a record. It is four o'clock in the morning. The sun is not yet up.

A baby girl was born 15 minutes ago.

May 11, 1778, Monday

We have all had some rest and so it is easier for me to write.

Helen is sleeping in Mama's bed, her tiny daughter at her side. She has named her Olivia and she is a beautiful pink with a crown of red hair. Now I remember her father, the poor soldier in the hut whose feet were cut off. He had red hair, too, and the most gentle blue eyes. I sorrow that he is not alive to see his family.

Mrs. Potter came by with a pot of stew and corn-cakes. Mrs. Adams brought three apple pies. I knew not what to say when we opened the door and saw Mrs. Fitzgerald standing there with a basket on her arm.

"For the new baby," she said. She turned and walked quickly down the road. We lifted the cloth. There inside was a small quilt, booties, and a rag doll with a pretty blue dress.

May 12, 1778, Tuesday

We are a day late doing the General's laundry, but Mama said sometimes that is the way of things. We have strung two lines outside between the trees and fence, to let the sun do its quick work. It is much more pleasant to iron and fold when shirts and such dry in the fresh air instead of a sooty house.

Mama is teaching Helen how to nurse her baby and keep her clean and warm. I held Olivia and rocked her. Oh, she's beautiful.

May 13, 1778, Wednesday

We heard today that a girl with shorn hair was seen at one of the hospitals, working as a nurse. Mr. Smith and Papa left immediately to find her, and everyone is praying that it is Lucy.

All day I worried if I should tell where Lucy really is and worried myself so much that I got a terrible stomachache.

Reverend Currie came for supper, but I stayed in my bed listening through the floor cracks. He said a drummer boy was given 50 lashes for trading shirts with a British soldier. How this was discovered, he didn't say. Also, a soldier was given 200 lashes after he was caught running away from his commanding officer.

Reverend Currie asked our prayers for the great number of soldiers who are sick. Many are dying of the Pox and other infections. They are being buried naked so that their clothes can be passed on to others in need.

May 14, 1778, Thursday

The girl with shorn hair was not Lucy, which I knew it wouldn't be. At breakfast we prayed for her and for the soldiers. I silently asked God to show me what to do.

There are Indians in camp! Oneidas and Tuscaroras. I saw them walk along the road toward Headquarters, dressed in a curious assortment of deerskin leggings and soldier coats, feather ornaments and tricorns. They have volunteered to help General Washington.

"I want to see the Indians," Sally demanded. "Up close, please!"

I was fearful, but Papa said not to be. "There are Mohegan and Stockbridge Indians already serving the brigades from Massachusetts and Connecticut, Abby. And they are as loyal as any of the other men."

Still, I stayed home. Two hours later Sally burst in the front door.

"Abby, I saw one. He had tattoos on his arms and face and guess what he did!"

"What."

"He walked into Mrs. Washington's kitchen. There was a hot roast beef on the table and he grabbed a chunk of it with his finger and thumb and he twisted it out and he walked to the front door right past me — right past me — and he began to eat and dripped grease all over the floor. Abby, I saw an Indian and I feared not."

Sally is now in Mama's room telling her adventure to Helen and Elisabeth.

When I see how tenderly Helen holds her new little daughter, I wonder if I must now go to Mrs. Smith. How she must ache for Lucy.

May 17, 1778, Sunday

Baby Olivia is now seven days old and it is so warm and pleasant out Helen brought her to church.

Mrs. Hewes told us afterward that there was another theatrical production at the Bakehouse last Monday and the audience was most lively. The play was *Cato*. I wish I could go see the next one, but no children are allowed.

May 18, 1778, Monday

Washday.

We put Olivia in the cradle and Johnny in the pen, which makes him mad. He hollers and bangs his spoon against the wood.

I carried him outside so he could crawl in the grass while we hung the wash. I turned my back on him for just a moment and when I looked there he was in the middle of the road and horses were coming.

"Johnny, thou art too little to play here," I scolded as I lifted him to my hip. His mouth turned down and he let out such a wail Papa came over. Papa clapped his hands and set Johnny on his shoulders for a "Bumpity Ride." Soon he started laughing and I was able to finish with the clothesline.

At sunset I hurried down the lane to the Smith cottage. I had made up my mind. In a quick breath I told them Lucy is safe, that she shall return when her hair has grown to her shoulders.

Mrs. Smith wept with relief and her husband wiped his own cheek.

"Thank you, Abigail," he said.

After supper I wrote a letter to Lucy, saying I could no longer bear to see her parents' sorrow.

"But they know not where you stay," I wrote, "and for now I shant tell a soul."

May 19, 1778, Tuesday

General Lafayette and some of our troops are marching toward Germantown. They crossed the Schuylkill at Swede's Ford last night about midnight. Papa said 100 Indians came, too, and they are all camped at Barren Hill, twelve miles from Philadelphia. He said there may or may not be a battle.

General Washington says from now on the soldiers are free on Fridays, they don't have to drill. This is because the streams are warm enough to wash clothes and to bathe — but they may stay in the water no longer than ten minutes so they do not get a chill.

Oney came to say Mrs. Washington would enjoy the company of one of us to visit some hospitals at the southern edge of camp. Elisabeth refuses to go anymore, Helen has a baby to care for, and the three Potter girls have not been vaccinated for the Pox (we were last year).

Now that I'm ready to go to bed and am

remembering the last time I visited sick soldiers with Mrs. Washington, I'm sorry I said yes.

May 20, 1778, Wednesday

A lieutenant drove us in the wagon, south along Gulph Road to the Quaker meeting house. There were cots from one end of the room to the other.

The stench was worse than a latrine and there was a sharp odor I could not recognize. To keep from gagging I covered my mouth and nose with my shawl. Why the windows and doors were not open to let in fresh air I know not. I followed Mrs. Washington as she worked her way down the crowded rows, talking to the soldiers who were awake and praying with them. She drew not away from smells or the sight of amputated feet.

In a corner of the room a doctor was giving inoculations for the Pox. One soldier whose cheeks were covered with sores tossed on his bed in a fever, moaning and crying out. He was shivering even with a blanket over him. The doctor took a feather and with the sharp end of the quill, scooped it into one of the man's oozing pox. Then he turned to a waiting soldier who had his sleeve rolled up and a fresh cut on his arm from the doctor's pen knife (I was sickened, watching).

Into this fresh cut the doctor dabbed a bit of the goo and said, "There you go, friend. Thou shalt soon have a fever, but worry not. More die from the disease than vaccinations."

This was repeated with nine soldiers who'd been waiting outside in the sunshine.

When we climbed up to the wagon seat we saw a graveyard across the lane. Two men were finishing digging a grave. Beside them lay the thin shape of a body rolled into a blanket. Without a word the men lifted, then dropped the body — naked — into the grave, each holding an edge of the blanket. While one shoveled dirt, the other carried the blanket to the hospital and handed it through the door.

Our wagon dipped down into a gully and as it rose again over a hill I turned around. I could see through a window that the blanket was being spread over one of the sick men. I glanced back at the cemetery.

"Why are there no names on the graves?" I asked Mrs. Washington.

She smiled. Sunlight was on her face and she closed her eyes to enjoy the warmth. "My dear, it is one of those puzzles. Quakers, God bless them, are against war. They do not honour soldiers, so that is why their graves are marked not."

May 21, 1778, Thursday

Elisabeth and I were with Papa at the north end of our orchards, trimming branches that had broken in the winds last month. A coach passed us, its horses at a high trot with a coachman riding above the rear wheel. Sally was already running from the house (barefoot still, as Papa has had no time to make her shoes).

Papa laughed and said, "Go on, girls," and we, too, ran with Sally.

When we saw the very plump lady stepping down from the coach with a tiny infant in her arms, we cried "Hello, Mrs. Knox!" She waved and called us over to look at her new baby.

A handsome soldier inside the coach helped her down then stepped out with a cane. He wore high-heeled boots and was limping quite a bit. He took Mrs. Knox's elbow to guide her into Headquarters.

"Girls," she said to us, "this is Mr. Benedict

Arnold, my official escort. Would you like to take turns holding the baby when we get inside?"

Sally went first, sitting on the stool by the kitchen hearth. Mrs. Washington cooed and fussed over the tiny thing, and not until we were home did I realize no one said if it was a boy or a girl or what its name was.

While Elisabeth held the baby, we could hear Benedict Arnold in the parlour talking to General Washington. He was describing his horrible wound from the Saratoga Campaign seven months ago and how he is only now able to hobble about with great pain.

While I held the baby — only for a quick moment — Mrs. Washington told us there will be no more plays at the Bakehouse.

"Can ye imagine?" she said. "Of all the things Congress has to worry about and they pass a silly resolution. This is what it says." She pulled a piece of parchment from her apron pocket, unfolded it, and held it at arm's length to read: "'Any person holding an office under the United States, who shall attend a theatrical performance shall be dismissed from service.'" Mrs. Washington handed the page to Mrs. Knox so she could read for herself then said, "Sometimes government has the most ridiculous notions."

May 25, 1778, Monday

When Elisabeth and I arrived at Headquarters to pick up the laundry, there were several ladies dressed in their best, saying farewell to one another.

Billy Lee told us, "There's soon to be a battle, so the wives are going home."

"Battle?"

"Oh, not here, Miss. General Wash'ton will take his soldiers somewheres else to fight the Redcoats, don't you worry none. Not here, nosir."

May 26, 1778, Tuesday

Elisabeth and I were putting clean linen on our beds when Sally stomped upstairs, excited and out of breath.

"A soldier is here asking for thee, Beth. Hurry."

I looked at my older sister and could see her eyes brighten. "Is it Pierre?" she whispered.

"He said naught." Sally was already hurrying

downstairs, making a lot of noise for someone with bare feet.

Elisabeth smoothed her skirt. She smiled tenderly at me before turning for the stairs.

The soldier standing by the hearth looked proud in his uniform, white stirrups over new shoes, a tricorn under his arm, a handsome coat. When he smiled at her and I saw his top teeth were missing, I knew the handsome coat was the one made by Elisabeth.

I could not see her face.

"Yes?" she said softly.

We all dared not breathe. Helen was in the rocker with Johnny on her lap, Mama at the fire, Papa was sewing a piece of leather.

Sally stared at the soldier, then said, "Canst thou do this?" She stuck her tongue out through the space where her two new teeth were barely showing. "Look." But she spit by mistake and we all in one voice said, "Sally!"

The soldier laughed and reached over to pat her head. "I jess come by t' thank Miss Elisabeth Ann for making me a coat. No one ever done such a nice thing for me ever. Thank you, Miss. I'll be going now."

He shook Papa's hand, smiled again at Elisabeth, then stepped outside.

"Mister!" called Sally. "What is thy name?"

"Ben," he said. "Ben Valentine, Second Pennsylvania Brigade."

May 27, 1778, Wednesday

The soldiers who camped with General Lafayette outside Philadelphia a few days ago returned this morning in a drizzle. No shots were fired. Papa said it was just a drill.

It rained all day and was cold enough to wear our wool stockings.

Elisabeth was gloomy. "I wish I had been kinder to Ben Valentine," she told me in the barn while we milked Brownie.

"Thou wast not mean to him, Beth."

"No, but I could have offered him tea. He was good to come by, was he not, Abby?"

Odd, but I am no longer jealous of Elisabeth. She is much prettier than I, but she is not perfect. Today, I think she is even a bit heartsore.

May 28, 1778, Thursday

Rain and wind.

May 31, 1778, Sunday

It has been dark and rainy for five days. We all have colds so we stayed in. Papa led us in prayers and hymns instead of taking us to church. We can see that the soldiers are also inside. The valley is quiet with chimney smoke coming from the huts.

Johnny kept us amused by a new trick he's learned. He pops his lips. Also, he now can climb to the top of the stairs. He stays on his stomach and tries to crawl down backwards, but twice he bumped his chin and cried so loud, we carried him back to the rug. Papa made a gate at the bottom of the stairs from one of the cupboard doors so now Johnny must find something else to do.

Sally keeps asking me to tell more about Lucy.

"Do not worry, Sally. I promise she's safe."

June 1, 1778, Monday

The roads are muddy again, but now the sun has returned, warmer than before.

The soldiers practice until sundown so we are hearing cannons and muskets fired all day. Papa said General Washington is getting ready to move the Army to battle, but nearly 4,000 will stay behind — those who are sick or crippled.

Because the air is warm, there is a terrible stench as we ride at the edge of camp. Dead horses need to be buried — Papa said 1,500 have died! At night we hear crows and owls fly from their nests in the dark hillsides to pick at their carcasses and other butchered animals.

Washday.

June 2, 1778, Tuesday

We took Johnny to the creek after delivering the laundry to Headquarters. I held him while he kicked his chubby legs in the water and shrieked. He is six months old and will stand up and take a step if someone holds his arms. In his mouth, on his bottom gum, is a tiny white bulge where a tooth is trying to grow.

I like to hug him and twirl him over the stream so his feet skim the water. When he laughs I am so thankful he's alive — our first brother to make it through the winter.

I find myself more patient with Sally because my worry for Johnny has passed.

June 3, 1778, Wednesday

Reverend Currie delivered a letter for Mama. She sat at the table where there's light from our window, and carefully broke the seal. Her eyes fell to the signature.

"It's from Philadelphia, from your Auntie Hannie," she said. I watched Mama's face as she read silently. Finally she looked up.

"Girls, ye have a new cousin. His name is Matthew Robert and all is well. Bless Hannie, she's now got six little ones, my goodness. But here is the best part, listen:

'The baby is ever so tiny and needs constant attention as do the five others. I thank God your friend Lucy is here to help, for I know not how I would rest otherwise . . .'"

All heads turned to me as Mama continued to read.

"'. . . Lucy has asked me to relay her where-abouts to you. She is terribly quiet and I worry about her cough and lack of appetite. She was several days without food or shelter while making her way here, hiding in the forest from soldiers. Lucy begged to stay with us, until her hair has grown, for she is too full of shame to face her parents otherwise. I pray, for her mother's sake, that her hair grows quickly. Your loving sister, Hannie.'

"Why did she go all the way to Philadelphia?" Mama asked me.

I took a deep breath. "Lucy knew Hannie would not turn her away for they became fast friends when we visited in January. She knew she would be safe." Here I burst into tears, finally free of Lucy's secret.

Mama put her arms around me. "It's all right, dear."

June 4, 1778, Thursday

I was so happy yesterday but I'm not happy today.

We saw with our own eyes a soldier being hanged. We happened along the road just as the horse bolted from under the tree and the poor man kicked and struggled. His hands were tied behind his back, but he managed to free one hand and try to grab the noose. I burst into sobs, Elisabeth did, too. Oh, it was horrible, horrible — the poor man.

Talk on the road was that he was a spy and that one of his friends shall be hanged tomorrow. I hate the Army—I want them to leave!

June 7, 1778, Sunday

Beautiful drive to church. Daisies, white and yellow, are in bloom along the road and up the hillsides. We are a large family now with Helen and baby Olivia, Mama and Papa, Elisabeth, Sally and I, and our wiggly Johnny.

An announcement from the pulpit made us all break into cheers (something I have not before heard in church): The British have released six patriots from the Walnut Street jail in Philadelphia, they are in reasonably fair health, and they shall return to Valley Forge tomorrow. The name that made me want to cry for joy was this one:

Mr. William Fitzgerald.

June 8, 1778, Monday

Mrs. Fitzgerald was standing in the road looking south when we passed her on our way to pick up the wash from Headquarters. With her were her three littlest boys, standing straight, their faces clean and hair combed. They were about five, six, and seven years old, and the sight of them made my heart squeeze tight.

How brave she was to stand there, ready to meet her husband, to give him the tragic news about their five older sons. She seemed a different woman now that she knew she must be brave.

When Buttercup pulled the wagon around the bend and out of her sight, I broke down weeping, heavy sobs that would not stop. I was heartsore for Mrs. Fitzgerald, but thrilled her husband was safe. I felt sad for also hating Tom and that he'd not had a chance to grow up and be the good man his father is. I am very blue . . .

June 9, 1778, Tuesday

I am even more heartsore than yesterday.

Mrs. Washington left a few hours ago.

She is traveling back to Mount Vernon and I shall probably never see her again.

Elisabeth and I returned the wash about half-past nine this morning. Oney and Billy Lee were packing trunks and the other servants were up and down the stairs with things. The kitchen smelled of fresh apple pie and coffee, and several officers — I remember not their names — were talking with General Washington in the front room.

Billy Lee said to us, "Lady Wash'ton will be down soon, after her devotions, Misses. Then yous can say good-bye."

But I wanted not to say good-bye. So much kindness had come from her kitchen and her words. The long, cold winter had not seemed so lonesome because of her.

"Dear girls." We turned to see her coming down the stairs. She wore a dress of blue muslin with tiny white buttons up each sleeve. She seemed beautiful to me, though I remember how plain I'd thought she was at first.

We've known her just four months and I can say she is the most cheerful, loving person I have ever met. Never did I hear her say a cruel word or complain about her surroundings. Mama said at Mount Vernon Mrs. Washington has more than 300 slaves and a luxurious mansion. We are not of her social class and we had little to offer her, yet still she welcomed us as friends.

She gave us a small basket as we curtsied out the

door. "Inside there ye shall find a little something for your mother and yourselves, too. God bless ye, dear girls."

We hurried home. Mama put the basket on the table, and removed the cloth. Inside was a small leather pouch that jingled with coins. She peeked inside and read the attached note: "'40 shillings per month for Headquarters' laundry in addition to 4 shillings per dozen pieces for Mrs. Washington.'

"Why there must be a fortune here, my goodness. And what's this?" Mama lifted out a small stack of handkerchiefs, tied with a red satin ribbon. They were cotton trimmed with lace, folded neatly. There were ten, two for each of us and with them this note: "With fond wishes to Mrs. Stewart, Elisabeth, Abigail, Sally, and Helen Kern. We spent just a brief time together, but I shall always remember ye. Martha Washington."

June 10, 1778, Wednesday

The days are warm and drowsy.

We made soap with beet juice so it would turn pink, then we scented it with lavender. Helen and Sally gathered the flowers from along the creek then crushed the petals into a sweet-smelling oil. After mixing, we poured it into our wooden mould that we'd lined with a damp cloth. It must set 24 hours.

June 11, 1778, Thursday

By noon the soap was dry so we cut it into cakes with a wire. This is the most pleasant chore of them all. We boiled more lard and this time added carrot juice to make it yellowish, and crushed rosemary leaves for perfume.

Tomorrow Sally wants to use spinach for green, then add rose petals for scent. My opinion of green soap is this: It looks like something from the bottom of our well, but I wanted not to hurt Sally's feelings so kept this to myself. (My favourite is pink with a rosemary fragrance.) What a luxury to again have soap. I shall appreciate my bath even more, knowing our soldiers shant see their own homes for weeks to come.

June 12, 1778, Friday

Mama says the best thing about the Army leaving soon is that there shall be no more drums and whistles at five o'clock in the morning.

I shall be glad to see no more hangings.

Cannons and muskets still fire throughout the day.

Papa made a new butter churn. It hangs in the kitchen from a rafter by the front door. Every time one of us walks by we push it to swing. Sally finds this most amusing and because she is bossy, she has assigned us each a task:

I set aside the cream from Brownie's milk; Helen pours it in the top of the churn; Elisabeth corks it; then Sally gets to swing the barrel first. She pushed it so hard though, it banged into the wall. Papa has now re-hung it further into the room and raised it several inches so we won't bump our heads. He gave Sally a stick so she can reach it.

June 13, 1778, Saturday

We bathed today at the stream. Johnny thinks he can swim. He crawls fast from the bank, across the narrow sandy beach, then into the water. He cries not when his head goes under or when the current tries to carry him away. We must watch him every moment.

Next week we will leave him home with Mama so we can swim without worrying about him.

June 15, 1778, Monday

Our wash dries fast in the sun and breeze. The grass is wonderful under our bare feet.

Sally stepped on a wasp and it kept stinging her and even crawled up her ankle to sting her there several times. How she wailed! Papa carried her inside where Mama smoothed baking soda on all the bites. All of an instant Sally stopped crying, that is how fast soda works. Mama said if it happens again when we're out in the field to use mud.

Tomorrow and Wednesday we will make our candles, enough to last through next winter. When I carry mine upstairs and look out a snowy window, I shall remember our soldiers. I shall remember to complain not about being cold or having unpleasant chores.

June 18, 1778, Thursday

Riders galloped through Valley Forge early this morning, crying out, "The British are leaving Philadelphia!"

Where they are going, Papa knows not. Moments later our soldiers began forming ranks. The generals are on horseback and we've seen Baron von Steuben riding next to General Washington. Tents outside camp are coming down as it is warm enough to sleep without shelter, and there is much shouting of orders and busyness.

June 19, 1778, Friday

We woke at five o'clock this morning to a drumbeat, a quickstep. We hurriedly dressed — Mama held Johnny, Helen carried Olivia in her shawl — and we ran into the road. It was dark save for a few distant torches.

"The Army is leaving," said Papa. "God bless them and God bless America."

By noon the huts were deserted, the valley was quiet. We could see the camp followers straggling out with hand-carried belongings and a noisy assortment of children and dogs.

Papa rode into the encampment with Mr. Potter and Mr. Adams. "It is a mess," they said when they returned. "It shall take weeks to bury the garbage and dead animals."

Before Mrs. Hewes could move back into her house, Mama and us girls went to clean. What a sight. All I can say is there were many muddy boots that went in and out, and many chairs and tables that banged against the walls and scraped the floors. The entire house needs paint.

And I suspect Mrs. Hewes will be disappointed the officers used her parlour to powder their hair and wigs, for the walls are covered with white dust. (I think a respectable home should have its own little powder room with looking glass, combs, etc., for neatness' sake.)

Mrs. Adams brought two of her roosters to clean the chimneys. Her husband climbed onto the roof and into each cold chimney he dropped one of the birds. They flapped their wings frantically, brushing the stone insides until chunks of soot began raining down. After a few minutes they were so tired they dropped into the empty hearths. The birds did not die, but they looked like they wished to.

I suspect the Adamses will have roast chicken for supper tonight.

June 20, 1778, Saturday

A hush has fallen over the valley. I'd forgotten how quiet it used to be and how much I love the stillness.

Where the Army has marched we know not. Every meal Papa leads us in prayer for the safety of our soldiers and victory for General Washington.

Just before sunset a letter arrived for me. I quickly broke the seal. After reading, I did not throw it into the fire, but pasted it onto this page:

Dear Abigail,

I must tell you some surprising news . . .

Yesterday I visited the wigmaker, remember his tiny shop next door to Auntie Hannie? He said my hair was made into a beautiful wig for the wife of a general who wintered at Valley Forge. When I inquired "who is she?" he looked through his papers and showed me the order. Do you know, Abby, that the note was signed by Martha Washington herself? Now I can sleep again. Thank God my foolish mistake did not land my hair on the head of one of those plump British officers.

How I miss you, Abby, and my own family as well. I shall soon be home.

Your loving friend, Lucy

June 22, 1778, Monday

Papa has gone with the other men to reclaim their fences. All day they worked at tearing down huts and loading wagons with wood.

The children comb the grassy fields for musket balls to use for marbles. Mama says the flat ones she can make into buttons by drilling two holes in the center.

Elisabeth and I walked to the schoolhouse. It's being used still as a hospital, which pleases me. Everywhere we look are signs of fresh graves. Papa said nearly 3,000 soldiers died this winter and there was not even a battle.

At supper Papa poured each of us a toddy and held up his mug to toast. "To our new Army," he said. "Six months ago all we had was a bunch of volunteers from the 13 colonies and now look at them, ye saw them, girls. We have a real Continental Army now, ready to send the Redcoats back to King George, hip hooray! May God bless our every man."

June 23, 1778, Tuesday

The sun is hot.

I saw Elisabeth sitting under our big oak tree,

writing a letter against her knees. Her ink jug was burrowed in the dirt beside her so it wouldn't tip over.

I sat in the shade and leaned against the trunk so I could spy at her paper. She covered it with her hand, then turned to me with a laugh.

"Since thou must know, Little Sister, I am writing to Ben Valentine."

"Why?"

"Abby, he was kind and gentle, he appreciated my coat even though I had sewn it with selfish motives. I'm writing to tell him I shall pray every day for his safety and well-being. And when the war is over I shall cook him dinner."

I knew not what to think so I said something silly. "Well, then, why do thee not also write a letter to Azor?"

Elisabeth laughed again. "Oh, Abby."

June 26, 1778, Friday

This has been the hottest summer I remember. The nights are so steamy we sleep on cots outside, but the mosquitoes are vicious. They do not bother us if we stay in with the doors and windows fastened, but then the heat is so heavy we cannot sleep.

So Mama has taken to rubbing laurel leaves and mint on our faces, hands, and necks, and having us sleep in long-sleeved dresses with cotton leggings. This way we can lie on our cots and stare at the sky. The stars are so bright we can see the dark hillsides and the shadows of bats as they fly about. All night there is a faraway murmur from the creek.

I think about Mrs. Washington. Somehow I feel not so lonesome for her, knowing she may be wearing Lucy's beautiful brown hair. I'm beginning to believe that unpleasant events often work together for good, like a coat of many colors.

June 29, 1778, Monday

Criers rode through Valley Forge this morning with news of a battle yesterday near Monmouth Courthouse. While our Army fought the British, General Washington rode back and forth among the ranks of his soldiers until his horse dropped dead from exhaustion. At sunset both armies stopped fighting so they could rest, then after midnight the enemy snuck away.

We know not how many of our soldiers were wounded or killed, but we worry for them. They are like family to us now. Elisabeth must wait patiently for word about Ben Valentine.

I watch her wait and I puzzle how it has happened that strangers from last winter have become so dear.

June 30, 1778, Tuesday

More news about the Battle of Monmouth:

Three women stepped in to help with cannons after their husbands fainted from the heat. It has been the hottest June in memory and even some of the horses collapsed.

Other news pleased me: General Charles Lee was stripped of his command by General Washington, because he disobeyed orders and retreated in haste.

Papa said, "Bravo. The man is a coward, an embarrassment to the Patriots."

July 3, 1778, Friday

Much pie baking and visiting between the farms to borrow eggs, flour, sugar, bacon, and so-forth. We are all very much glad to replenish our larders and not worry about thieves, although if our soldiers should again be in need, I think I shall be one of the first to share.

Tomorrow is a celebration for Independence Day. It has been two years since the Declaration was signed and even though the British shant leave us alone, we shall still have a party!

Papa sawed our front and back doors in half, then re-hung them so we can latch the lower half. With the tops open we catch a breeze, but Johnny can't crawl out and no wild animals can crawl in.

July 4, 1778, Saturday

It is late and I am tired.

A breeze rose this afternoon that made the heat bearable. We are sleeping inside with windows open and the upper doors open. The breeze is pleasant and not allowing mosquitoes to land on us. I am dead sleepy, thus shall be brief.

Some of the soldiers' May Poles were still in camp, so much of the day we children played and ran around them, using rope to swing on. There are still many trinkets to be found in the grass and dirt, even enough cannon balls to play Long Bullet.

At noon, blankets were spread in the shade along the banks of the Schuylkill. A finer barbeque I've not enjoyed — Mr. and Mrs. Fitzgerald butchered two of their cows to share with everyone, so grateful they are for all our prayers and concern. There also were dozens of meat pies, fruit pies, and pumpkin pies passed around; cider and sweet lemonade, too.

Baby Olivia is nearly two months old and is quite content. No wonder. There is always someone wanting to hold her and kiss her. Johnny looks like a giant next to her. He now pulls himself up and with one hand on a tree trunk walks around it in a circle, around and around. He is sore proud of himself.

Colonel DeWees gave a patriotic speech, but I did not listen. It was hot and I wanted to play in the stream.

Tomorrow I shall have to ask Mama for more paper to sew together, so I can keep writing my journal . . . I want to record every word we hear about our Army. Papa says the war might continue many more months, but he's not worried. He has so much confidence in General Washington and our newly trained soldiers, that he says we shall beat the British for sure.

The crickets are loud tonight! And there is an owl nesting in our barn. When he flies out to do his night hunting he passes our window, his wings like a whisper

One more thought before I blow out my candle. I do hope Ben Valentine receives Elisabeth's letter.

Epilogue

During the Battle of Monmouth, Ben Valentine was shot in the left wrist. His arm was amputated on the field, then he was sent to Philadelphia to recover. Over the weeks, Elisabeth visited him, a romance developed, and they were married in the summer of 1779.

Two summers later, at the age of 15, Abigail married a blacksmith named Willie Campbell. Another wedding took place at this time: The young widow, Helen Kern, married Daniel Kern, her deceased husband's brother, so she remained "Mrs. Kern." They eventually had five children together.

In 1787 the Valentines and Campbells, the Stewarts and Kerns, moved west to homestead in the Ohio River Valley.

Abigail and Willie had nine children. Their daughter, Hannah, became the first woman doctor in Philip's County, and three sons became lawyers; one moved to Washington City to be President Thomas Jefferson's personal counsel.

Abigail died in 1823 at the age of 57, after being

thrown from her horse. Willie died two years later...
some say from grief.

Elisabeth and Ben had four daughters who died in infancy, but their sons, Paul and Nathaniel, grew up to be explorers. Paul helped map the Missouri River and its surrounding territory. He was good friends with Daniel Boone.

At the age of 13, Nathaniel ventured to Boston and signed on as a cabin boy aboard the ship Otter, captained by the legendary China trader Ebenezer Dorr, Jr. They sailed into Monterey Bay in October of 1796, the first American vessel to anchor in a California port.

Elisabeth and Ben died together when their house caught fire in 1825.

Life in
America
in 1777

Historical Note

The American Revolution, also known as the War for Independence, was fought between 1775 and 1783. For the first time in history, the thirteen American colonies banded together as a nation so that they could fight against Britain and achieve their own independence. Over the years, Britain and their ruler, King George III, had given the colonies a lot of freedom to govern themselves by allowing each colony to have its own legislature. In return, the colonies were given the protection of the British Empire and its famous Royal Navy.

But then, in 1764, Britain imposed the Sugar Act and, a year later, the Stamp Act on the colonies. These acts forced Americans to pay very high taxes on sugar, legal documents, newspapers, and other items being imported into the colonies. Since the colonies had not been consulted about this, there were many riots and protests. This was "taxation without representation," and the colonists had no intention of cooperating. In 1767, Britain's Parliament passed the Townshend Acts, which placed outrageously high taxes on items such as paper, glass, paint, and tea.

The colonists continued to protest and tried to boycott British products. Finally, in late 1773, some rebellious citizens in Boston crept onto a British supply ship in Boston Harbor. They found more than three hundred chests of tea and dumped them into the water. Britain was furious about this and began to pass even more punitive laws, which the colonists described as the Intolerable Acts.

For many years the colonies had acted like thirteen little countries, but now it was time to work together. In 1774, the First Continental Congress met in Philadelphia, with representatives from twelve of the thirteen colonies. They agreed to remain under British authority, but decided that they wanted the right to create their own laws and taxes, without British interference. They also agreed to ban most imported products from Britain. Britain's response to this was to bring troops, the Redcoats, into the colonies. While the colonies had no army of their own, small local volunteer groups began to form militias, so that they would be able to defend themselves.

Then, one night in April 1775, British troops

were ordered to march from Boston out to Concord, Massachusetts, where they were planning to arrest rebel leaders and seize weapons and ammunition. That was the night Paul Revere crossed Boston Harbor and took his famous ride on horseback through the nearby towns, shouting a warning to one and all. When the Redcoats arrived in Lexington, the rebels — also known as the "patriots" — were there to greet them.

Nobody knows who fired that first shot, but it is called "the shot heard 'round the world." The rebels ended up chasing the Redcoats all the way back to Boston. Considering how many thousands of shots were fired that day, surprisingly few people were killed, but the war had now begun.

A few weeks later the Second Continental Congress met and decided to form a Continental Army. They selected a man who had been a great hero in the French and Indian War to be their general. His name was George Washington. He had never run an army before, but he turned out to be a born leader.

Early in 1776, a writer named Thomas Paine published a pamphlet titled *Common Sense*. In it, Paine described the terrible tyranny King George III was forcing on the colonies and called for complete independence. The Continental Congress agreed. They appointed a small committee to draft some resolutions for the colonies, now to be described as "states." Three of the five men on the committee were Thomas Jefferson, Benjamin Franklin, and John Adams. It was primarily Jefferson who wrote a document called the Declaration of Independence, and the Congress voted it into law on July 4, 1776.

There seemed to be very little chance that these tiny united states could defeat the great British Empire. Britain had a population of eight million people, a thriving economy, and the finest naval and armed forces in the world. The total population in the colonies was only two and a half million, and half a million of these citizens were still pledging allegiance to King George. They were called "loyalists" or "Tories," and they refused to help the patriots in the war against Britain. There were also half a million slaves, who were not allowed to fight, and two hundred thousand more people who were "neutralists" and would not fight at all. The colonies were not only outnumbered, but they also had no army, no navy, and almost no factories to manufacture the weapons and other supplies they would need. The only advantage they did have was that Britain was three thousand miles away, across the Atlantic Ocean, and would have a hard time supplying its own troops.

Britain's goal in the war was to squash the rebellion and force the colonies back under British rule, while America's goal was to gain total freedom and independence. The first major skirmish was the Battle of Bunker Hill—which actually took place on nearby Breed's Hill, in Boston. Neither side won. The British should have easily defeated the small amateur militia but, because the undermanned patriots fought so well, the British knew they were in for a difficult fight.

The British decided that if they could capture New York and the Hudson River, they could cut the colonies in half. During the lengthy Battle of Long Island, British General Sir William Howe almost managed to do just that. He was able to chase General Washington and his untrained soldiers from Brooklyn Heights all the way to Pennsylvania and probably could have defeated the colonists once and for all. But wars were fought very differently in the 1700s and, among other things, most armies took the winter off. Transportation was difficult under any circumstances, and the cold winter months made fighting almost impossible.

Having succeeded sufficiently for the time being, Howe withdrew back to New York. However, while Howe's army was resting and the general was busy going to parties and enjoying his holiday season, George Washington led his troops on a sneak Christmas attack. Washington and his militia crossed the Delaware River in boats, surrounded the British fort in Trenton, New Jersey, and forced the one thousand soldiers inside to surrender. Washington and his troops escaped before General Howe's army could retaliate.

The war continued in small, indecisive battles during 1777. The British were able to capture Philadelphia and won large battles at Fort Ticonderoga and Fort Edward in New York. But only a few weeks later, the Americans forced over 5,000 British soldiers to surrender at Saratoga. It was the first genuine victory for the United States and the turning point of the war. France, which had remained neutral, now decided that the United States would ultimately prevail, and the French agreed to become an ally. Throughout the rest of the war, the French were often able to provide desperately needed supplies and financial assistance to the colonists. Without this help, the Americans might not have been able to hang on long enough to win the war.

The winter of 1777–1778 is famous because Washington brought his troops to Valley Forge, Pennsylvania, for the winter. Food and clothing were so scarce that as many as 4,000 soldiers — about a third of the army — were barefoot and starving. While this could have permanently destroyed the soldiers' willpower, these struggles ended up making them stronger. The troops spent the long, cold months being drilled and trained in military tactics. By the time spring arrived, the motley Continental Army had become a group of skilled professional soldiers.

The war continued on for the next several years. Britain couldn't manage to win, and the Americans would not give up. Finally, in late 1781, with France's help, America won a crucial victory at Yorktown, Virginia. They defeated British General Cornwallis, who was forced to surrender his entire British Army of 8,000 men. It was the last real battle of the war.

The next spring, peace talks began in Paris. Britain officially agreed to grant America its permanent independence and to withdraw all of its remaining troops from the country. America's victory was complete, and the Treaty of Paris was approved by the Continental Congress on April 15, 1783, and signed in September. It was almost exactly eight years after "the shot heard 'round the world," and the thirteen colonies had finally become a free and independent nation, the United States of America.

Typical dress of an eighteenth-century man. The tailored coat buttoned to the waist and then curved away to allow for freedom of movement.

Eighteenth-century women often wore shawls to fill in the low necklines of their gowns. Aprons were considered fashionable decorations, and caps or bonnets were also popular.

The main room in an eighteenth-century home, where the family cooked, ate, and worked. The fireplace provided some warmth, but the houses were still quite cold during the winter.

*Teaching manners
to children was very
important in Colonial
America. Many books
contained rules of courtesy
and behavior, such as*
The School of Manners,
*first published in London
in 1701.*

17. Bite not thy bread, but
break it, but not with flovenly
Fingers, nor with the fame where-
with thou takeft up thy meat,

18 Dip not thy Meat in the
Sawce.

19. Take not falt with a greasy
Knife.

20 Spit not, cough not, nor
blow thy Nofe at Table if it may
be avoided ; but if there be ne-
ceffity, do it afide, and without
much noife.

21. Lean not thy Elbow on
the Table, or on the back of thy
Chair.

22. Stuff not thy mouth fo
as to fill thy Cheeks ; be content
with fmaller Mouthfuls.

23. Blow not thy Meat, but
with Patience wait till it be cool.

24. Sup not Broth at the Table, but eat it with a Spoon.

An excerpt from The
School of Manners.
*The rules for etiquette are
borrowed from a famous
earlier book called* Youths'
Behaviour, or Decency
in Conversation
Amongst Men. *Note that
S's look like F's.*

172

Charles Willson Peale was one of the most famous portrait painters of the eighteenth century. He painted some of the best-known portraits of George Washington, such as the one from which the illustration shown here is drawn. His son, Rembrandt Peale, painted this portrait of Martha Washington.

Martha Washington arrives in her carriage at Valley Forge.

The young American soldiers slept in tents until they could build log huts. Without proper shelter, enough food, or shoes, the troops were poorly prepared to fight the able British Army.

The British soldiers were outfitted in formal uniforms.

GEORGE WASHINGTON, Esquire,

GENERAL and COMMANDER in CHIEF of the Forces of the United States of America.

BY Virtue of the Power and Direction to Me especially given, I hereby enjoin and require all Persons residing within seventy Miles of my Head Quarters to thresh one Half of their Grain by the 1st Day of February, and the other Half by the 1st Day of March next ensuing, on Pain, in Case of Failure of having all that shall remain in Sheaves after the Period above mentioned, seized by the Commissaries and Quarter-Masters of the Army, and paid for as Straw

GIVEN under my Hand, at Head Quarters, near the Valley Forge, in Philadelphia County, this 20th Day of December, 1777.

G. WASHINGTON.

By His Excellency's Command,
ROBERT H. HARRISON, Sec'y.

LANCASTER: Printed by JOHN DUNLAP

Commander in Chief George Washington issued this request, seeking aid for his men, to all people in the Valley Forge area.

Washington's Headquarters in Valley Forge.

The Declaration of Independence, written primarily by Thomas Jefferson over the course of seventeen days, explains why Americans should fight for their freedom from the oppressive British king. "We hold these truths to be self-evident," it decrees, "that all men are created equal."

The Yankee's RETURN FROM CAMP.

FATHER and I went down to camp,
  Along with captain Gooding
There we see the men and boys,
  As thick as hasty-pudding,
    Yankee doodle keep it up,
      Yankee doodle dandy;
Cho.—*Mind the Music and the step,*
      And with the girls be handy.

And there we see a thousand men,
  As rich as 'Squire David;
And what they wasted every day,
  I wish it could be saved.
    Yankee doodle, &c.

The 'lasses they eat every day,
  Would keep an house a winter,
They have as much that I'll be bound,
  They eat it when they're amind to,
    Yankee doodle, &c.

And there we see a swamping gun,
  Large as a log of maple,
Upon a duced little cart,
  A load for father's cattle.
    Yankee doodle, &c.

And every time they shoot it off,
  It takes a horn of powder;
It makes a noise like father's gun,
  Only a nation louder.
    Yankee doodle, &c.

I went as nigh to one myself,
  As 'Siah's under-pinning;
And father went as nigh again,
  I thought the duce was in him.
    Yankee doodle, &c.

Cousin Simon grew so bold,
  I thought he would have cock'd it;
It scar'd me so I streak'd it off,
  And hung by father's pocket.
    Yankee doodle, &c.

But Captain Davis has a gun,
  He kind of clap'd his hand on't,
And stuck a crooked stabbing iron,
  Upon the little end on't.
    Yankee doodle, &c.

And there I see a pumpkin shell,
  As big as mother's bason,
And every time they touch'd it off,
  They scamper'd like the nation.
    Yankee doodle, &c.

I see a little barrel too,
  The heads were made of leather,
They knock'd upon it with little clubs,
  And call'd the folks together,
    Yankee doodle, &c.

And there was Captain Washington,
  And gentlefolks about him,
They say he's grown so tarnal proud,
  He will not ride without 'em.
    Yankee doodle, &c.

He got him on his meeting clothes,
  Upon a slapping stallion,
He set the world along in rows,
  In hundreds and in millions.
    Yankee doodle &c.

The flaming ribbons in their hats,
  They look'd so tearing fine, ah,
I wanted plaguily to get,
  To give to my Jemima.
    Yankee doodle &c.

I see another snarl of men,
  A digging graves, they told me,
So tarnal long, so tarnal deep,
  They 'tended they should hold me.
    Yankee doodle, &c.

It scar'd me so, I hook'd it off,
  Nor stopp'd as I remember,
Nor turn'd about till I got home,
  Lock'd up in mother's chamber.
    Yankee doodle, &c.

Sold, wholesale and retail, at 132, Ann Street, Boston.

Lyrics to an early version of the popular song "Yankee Doodle." The expression Yankee Doodle, coined by the British soldiers, was meant to mock the young American army. But it quickly became the Americans' rallying cry — and their theme song.

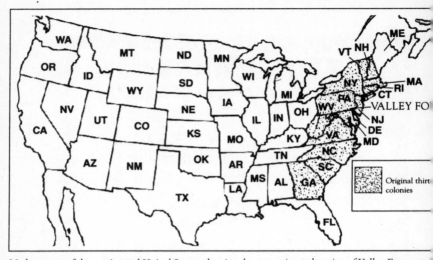

Modern map of the continental United States, showing the approximate location of Valley Forge, and the original thirteen colonies.

This detail of Valley Fo
and its outlying areas
shows important places
battles sites of the Amer
Revolution.

About the Author

KRISTIANA GREGORY is well-known for her accurate and compelling historical fiction for middle-grade and young adult readers, bringing the adventures and struggles of young people during many different times in American history vividly to life. The Revolutionary War period has always held a particular personal interest for her.

"I've always felt a kinship with this period of history because many of my ancestors fought in the Revolutionary War, including one who was camped at Valley Forge during the winter of 1777–1778. His name was William Kern, and he was a sergeant in Daniel Morgan's 11th Virginia Regiment.

"One of my visits to Valley Forge was on a Christmas Day. It was bitterly cold and the snow was knee-deep. Shivering, I peered inside one of the log huts and tried to imagine the poor soldiers without shoes or warm clothes. It fascinated me to realize that George Washington had ridden his horse along that very road. My ancestor may have spoken to him."

Writing *The Winter of Red Snow* allowed her to imagine what it really would have been like to watch the young American soldiers prepare for war and also to experience the excitement of meeting George Washington. And though the diary is a work of fiction, most of the events and characters are real, including von Steuben's 17-year-old interpreter, Pierre Etienne Duponceau, and his polite greyhound, Azor, as well as George Washington's expense account, which records a payment of "40 shillings a month, plus 4 shillings per dozen pieces" to a laundress named Peggy Lee.

Ms. Gregory discovered that, "After the war, William Kern's brother, Adam, married a young woman named Christiana, coincidentally my namesake."

Ms. Gregory's historical fiction novels include *Jimmy Spoon and the Pony Express* and *The Stowaway*, as well as *Clementine*, *Jenny of the Tetons*, *The Legend of Jimmy Spoon*, and *Earthquake at Dawn*. She lives in Idaho with her family.

Acknowledgments

I'm deeply grateful to Pennsylvanians Betty Page of the Valley Forge Historical Society and Elsie Mullin, for their help with research.

The recipe of "Martha Washington's Great Cake" was provided by The Women's Committee of the Valley Forge Historical Society, Valley Forge, Pennsylvania.

Grateful acknowledgment is made for permission to use the following:

Cover portrait by Tim O'Brien.

Cover background: *Washington's Headquarters—Valley Forge*. Watercolor painting by Roland Lee, www.rolandlee.com. Used with permission.

Page 171 (top): *Everyday Dress of Rural America*, Dover Publications, Inc., New York.

Page 171 (bottom): *A New England Kitchen*, Art Resource, New York.

Page 172 (top): Title page from *The School of Manners, or Rules for Children's Behaviour*, John Garretson, London: Oregon Press for the Victoria and Albert Museum, 1701, 1983.

Page 172 (bottom): Excerpt from *The School of Manners*, ibid.

Page 173 (top): Illustration of George Washington after a portrait by Charles Willson Peale, *The American Revolution: A Picture Sourcebook*, Dover Publications, Inc., New York.

Page 173 (top): *Martha Washington* by Rembrandt Peale, © The Metropolitan Museum of Art/Art Resource, NY.

Page 173 (bottom): *Martha Washington Arrives at Valley Forge* by Henry Alexander Ogden. Collection of The New-York Historical Society, 1936. 850.

Page 174 (top): *Washington and Lafayette at Valley Forge*, Culver Pictures, Inc.

Page 174 (bottom): British soldier's uniform, *The American Revolution: A Picture Sourcebook*, Dover Publications, Inc., New York.

Page 175 (top) George Washington's request, ibid.

Page 175 (bottom): *Washington's Headquarters at Valley Forge* by Henry Alexander Ogden. Collection of The New-York Historical Society, 1936. 849.

Page 176: Declaration of Independence, The National Archives.

Page 177: "The Yankee's Return from Camp," *The American Revolution: A Picture Sourcebook*, Dover Publications, Inc., New York.

Page 178: Maps by Heather Saunders.

THE UNTOUCHED KEY

ALICE MILLER

TRANSLATED FROM
THE GERMAN BY
HILDEGARDE AND
HUNTER HANNUM

*Tracing
Childhood
Trauma
in
Creativity
and
Destructiveness*

THE

UNTOUCHED KEY

DOUBLEDAY
New York London Toronto Sydney Auckland

PUBLISHED BY DOUBLEDAY

a division of Bantam Doubleday Dell Publishing Group, Inc.
666 Fifth Avenue, New York, New York 10103

DOUBLEDAY *and the portrayal of an anchor with a dolphin are*
trademarks of Doubleday, a division of Bantam Doubleday Dell
Publishing Group, Inc.

Originally published as Der gemiedene Schlüssel *by Suhrkamp*
Verlag am Main, copyright © 1988. Any variations from the
original German text are a result of the author's wishes.

Library of Congress Cataloging-in-Publication Data

Miller, Alice.
    [Gemiedene Schlüssel. English]
    The untouched key : tracing childhood trauma in creativity
and destructiveness / Alice Miller ; translated from the German by
Hildegarde and Hunter Hannum.
        p.   cm.
    Translation of: Der gemiedene Schlüssel.
    Includes bibliographical references.
    1. Child psychology.   2. Parent and child.   3. Psychic
trauma in children.   I. Title.
    BF721.M539713   1990
    155.4—dc20   89-25623
                                                        CIP

ISBN 0-385-26763-0

Translation copyright © 1990 by Alice Miller

FRONTISPIECE: Picasso, Guernica
                    1990 ARS N.Y./SPADEM

All Rights Reserved
Printed in the United States of America
March 1990
FIRST EDITION IN THE UNITED STATES OF AMERICA

Contents

Preface

*W*henever I leaf through a biography of a creative person, I find information on the first pages of the book that is especially helpful in my work. The information has to do with one or more childhood events whose traces are always apparent in the person's creative work, usually running through it like a continuous thread. In spite of this, the individual childhood events usually are not given any prominence by the biographer. The facts surrounding them could be likened to a key ring we have found but have no use for. We don't know who the owner is, and we suspect the person has long since moved to another house and therefore will no longer have the slightest interest in the lost keys.

Is it permissible, then, for me to take these keys and try to match them to the doors of old houses to discover a life that has long been waiting to be recognized? It may be considered indiscreet to open the doors of someone else's house and rummage around in other people's family histories. Since so many of us still have the tendency to idealize our parents, my undertaking may even be regarded as improper. And yet it is something that I think must be done, for the amazing knowledge that comes to light from behind those previously locked doors contributes substantially toward helping people rescue themselves from their dangerous sleep and all its grave consequences.

ONE

Repressed Childhood Experiences in Art

1

PABLO PICASSO:

The Earthquake in Málaga and the Painter's Eye of a Child

*T*he throngs of people at the exhibit of Picasso's late works in Basel make it difficult to get a good look at the pictures. Groups of students are being told by experts how they should interpret Picasso. They are trying hard to understand something they could learn about just as well at home from Picasso reproductions—for example, his skill in composition. Many of them yawn, turn away from the pictures, look at their watches, and probably think of the cup of coffee that will come to their rescue. The expert who is instructing them doesn't give up; he tries the theory of color, explaining how the orange makes the blue stand out and how well Picasso knew which colors to use for a strong effect. This too seems to bore the students. They are making a visible effort to take in what their instructor is saying and to be sure not to forget it, but the Picasso who is being explained here is somehow dead, one artist among others who have great skill and a mastery of color and form.

Yet along with the many bored and yawning faces, I think I can detect some that are curious, fascinated, and disquieted. I myself feel something like gratitude for this great festival of color I am permitted to feast my eyes on and for Picasso's courage, from which I take inspiration. This man, nearly ninety when he painted these pictures, disregarded all convention as well as his own technical ability and attained what he had wished for all his life: the spontaneity and freedom of a child, which his perfectionism robbed him of in childhood.

It may have been precisely this inspiring power of Picasso's late works that helped me gradually forget the great crowds of bored people around me until finally I was fully able to enter inwardly on this adventure. I seemed to be sensing a man's last strenuous efforts to express the most hidden secrets of his life with every means at his disposal before it's too late, before death takes the brush from his hand.

A great deal has been written about the sexual themes in Picasso's work, and they have always been understood as a sign of his virility. The fact that he depicted male and female genital organs with increasing frequency as he grew older, even right up to his death, has been attributed to his declining libido and a longing for pleasures no longer attainable. But anyone who makes the effort to discover the emotional content of Picasso's last pictures of nude men and women will probably sense a sorrow that is much deeper and whose roots reach back much further in Picasso's life than can be explained by an aging man's regrets at his waning sexual vitality.

But what is the origin of his suffering? I asked myself as I walked through the exhibit, and at first I found no answer. I sensed his suffering not only in the themes but also in the force of the brush movements, in the vehement way he sometimes applied the color and conjured up new feelings that had to be given form. I had the impression that these paintings express a struggle between what Picasso *must* do and what he *is able* to do, between the necessity of making these strokes and no other, of using this color and no other, and a highly conscious, masterful eye that cannot unlearn the laws of color theory and composition even if it would like to. The force of necessity increases with such intensity in Picasso's late works that his ability becomes secondary. Feeling is no longer given a shape, as it was in the painting *Guernica*; now it is lived and becomes pure expression. He no longer does drawings, he no longer counts on the viewer's comprehension; there remains only his haste to produce the unsayable, to say it with colors. But what was the unsayable for Picasso?

I viewed the exhibit of his late works with this question in mind and found no answer. I leafed through an endless number of Picasso biographies, searching for traumatic experiences in his childhood. Since the efficiency of defense mechanisms decreases in old age, since repression works with less ingenuity, it was possible, I thought, that traces of childhood trauma not evident before might become visible in his late works. But at first such traces were undetectable; here was a child who was loved, who had a happy home life. . . .

Even though I know that biographers are seldom interested in their subjects' childhood, I nevertheless found it astonishing that in so many books about such a famous man of our time there was very little—and always the same—information about Picasso's first years: he was born in 1881 in Málaga; his father taught drawing; his mother loved him above all else; at the age of ten he moved to Barcelona; at age fourteen he entered an art school in Madrid and was the best student there; when he was seventeen, his father gave him his palette and stopped painting. This chronology is repeated in all the biographies. Then events that took place in the Spain of that day and in the rest of the world are described in great detail. The financial difficulties of his forebears are also thoroughly discussed, but Pablo Picasso the child is scarcely to be found. The biography by Josep Palau i Fabre was the only one in which I found a few pages that could give me some insight into Picasso's childhood. Although the facts were scattered here and there, with time they took on meaning and revealed the logical connections I was looking for. I read with amazement, for example, about Picasso's behavior in school:

It appears that Picasso's reluctance to go to school was so great that it finally caused him to fall really ill. The doctor said that he had an infection of the kidneys and could not continue to attend classes in that dank building. This news was received with great enthusiasm by little Pablo, for he thought that it meant he would never have to go to school again. And even at the fairly ripe age of eighty-six, Picasso told me that he could never remember the sequence of the alphabet and could not understand how he had ever learned to read and write—or, above all, to count.

When we look back on this childhood situation from the perspective of a famous painter, it seems understandable that the monotonous routine of school would not meet the needs of a child of genius. But it is not that simple. It may be that an alert child is not interested in the multiplication tables or in lists of spelling words because he has already mastered them, whereas the other children are still having trouble. But Picasso *was* having difficulty learning his *ABC*'s. The description of his behavior in school indicates that something entirely different was bothering him. But what?

I continued reading and learned that a second sister was born when he was six and was just starting school. This in itself need not cause problems in school, one might argue, for his mother idolized him and his father was extraordinarily supportive. But what did the birth of his second sister mean for Pablo? Could this event have reminded him of an earlier one? One would have to know the conditions surrounding the birth of his first sister, I thought. I continued my search and was amazed when I found the answer. How is it possible, I wondered, that these facts did not find their way into all the Picasso books, that they were never linked to *Guernica*? Palau i Fabre writes:

> One evening in mid-December 1884—when Picasso was just three years old—there was an earthquake in Málaga. Don José was chatting with some friends in the room behind the local chemist's shop when he saw the rows of jars on the shelves crashing to the floor. The party broke up immediately, its members hastening to their various homes. Don José was in his apartment in a very few moments and said to his wife: "These rooms are too big, María: get dressed quickly! And you, Pablo, come along with me."
>
> Picasso's own account of this incident, as told to Sabartés, went as follows: "My mother was wearing a kerchief on her head: I had never seen her like that before. My father took his cloak from its hanger, flung it over his shoulders, snatched me up and wrapped me in its folds until only my head was peeping out."
>
> They then left the apartment and went to Muñoz Degrain's house, at No. 60 in the Calle de la Victoria. . . .
>
> The Calle de la Victoria, which is one of the longest streets in Málaga, runs parallel to the western slope of the hill of Gibralfaro. It does not exactly lean on this slope, as has been said, but almost certainly the foundations of its houses are set upon the rocky outcrops of the hill. This was the explicit reason that led Don José to seek a refuge for his family in that house. Muñoz Degrain himself was away from home at the time, having gone to Rome on a painting trip with Moreno Carbonero.

A few days after moving into this temporary home—
on 28th December 1884, to be precise, according to the
attached birth certificate—the couple's second child was
born, a girl who was given the name Lola (the most usual
diminutive of Dolores). . . .

The earthquake that led to the family's removal must
have been quite a considerable one, for a few days later
King Alfonso XII visited Málaga to see the extent of the
damage for himself.

I didn't find the exact date of the earthquake in any
of the numerous biographies, but after making some tele-
phone inquiries I finally learned that on December 25,
1884, Spain was shaken by a severe earthquake, with six
seismic shocks occurring between nine and eleven at night.
The epicenter was in Arenas del Rey, less than twenty
miles from Málaga. Many years later Picasso told his friend
Sabartés: " 'My father thought it safer to be near the
rocks.' " Sabartés himelf adds, "There [the family] spent
anxious days waiting for the earth to settle." Picasso's sister
was born three days after the earthquake; possibly labor
was induced by the fright his mother experienced. So in
the space of three days the three-year-old Picasso had to
cope with the shock of an earthquake and the birth of his
first sister in a highly unusual situation and in strange
surroundings.

This example made clear to me once again how fruit-
less historical research can be if the psychological significance of external events is not taken into consideration
simply because an adult is rarely able to understand the

feelings of a child. Just try to imagine what it must be like for a three-year-old to have his father take him and his pregnant mother through the dark city during an earthquake to a strange house and then to be present at the birth of his sister. In Picasso's case two additional factors were at work: being encouraged to see by his father and being told to be silent by his mother. As a little boy, he began to perfect his way of seeing, but he was not supposed to put what he saw into words. All his life, Picasso was proud of his "discretion," the result of his mother's warning—one of his earliest memories—"not to say anything about anybody or anything."

Picasso's mother liked to tell people that her son could draw before he could walk. His first word was *piz*, one of whose meanings in Spanish is "pencil" in baby talk. His father took the greatest pleasure in the little boy's progress in drawing, a fact that surely did not escape the son's notice. When he was drawing, Pablo no doubt received the most attention and encouragement from his father, attention that in an otherwise female household was naturally very important. His father's fondest wish was for his son to win the recognition as a painter that he himself, to his sorrow, had never been given. And the son's wish was for his father to love him.

By the age of three, Picasso was already drawing from his father's models; in particular he drew doves. This taught the boy to look very carefully, to observe an object closely, and to distinguish among the variety of forms. The earlier a child masters something, the more deeply it becomes imprinted and the more certain he is of success for the rest of his life. This is why, conversely, negative messages and experiences are so difficult to unlearn.

Picasso had just turned three in October 1884. What happens to a child who has learned so well at such an early age to use his eyes, to observe his surroundings very closely and register every change, when he is subjected to as terrible a trauma as an earthquake? Perhaps his poem about Spain, written in 1936, can give us a faint idea:

> Children's screams screams of women bird screams flower screams screams of beams and stones screams of bricks screams of furniture of beds of chairs of curtains of frying pans of cats and of papers screams of smells that scrape at one another screams of smoke that burns in the throats of the screams cooking in the pot and screams of raining birds who flood the sea which gnaws the bone that breaks its teeth . . .

Because I saw in these words the verbal and in *Guernica* the visual portrayal of an earthquake as experienced by a child, I thought my discovery would have to be equally exciting for others. But I was mistaken. Picasso experts said that it had happened too long ago and that biography had no significance for the work of such a great painter. Again and again, I am deeply affected by facts that do not count for others—at first. But years later, when resistance has somehow been weakened, it occasionally happens that what was once so vehemently disputed is then taken for granted by others too.

We don't know precisely what was taking place on the Calle de la Victoria as little Pablo was being carried down the long street by his father, but we have a good idea. No doubt the boy saw horses lying in the street, contorted faces, children wandering around; he must have heard terrible screams of fear. Unfortunately, no scholars have yet tried to find out how severe the earthquake in Málaga was, whether houses collapsed as well, and what scenes of human misery and suffering took place before the observant eyes of a child who was later to be a genius. For lack of this information, we can turn to *Guernica*, painted in 1937, in which Picasso portrayed the misery of a war he never was in. He painted the scene in such a way that those who see it can experience their own feelings of horror, terror, and helplessness in the face of total destruction—provided they do not let themselves be distracted by the opinions of art critics. He even painted himself over to the right as the bewildered child in the cellar.

Guernica owes the immediacy of its emotional impact on the viewer, it now strikes me, to Picasso's experiences during the 1884 earthquake in Málaga, experiences that affected his imagination so profoundly that they played an enduring role in his art. The crying, contorted female faces he painted in the period following *Guernica* can even be traced directly in theme to these experiences. He is not attempting to express his own inner state in the faces he paints, as is the case with Edvard Munch in *The Scream* or with various other expressionist painters; rather, Picasso's portrayals are of actual screaming and crying women, but their features cannot be clearly distinguished and their suffering, circumstances, and history are as incomprehensible to us as strangers screaming in the street must be to a child who doesn't know the reason for their terror.

As I looked at Picasso's paintings, I often felt I was seeing with the eyes of the confused, uncomprehending, disoriented, but interested and curious child. We try to distinguish the individual parts of the bodies of his nudes: Where is the foot? Where is the hand? Why are the eyes placed so that they aren't looking at us, so that they can't look at anyone? Art historians tell us that Picasso wanted to show both the front and the back of a head simultaneously because that was part of his "program" at the time. But why? Was Picasso a person who had to adhere to programs? After all, he always abandoned a style once he had developed it, since it bored him to be tied to any one in particular. But the theme of the distorted human body haunted him all his life. It seems to me that his brush was guided by a compulsion he neither understood nor recognized and indeed could not explain because it emerged from his unconscious, which had been imprinted with his earliest childhood experiences. If Picasso had felt constrained to show proof of his ability, he would have stayed with one of his successful phases, perhaps the cubist one. But he had proven his ability long ago when he was still a little boy. Therefore, as an old man he was free to paint what his repressed experience dictated without having to demonstrate his mastery of technique, color, and so on; only then was he able to let what was stored in his unconscious speak through colors.

Little children often express their traumas in a painting the moment a brush is put into their hand. They don't know what they are portraying, and unfortunately adults are practiced in overlooking the revealing content of children's art. Picasso, however, did not have the opportunity to express himself spontaneously as a child; he said that he always painted grown-up pictures, and it took forty years before he was able to paint like a child, that is, to let his unconscious speak. In the same way that adults often are deaf to the cry for help expressed in a child's drawing, taking pleasure instead in the pretty colors and broad strokes, the public received Picasso's later, incomprehensible works with favor, for he was, after all, already recognized as a master.

One can, if one must, see the twisted, distorted female nudes still being done by the artist at ninety simply as a sign of his preoccupation with sex. I prefer to picture the three-year-old boy who, in the midst of all the turmoil of the earthquake and the family's flight, was also witness to his sister's birth. Even if the adults had thought the boy might be traumatized, an awareness of psychology that would not have been likely in those days, probably in the family's temporary quarters no one could have kept this lively, curious child from witnessing the event around which everything now revolved. How does a woman giving birth look from the perspective of a three-year-old, and what happens in the young boy's psyche when this woman writhing in pain happens to be his mother? And all this in surroundings that have just been rocked by an earthquake. The little boy had to repress his feelings, but many images no doubt remained fixed in his memory, although separated from their context.

It is an open question how much viewers can recognize of these events of early childhood in Picasso's paintings. Such awareness should by no means be made into an obligatory program. I want only to indicate that even as severe a trauma as an earthquake need not be repressed entirely but can be represented in works of art if the traumatized child experienced his parents' love and protection when the catastrophe occurred. In addition, I want to point out how much we miss if we disregard the dimension of early childhood experience.

The artist is left with his loneliness as the child was with his: posterity does not concern itself with his trauma but only with his achievement. His paintings can bring in high prices the same way his childhood accomplishments brought him high praise. The more his pictures are praised, however, the more the artist who painted them remains alone with his truth, as I sensed so clearly at the exhibit in Basel. An earthquake in Málaga in 1884? Who cares about that today? Witness to the birth of his sister? What's so unusual about that? But if we put everything together —the earthquake and the birth, the plight of his parents and of the whole city, an upbringing of seeing but remaining silent—a particular constellation emerges that was of indelible significance for this particular individual, Pablo Picasso. Had Picasso not been carried along the Calle de la Victoria in the arms of the father he loved, he might have become psychotic or he might have had to repress the trauma so totally that he would have become an upstanding, compulsive functionary in Franco's Spain. Then it would have been no coincidence if he had taken a special interest in the production of weapons capable of destroying whole cities in one blow.

His father's sheltering arms made it possible for the little boy to overcome his terrifying experience in an optimal manner. Thanks to this protective care, he was able to store what he saw in a way that permitted him to keep expressing it in new forms in his art. Thus, he escaped psychosis as well as total emotional self-alienation (which characterizes the life of so many people) even though he suffered a severe trauma not only at the age of three but even at birth. Most biographers report major complications connected with Picasso's birth. "Apparently, Picasso had such a difficult birth that he was at first thought to be stillborn. Such was evidently the opinion of the midwife, at any rate, for she left him lying on a table in order to devote her attention to his mother. It was only thanks to the presence of mind shown by his doctor uncle, Don Salvador, that the baby came to life." Thus, Picasso, like so many babies, was deprived at birth of being held in his mother's arms, of finding comfort and reassurance there after surviving the struggle for life, and of storing up tenderness and a feeling of trust at this crucial moment. But the later affection shown by his parents, aunts, and cousins helped him to keep taking anew the step leading from death to life. Many of Picasso's contemporaries and friends report that he felt wholly alive only when he was painting. Only then was it possible for him to escape the lethal compulsion to achieve and instead to taste the freedom of inspiration, feeling, and impulse—that is, of life.

The three-year-old Picasso was painfully reminded of the trauma of his own birth by the horrors of the earthquake, the proximity of death, *and* the birth of his sister. But these shocks to his psyche subsided, since the boy's home life was happy and he was permitted to play. It was the discipline and constraints he experienced in school that reawakened his fears, especially since another birth, that of his second sister just as he was starting school, reminded him of his earlier trauma. This highly intelligent child at first reacted to school with learning problems and a severe illness, but as a result of the love and support of his family he did not succumb. He was allowed to rebel against the stultifying constraints confronting him and, even in the Spain of that day, succeeded in expressing his needs.

> When taken to school Pablo always demanded, especially from his father, some sort of pledge or token; and quite frequently this was the pigeon he used as a model. And the teacher . . . was quite willing to let him keep this pigeon on his desk and draw it to his heart's content. Nevertheless, the little boy had such an independent character that whenever he felt inspired to do so he would leave his place, walk over to the window, and tap on the glass on

the off-chance of being noticed by somebody who might get him out. His uncle by marriage, Antonio Suárez Pizarro (the husband of Don José's sister Eloisa Ruiz Blasco), since he lived opposite the school, used to keep an eye open for these appearances and would call for his nephew after *one* hour. This figure—one—seemed to Picasso, according to what he had been taught, to be the smallest possible unit, which was why he insisted on it. But how long the waiting felt, how long an hour could seem!

Even today, one hundred years later, parents still believe they must teach their little children discipline, for if the children are already used to being obedient, then they supposedly won't have to "suffer" in school. It is fortunate that there are some children, like Picasso, who do not submit when confronted with rigidity because they haven't experienced it at home. Pablo's revolt against his school harmed no one, even if it did cause headaches for a few adults. It was the first step on the artist's long journey leading away from constricting conventions to the freedom to create, to think, and to feel.

2

KÄTHE KOLLWITZ:

A Mother's Dead Little Angels and Her Daughter's Activist Art

The following observations are a result of my participation in a discussion about Käthe Kollwitz in conjunction with an exhibit of her works in Zurich in 1981. She is not a painter who moves me deeply enough that I would have felt compelled on my own to become involved with her art. For me, the political effect and power of a work do not depend on its conscious themes. Some pictures can arouse my anger, can give me a feeling of wanting to resist or take action without their having to be regarded as political. In the case of Käthe Kollwitz, on the other hand, when I look at her pictures I am inclined to see hopelessness and despair but not a powerful political statement.

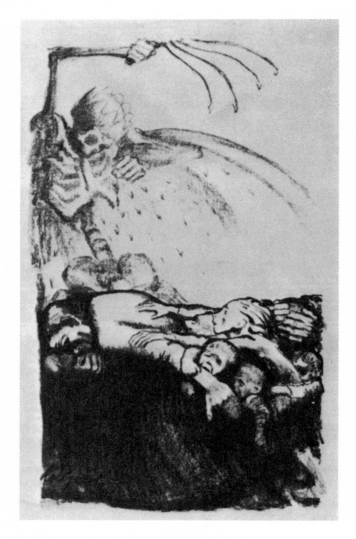

Käthe Kollwitz, Vienna Is Dying! Save Her Children!
VAGA New York 1989

But now that I had told the Kunsthaus, the museum where her works were on display, that I would take part in the discussions, I tried to figure out why I found her pictures so depressing (as well as expressive of depression) and why a mother mourning over her dead child appeared so frequently in them. Art historians find what they consider adequate explanations for this, but I was not convinced. They emphasize, for example, that as a doctor's wife, the painter was often confronted with the tragedy of mothers losing their children. In addition, she herself lost her son Peter in 1914 just a few days after he had gone to war as a volunteer, which had been a matter of great pride to her.

Yet Käthe Kollwitz had already been obsessed with the theme of death and the dead child in the arms of its mother long before the death of her son. Simple causality was therefore not the answer, and yet I didn't want to exclude her personal fate as the explanation. I began asking myself how these facts related to one another and whether they might gain new significance if they were placed in a larger, more comprehensive context.

Before turning to Käthe Kollwitz's childhood memories contained in her diaries, I walked through the exhibit and was attentive to the content of her work and its effect on me. Again and again I saw a dead child or a figure of death coming to take the child away from its mother or of death as lover, comforter, or friend who snatches the mother from her terrified children. I also saw death depicted as violently assaulting the children. Then I saw sad figures, prisoners bound with ropes, and revolutionaries whose faces very rarely expressed anger but rather resignation and hopelessness.

I left the exhibit with many unanswered questions. What kind of images did the eyes of Käthe Kollwitz the child take in from her surroundings and store up? Who is the bent, lost-looking, depressive woman to be seen in almost all the pictures? It can't be the self-portrait of a painter who was capable of that much expression and who showed such strength in the strokes of her brush. Could it be her mother, who did *not* have this outlet for self-expression? What role did death play in the artist's childhood? What concrete experiences relate to the idea of death as a child pictures it? What riddles were there for the child to solve? With these questions in mind, I finally opened the pages of Käthe Kollwitz's diaries.

The entries about her childhood were very illuminating. Käthe Kollwitz, born Käthe Schmidt in 1867, grew up in Königsberg in a religious sect called the Free Religious Congregation, which had been founded and run by her maternal grandfather, Julius Rupp. After her grandfather's death, Käthe's father took over leadership of the group. His writings plainly show a mixture of naiveté, coerciveness, and scrupulousness. Käthe was raised to follow rules and orders to the letter and to suppress her feelings in the service of religious values, self-control chief among them. Since she was a very alert and high-spirited child, strict measures and severe punishment were required for her upbringing. The artist describes being locked up by herself for a long time as punishment for screaming, with no one coming to talk to her. Once, a night watchman going by on the street even came to the door because he was alarmed by the child's "bawling." As is so often the case, her older siblings adopted the parents' ways and used similar methods to train the younger child.

I do not remember much about my sister Julie at that time. Later Mother told me that Julie had always been a solicitous child. Two years younger than Konrad, she was always trailing along behind her brother to save him from mischief. Even at that early age she had begun her mothering of us which we later so rebelled against.

Once Mother sent the two of us to visit Ernestine Castell. As Julie was preparing to leave with me, she took a lump of sugar out of the box and pocketed it. "What is that for?" Aunt Tina asked. "To cram into Kaethe's mouth if she starts to bawl," Julie answered.

This stubborn bawling of mine was dreaded by everyone. I could bawl so loudly that no one could stand it. There must have been one occasion when I did it at night, because I remember that the night watchman came to see what was the matter. When Mother took me anywhere, she was thankful if the fit did not come over me in the street, for then I would stop dead in my tracks and nothing could persuade me to move on. If the fit came over me at home, my parents would shut me up alone in a room until I had bawled myself to exhaustion. We were never spanked.

Her stored-up rage led to physical symptoms, whose significance no one could be bothered about.

Käthe Kollwitz, Death Reaches for the Children
VAGA New York 1989

[My] stomach aches were a surrogate for all physical and mental pains. I imagine my bilious trouble began at that time. I went around in misery for days at a time, my face yellow, and often lay belly down on a chair because that made me feel better. My mother knew that my stomach aches concealed small sorrows, and at such times she would let me snuggle close to her.

Käthe was allowed to snuggle close to her mother as long as she was quiet and behaved herself and above all didn't say anything about what was troubling her. This resulted in loneliness, self-accusations, and depressive moods beginning in childhood.

On the whole I was a quiet, shy child, and nervous as well. Later on, instead of these tantrums of kicking and roaring I had moods that lasted for hours and even days. When in these moods I could not bring myself to use words to communicate with others. The more I saw what a burden I was being to the family, the harder it became for me to emerge from my mood.

I needed to confide in my mother, to confess to her. Since I could not conceive of lying to my mother, or even of being disobedient, I decided to give my mother a daily report on what I had done and felt that day. I imagined that her sharing the knowledge would be a help to me. But she said nothing at all, and so I too soon fell silent.

There is a picture of [my mother] holding on her lap her first child, which was named Julius after my grandfather. This was the "firstborn child, the holy child," and she had lost it, as well as the one born after it. Looking at her picture you can see that she was truly Julius Rupp's daughter and would never let herself give way completely to grief. But although she never surrendered to the deep sorrow of those early days of her marriage, it must have been her years of suffering which gave her for ever after the remote air of a madonna. Mother was never a close friend and good comrade to us. But we always loved her.

Käthe Kollwitz describes her love for her mother as "tender and solicitous." She was often fearful that her mother might "come to some harm," "get lost," "go mad," or die. Sometimes she wished her parents were already dead, "so that it would all lie behind me." It was inevitable, with all her desperate attempts to hold back her true feelings, that she suffered not only from physical symptoms but from psychic ones as well. She writes:

> I don't know just when I began to suffer from nocturnal frights. . . . Nights I was tormented by frightful dreams. . . . Then there was a horrible state I fell into when objects would begin to grow smaller. It was bad enough when they grew larger, but when they grew smaller it was horrifying.
>
> I experienced such states of unfounded fear for many years; even when I was in Munich [in her early twenties] they occurred, but in far feebler form. I constantly had the feeling that I was in an airless room, or that I was sinking or vanishing away.

Her belief in her own guilt and in the value of a strict upbringing for a person's later life would in itself be sufficient to explain the depressive cast to Käthe Kollwitz's pictures. For if a child is forbidden to express her true feelings, observations, and thoughts because only good, kind thoughts that are pleasing to God are permitted, then everything that has no place in this "good" world is relegated to the realm of death. As a child, Käthe Kollwitz often dreamed she was dead; this was because the uncomfortable, intense side of her nature was not allowed to live. Since I regard depression as the consequence of attempts, such as she was subjected to, to smother life, at first I was inclined to interpret the many depictions of death in her graphic work as the symbolic manifestation of her suffering. Gradually, however, it became clear that the theme of death in her art had other sources as well.

Käthe was one of four siblings—Konrad, Julie, Käthe, and Lise—to live beyond childhood. Her mother's first two children died at a very early age. The last-born child, Benjamin, born after Lise, died of meningitis when he was one year old. This information held great significance for me. Experience shows that the death of a child, especially the firstborn, plays a very important role in a mother's life. The birth of every child inevitably awakens or reawakens desires in the parents that somehow are connected to making up for their own childhoods. Either they look to the child to compensate for their not having had good parents ("At last here is someone who will show concern for me, who will treat me with consideration and respect") or to be the child they once were ("Now I shall have someone to whom I can give all that my parents had to deny me").

If the child dies soon after birth, before the parents' expectations are disappointed by the child's desire for autonomy, the mother may idealize her lost child and thereby preserve its central importance for the rest of her life. Often after the death of an infant, there is no real period of mourning that runs its course; instead, the parents' hopes become attached to an "if": if only the child had lived, the parents think, their expectations would have been met. The belief in the fulfillment of all their hopes, originating in their own childhoods, is associated with the memory of this child, whose grave they visit and tend for decades after.

Superhuman, even divine, qualities are attributed to the dead child; at the same time, the other children in the family grow up in the shadow of this cult. They must be dutifully cared for and raised in a way to rid them of their bad behavior and make them acceptable in the future. To be too affectionate would be dangerous, for too much love could ruin them. The parents seem to think that affection and tenderness should be carefully measured out in the child's best interest. And so the poor well-raised mother feels a duty toward her living children to train them well and to suppress their true feelings. But it's a different matter in the case of her dead child, for that child needs nothing from her and does not awaken any feelings of inferiority or hatred, does not cause her any conflict, does not offend her. Since she need not be afraid of spoiling the child with her love, when she goes to the cemetery she feels genuine inner freedom in her grief. Compared with that feeling, being with her other children can make her suffer because they clearly do not measure up to the dead child and its fantasized goodness and wisdom. Their vitality, their demands and claims on her can make a mother in love with her dead child feel distinctly insecure. They can cause feelings of helplessness and despair if she sees her pedagogical principles called into question.

This does not mean that the mother consciously wishes her children dead. Quite the contrary, she is even anxiously concerned that nothing happen to them; she paints them a picture of the constant danger threatening them, and she is apparently right about the danger, for something terrible has already happened. She must always keep an eye on her children, plaguing them with her close supervision and restricting their freedom. As a result, she has long since unavoidably forfeited her own vitality and spontaneity and in her depressed state is ultimately serving death.

We can imagine such a fate as this in the case of Käthe Kollwitz's mother. But how did the situation look from the child's perspective? Her mother's concern for her children's physical survival was a constant accompaniment for Käthe at play. In her memoirs Kollwitz mentions a pit that would make one blind if one fell into it, a sign that she took her mother's warnings to heart. She was also always attempting to satisfy her parents' pedagogical desires and become a quiet, well-behaved, uncritical, psychically dead little girl. Even if there are no dead siblings involved, such an attempt to suppress a child's spontaneity

Käthe Kollwitz, A Woman Entrusts Herself to Death
VAGA New York 1989

will intensify the child's depressive tendencies, because depression is an indication of the loss of vitality. When, however, as in the case of Käthe Kollwitz, three dead siblings are held up as model children, serving as proof of the mother's supposed capacity for love, then the daughter will do everything in her power—will readily sacrifice all her own feelings—to show herself truly "worthy" of her mother's love. Thus, psychic death, whose price is depression, gains double significance: it brings promise of the mother's unconditional, unlimited love, which the daughter has observed but has not experienced herself, and it satisfies the longing for death on the part of the mother, whose face looks transfigured, soft, almost happy only when she is standing by her children's graves.

I had reached this point in my thinking when I returned to the Kunsthaus in Zurich to see the exhibit of Kollwitz's graphic art. Now I felt that I had found my entirely personal—purely subjective, if you will—key to these pictures. For what had previously seemed rigid and difficult to empathize with now had gained life and meaning. And my hypotheses, based on the autobiographical material I had read, were fully confirmed by the pictures I saw.

In one picture a mother is stretching out her hand to greet Death (of whom we see only the right hand). Two little children with terrified faces are clinging to her skirts; their expression is in striking contrast to their mother's. Her look and her handshake are calm and friendly in a conventional way, as if she had opened the door to find a familiar face, a friend or neighbor and not Death, and were saying, "Good evening, Mr. Jones. Please come in."

The theme "Mother with Dead Child" keeps reappearing in different ways. At the same time, death is shown as redeemer (transforming the child from an object of censure into one of love), as comforter (which the grave was for the mother), and as lover. This is how the daughter must have pictured death, I thought, when she heard her mother speak of it and watched her face. Now it was also clear to me that the stooped and lifeless woman I kept seeing, in group depictions as well, is not Käthe Kollwitz but her mother, as seen by one of her still living children. I also began to comprehend why so much resignation and hopelessness emanates from the group scenes, which lack the feeling of genuine anger one would expect from their theme: as a very young child, Käthe Kollwitz was threatened with punishment if she showed anger. The dead child being mourned is actually angry little Käthe herself.

As an adult Kollwitz was aware of the injustice of oppression, imprisonment, and exploitation on all sides, but she did not permit herself to cry out, just as she was not permitted to cry out as a child. Her socialism was not a revolutionary step for her; her father, brother, and husband were all socialists. By being one herself, she was in no way rebelling against her family but was, rather, in harmony with it; she had also tried to be pious in the pious setting of her childhood. She never freed herself from this dependency on her family's values and expectations of her. Her pictures express the hopelessness and resignation of

Käthe Kollwitz, Sitting Woman
VAGA New York 1989

a person who was not permitted to articulate her strong feelings because they made those around her uncomfortable. And because anger is missing from her works, it is not the feeling of pain that speaks in them but depression. The oversized figure of the mother mourning over Peter's grave also shows the familiar bent-over, depressed stance, but no pain. The father in Käthe Kollwitz's pictures hardly ever expresses anything but self-control.

Since I had now answered my questions in my own way, I no longer felt the need to track down all the details of this artist's life. I was about to return her diary to the library, having read only the sections about her childhood, when my eye was caught by a passage that confirmed my conjectures. Reminiscing about her mother, she writes:

> She often speaks of her first baby, who died a year after he was born. . . . The death of her first child must have been the most powerful experience in her life; that is why it is still so present for her now after fifty-five years.

And a little later she puts it even more plainly:

> Her awareness that her own child is now dead is blurred. She looks at the pictures of her babies, speaks in a tender voice of her "babies," and her eyes grow moist when she speaks of the first one who died. That happened nearly sixty years ago, but she still can't speak of him without being moved—and Julie dies and she grasps it only momentarily.

Her mother's eyes grow moist when she thinks of her child who died so long ago. Another daughter has just died, but this fact scarcely penetrates her consciousness. In the shadow of such a mother Käthe Kollwitz lived and painted her pictures of the dead child, which posterity would like to interpret simply as the expression of her social conscience and political commitment.

Buster Keaton with his parents

3

BUSTER KEATON:
Laughter at a Child's Mistreatment and the Art of Self-Control

*B*uster Keaton, the famous comedian of the twenties and thirties, could make people burst out laughing at his antics without cracking a smile himself. I can remember being bothered by this discrepancy as a child, and I wasn't able to find his antics funny when I had to look at that sad face. Lately, I chanced upon his biography by Wolfram Tichy and found in it the explanation for my discomfort. When he was only three, Buster Keaton started appearing on the stage with his parents, who were vaudeville performers, and helped to make them famous by taking severe abuse in front of an audience without batting an eyelash. The audience would squeal with delight, and by the time the authorities would be ready to intervene because of the physical injuries the little boy sustained, the family would already be performing in another city. In his autobiography, *My Wonderful World of Slapstick*, Keaton describes his situation plainly enough, but he describes only the *facts*, whose significance remained hidden to him. That this was the case can be seen from the following passage:

> *My parents were my first bit of great luck.* I cannot recall one argument that they had about money or anything else during the years I was growing up. . . . And from the time I was ten both they and the other actors on the bill treated me not as a little boy, but as an adult and a full-fledged performer. [Italics mine]

Had Buster Keaton realized that his parents were exploiting him shamelessly and brutally injuring not only his body but also his emotional life, he surely wouldn't have made a career of entertaining other people when he didn't feel like laughing himself. Keaton, quoted in Tichy's biography, reveals how he became the person he did:

> A child born backstage gets makeup smeared on his face by his parents as soon as he can walk . . . sometimes only for fun, for their own pleasure, and sometimes to see if the child is ready for an audience. . . . My father dressed me up in funny clothes, similar to the kind he wore himself. So from the beginning I wore pants and shoes that were too big for me. They brought me onstage when I was three, at first for matinées. When I had just turned four, a theater owner said, "If you bring him on for the evening performance, I'll pay

you $10 more." . . . From then on, I was part of the show, for $10 a week. . . . The first time I got paid was in 1899.

I appeared . . . before many different kinds of commissions, and in some cities before the mayor. In two states it was the governor who looked me over to see if I were being injured by the work that I did on the stage. Sometimes I was barred from appearing, but as our engagements were short, we would soon be in another town where the laws might be less strict.

In most cities and states, the laws specifically prohibited a child under sixteen doing juggling, wire work or acrobatics of any kind. This afforded a loophole for me, as I was not an acrobat. I did nothing except submit to being knocked about. When I went outside the theater, they used to dress me in long trousers, derby hat and hand me a cane to carry. In this way they fooled some people into believing that I was a midget.

In this knockabout act, my father and I used to hit each other with brooms, occasioning for me strange flops and falls. *If I should chance to smile, the next hit would be a good deal harder.* All the parental correction I ever received was with an audience looking on. *I could not even whimper.*

When I grew older, I readily figured out for myself that I was not one of those comedians who could jest with an audience and laugh with it. My audience must laugh *at* me. [Italics mine.]

One of the first things I noticed was that *whenever I smiled* or let the audience suspect how much I was enjoying myself *they didn't seem to laugh as much as usual.*

I guess people just never do expect any human mop,

39

dishrag, beanbag, or football to be pleased by what is being done to him. [Italics mine]

> If something tickled me and I started to grin, the old man would hiss, "Face! Face!" That meant freeze the puss. The longer I held it, why, if we got a laugh the blank pan or the puzzled puss would double it. He kept after me, never let up, and *in a few years it was automatic* [italics mine]. Then when I'd step onstage or in front of a camera, I *couldn't* smile. Still can't.

In view of his unwavering idealization of his parents, surely no one can doubt that the scenes described by Buster Keaton himself really took place. Nobody could make up anything so horrifying, especially not someone who claims to have had an ideal childhood. Yet he completely missed the *significance* of these scenes for his whole later life and for his art. The biographer misses it too. After he has put the facts together, Tichy writes, *"It is certain that Keaton's parents loved their son no less than other parents love their children* and treated him the way they subjectively thought right for everyone's interests" [italics mine].

This same biographer tells about the numerous times the father inflicted severe physical injury on his son and then even talked about it boastfully, proud that the boy put up with such treatment without complaining.

In spite of remembering what happened to him, Buster Keaton undoubtedly repressed the trauma of being abused and degraded. That is why he had to repeat the trauma countless times without ever *feeling* it, for the early lesson that his feelings were forbidden and were to be ignored retained its hold on him.

I have observed young people in the cafés and bars of a small city who also must have learned this lesson. They stare dully into space, cigarette in hand, sipping a glass of something alcoholic if they can afford it, and biting their fingernails. Alcohol, cigarettes, nail biting—all serve the same purpose: to prevent feelings from coming to the surface at any cost; as children these people never learned to experience their feelings, to feel comfortable with them, to understand them. They fear feelings like the plague and yet can't live entirely without them; so they pretend to themselves that getting high on drugs in a disco can make up for all they have lost. But it doesn't work. Cheated of their feelings, they begin to steal, to destroy property, and to ignore the feelings and rights of others. They don't know that all this was once done to them: they were robbed of their soul, their feelings were destroyed, their rights disregarded. Others were using them, innocent victims, to compensate for the humiliation they had once suffered themselves. For there is no way for mistreated children to defend their rights.

Society shares their ignorance. It puts these young people in reform schools, where they can perfect their destructive behavior at the expense of others while continuing to destroy themselves. We often hear people say that vandalism is on the increase nowadays, that young people were not always as violent, inconsiderate, and brutal as they are today. It's hard to say whether this is indeed

Buster Keaton with his parents

the case, because now certain forms of state-organized brutality such as war have disappeared—at least in Europe. But if it is actually true that today's youth are becoming increasingly unstable, then I wonder if it might not have something to do with the advancing technology surrounding childbirth and the manipulation of babies through medication, which make it impossible for newborns to experience their feelings and to orient themselves in terms of those feelings. I see a direct connection between infants tranquilized with drugs who can find no better alternatives in later life, and the adolescents in the bars whom I have just described.

What are young people to do with feelings that have been totally repressed but are still strongly active in the unconscious if the whole society ignores these feelings or denies that they are caused by child abuse? The only legal way to act out rage openly and violently in peacetime is in disciplining one's children. Since this outlet is not available to young people who have no children, they must look for another one. Suicide, addiction, criminal behavior, terrorism, and participation in organizations that sexually exploit children all can provide this kind of outlet—unless, like Buster Keaton, one can find it in creativity. Although creativity permits survival and helps a person to live with psychic damage, it still conceals rather than reveals the truth. Thus, it cannot protect the person from being self-destructive. As later chapters will show, Friedrich Nietzsche needed his entire philosophy to shield himself from knowing and telling what really happened to him.

Similarly, Buster Keaton learned to be creative without being able to laugh spontaneously. Neither of them became murderers or ended in prison, but they paid a great price for their denial of the truth. In addition, they were unable to help society understand the roots of destructive behavior and change its attitude toward children.

Chaim Soutine, Motherhood
1990 ARS N.Y./SPADEM

Chaim Soutine, Landscape
1990 ARS N.Y./SPADEM

4

Despot or Artist?

About five years ago I went to an exhibit of Chaim Soutine's paintings. I had felt very drawn to this painter for some time and had always had the impression that the great intensity of his work undeniably had its roots in childhood pain. The exhibit confirmed my impression and also provided me with important information. Along with the many portraits on display were numerous landscapes, which at first I didn't even look at because it was primarily the people—the strange, twisted, tormented figures—that fascinated me so. But when I did turn to the houses, streets, and squares, it struck me that they looked as though they might start to quiver at any moment.

I learned from the catalogue that Soutine was a Rus-

47

sian Jew who died in Paris in 1943. I asked myself whether the extremely threatening situation of the Nazi Holocaust had motivated, or even compelled, Soutine to paint the world as shaking and falling apart. Then I thought of Kafka and the discovery I had made in his case that visions of the future have to do with one's earliest experiences and that the repressed suffering of childhood can lend intensity and expressiveness to an artist's work without his even realizing what he is portraying. I wondered what it must be like for a little child who is being beaten, lying across someone's knee, head down so that the world looks upside down. And this upside-down world is quivering, for his body is shaken with every blow. That is how I experienced Soutine's paintings even before I learned from the catalogue that he was frequently beaten by his parents and brothers and could count on being punished regularly because he liked to draw so much, something that was forbidden by Orthodox Jews. The biographer who presented these facts did not attribute any significance to them; he defended the thesis that Soutine had a "narcissistic and necrophilic character" and therefore loved to portray death. The following passage, quoted from *Soutine* by Andrew Forge, appeared in the catalogue:

> Smilovitchi, the Lithuanian village where [Soutine] was born [in 1893] the tenth son of the village tailor, was absolutely without culture. The very thought of painting pictures was heretical in such an orthodox community, and from the first Soutine was made to know that he was sin-

Adolf Hitler, A Church in Flanders
Archiv für Kunst und Geschichte, Berlin

ning: "Thou shalt not make unto thee any graven image or any likeness of anything that is in heaven above or that is in earth beneath or that is in the water under the earth." His struggle to find ways of breaking the Second Commandment is part of his legend: he stole from the household to buy a coloured pencil and was locked up in the cellar as punishment; he made a drawing of the village idiot, then asked the rabbi to pose for him. The aftermath reads like a parable: the rabbi's son beat him up severely, the rabbi paid Soutine's mother damages and with the money he was able to leave Smilovitchi to study at art school.

These details about Soutine's childhood traumas brought me back to the old question of why all battered children don't turn into monsters like Adolf Hitler, why some grow up to be brutal, unfeeling criminals and others highly sensitive people such as painters and poets who are capable of expressing their suffering. I detected the presence in Soutine's life history of a sympathetic and helpful witness who confirmed the child's perceptions, thus making it possible for him to recognize that he had been wronged.

Men of various professions frequently ask me why they didn't become a Hitler but have lived their lives as more or less peaceful physicians, lawyers, or professors, even though they, like Hitler, were beaten every day when they were children. They use this question to argue against my thesis that brutal, unfeeling, and thoroughly destructive treatment of children produces monsters—not by chance but of necessity. Then I always inquire about the details of the person's childhood, and on closer examination it turns out in *every* case that a particular witness helped the child experience his feelings to some degree. In Adolf Hitler's childhood, such a stabilizing witness was totally lacking. I have often compared the structure of Hitler's family to a totalitarian regime in which there is no possibility of recourse against the police state.

Hitler's father's arbitrary exercise of power was the highest authority, from which there was no escape. In the Third Reich, Adolf Hitler demonstrated the extent to which he had internalized this system. Not a single feeling or humane consideration existed that might have set limits to his cruelty once *he* achieved sole power. His use of power paralleled exactly the way he had been brought up. Whatever course of action his parents thought appropriate was carried out mercilessly with every measure of force possible. The boy was never permitted to doubt the rightness of his parents' decisions, for that would have resulted in unbearable torture. It was just as impossible for ordinary citizens in the Third Reich to question a decision made by the state or the Gestapo. If they tried, torture and death were the inevitable response. Brute force represented the ultimate power, and it provided its own "justification" for "maintaining order" and for the "legality" of its crimes; this practice, too, was borrowed from the structure of Hitler's family, in which everything—the stifling of feelings and creativity as well as the suppression of all the child's needs, indeed of almost every human emotion—was done in the name of a good upbringing.

Hitler's frenzied campaign against "degenerate art" also reflected what had been done to him: because colors awaken feelings in people, Hitler had to forbid them. Colors were dangerous, reprehensible, almost Jewish. So were vague lines, which excite the imagination. All signs of vitality had to be stamped out with the same thoroughness with which the child's vitality had been crushed by his parents for the sake of establishing order. Since order established by violent means was the highest value in this system, the annihilation of creativity was the obvious result. A student has investigated in detail the similarities between Hitler's upbringing and the concept of "degenerate art." Drawing on my writing and using pictures, including some done by Hitler, she presents convincing evidence that Hitler's attack on modern art was a continuation of the destructive process begun by his parents.

The Holocaust, the euthanasia law, and the concept of degenerate art are only a few examples of the way an adult perpetuates the destructive treatment he endured as a child. Hitler's aides accepted his methods without hesitation because for them too this system of coercion and enforced obedience had always been the only right one; they were comfortable with it and never questioned it. To combat cruelty, a person must first be able to perceive it as such. When someone has been exposed throughout childhood to nothing but harshness, coldness, coercion, and the rigid wielding of power, as Hitler and his closest followers were, when any sign of softness, tenderness, creativity, or vitality is scorned, then the person against

whom that violence is directed accepts it as perfectly justified. Children believe they deserve the blows they are
given, idealize their persecutors, and later search out objects for projection, seeking relief by displacing their supposed guilt onto other individuals or even a whole people.
And in this way they become guilty themselves.

An artist like Soutine couldn't possibly have come
from as destructive a totalitarian home setting as Hitler.
The very fact that the boy was given money as compen-
sation for being beaten and that his mother handed the
money over to him shows that, despite the primitive conditions, someone was there for him in his childhood who
helped him develop a sense of justice. Thus he did not
have to blame himself for his suffering, to say nothing of
globally displacing his guilt onto others later in life. Thanks
to the money he was given as atonement, Soutine was even
able to fulfill his fervent desire to take drawing lessons and
go on to become a painter.

But there must have been other differences between
Chaim Soutine's and Adolf Hitler's childhoods. Although
they were both battered children and were severely punished for wanting to become artists, it is inconceivable that
a person like Adolf Hitler could have grown up in the family
of a poor Jewish tailor in Lithuania. It is just as inconceivable that Soutine the painter could have developed his
subtle sense of color and his ability to express suffering as
the son of Alois Hitler in Braunau. The hostility toward
life and the destructive power of the Hitler family are
evident from the abundance of available documents. The

force of their message has now been brought to a wide audience in a stage drama that draws on many examples to show how any pleasure Hitler took in playing, in having ideas, or in being inventive was nipped in the bud by his parents' rigid emphasis on obedience and strict training.

Soutine did not grow up in an emotional desert as Hitler did. His upbringing was less systematic and consistent, less focused on obedience, for Jewish fathers in Eastern Europe were not trained to be harsh and brutal. They were not forced, like German fathers, to suppress their soft, helpless side from childhood on. It was quite natural for them to kiss and caress little children, and this was never called "monkey love."

Thus, the children of Jewish fathers were more likely to be shown tenderness, which undoubtedly contributed toward reducing the harm done to them. Without such tenderness and affection, children are unable to experience a feeling of pleasure that shows them what life is and lets them know that vitality is worth fighting for. This is a different kind of pleasure from that derived, for example, by tormenting animals, a means by which an abused child can act out humiliation. Even if children aren't given a love that is selfless, responsible, and protective, nevertheless physical closeness, caresses, and affection can arouse feelings in them—feelings such as longing, pain, loneliness, anger, and outrage but also delight in nature, in their own body, in the bodies of others, and especially in life. To be sure, this delight can be clouded or impaired by the way adults exercise their power, but again the emotional climate and the behavior of other people to whom a child is attached can make a difference. The poet Paul Celan's life is a good example. I found the following passages about his childhood in the biography by Israel Chalfen:

> Paul's father maintained strict discipline at home. He was not a good-natured person; he placed high demands on his son, punished him, beat him often for every minor childish infraction. Leo was small of stature, about a head shorter than his wife. One had the impression that he was attempting to compensate for his unimpressive appearance and his financial failures by being tyrannical at home. But he didn't quarrel with his wife—he was very devoted to her! It was his son who bore the brunt of his iron rule. Paul was a very sensitive child and no doubt suffered greatly from his father's severity. . . .
>
> Little Paul learned at an early age to be obedient and to behave in a way that corresponded to his parents' idea of a "good upbringing." He had to be fastidious about personal cleanliness, had to eat everything that was set before him, and was not allowed to ask superfluous questions. When he nevertheless did contradict, rebel, or display childish defiance, his father rebuked him roundly or even beat him. If the "offense" seemed especially grave, he shut the boy in an empty closet and took the key. Fortunately, the closet had a window opening onto the rear courtyard so that the women in the family could release the bitterly crying boy from his prison as soon as his father left the house on business matters. Usually it was his mother who came to the rescue, sometimes one of his aunts. . . .
>
> Paul encountered limits to his freedom of movement everywhere: he wasn't allowed to open doors from one room to another, nor was he allowed to go ouside without being accompanied by an adult. This also prevented him from being by himself on the quiet street, Wassilkogasse, with

its chestnut trees. On rare occasions he was permitted to play with the daughter, almost the same age as he, of a music teacher who lived in the same building, but only in the backyard, where there were a few trees and some sparse grass. Between the piles of wood stored there for the winter, between fence and back door lay the paradise of the first three years of Paul's life. It is not by chance that one of Celan's boyhood poems begins with the line "The world lies on the other side of the chestnut trees."

Even though Paul Celan's father ruled tyrannically, taking out on his son his own insecurity, the father was very devoted to his wife, and this in itself set limits to his tyranny. Mother and aunts could come to Paul's aid and let him out of the closet when he was imprisoned. These were the witnesses who rescued him, who helped him to understand that along with cruelty, rigidity, and stupidity there can also be mercy and goodness and that he was not guilty and wicked but was even lovable, although his father hadn't noticed.

Because of the women who came to his rescue, the boy was able to integrate into his consciousness the injustice he experienced, the pain of being imprisoned and tormented, without completely repressing it. But since he was raised so strictly, he was not permitted to see that he was being persecuted and held back in life by his own father. He had to keep his father's image sacred and displace his feelings onto other people and situations. All poets do this; they have to. That is why all his life Paul Celan could never break away from the theme of the concentra-

Chaim Soutine, Landscape with Houses
1990 ARS N.Y./SPADEM

tion camps, which were a menacing backdrop to his young adulthood and in which his parents died. He wrote poems about imprisonment that, significantly, were much admired in the postwar period, a time of strong intellectual defense against feelings in literature and art. These poems helped Celan express the sufferings of others in a masterful, restrained, and detached language. Yet his own childhood suffering, which was emotionally inaccessible, remained hidden from him.

The reason for Celan's suicide in 1970 at age forty-nine is not to be found in his war experiences, which he shared with many other survivors. If a person no longer has any room for hope, the cause—which has been repressed—lies in the far distant past. With his suicide, Paul Celan concluded the destructive work begun by his father, who denied his son the simplest, most harmless pleasures, even if they would not have cost anything, out of sheer meanness and for no apparent reason. It is so easy to do this to children because they are defenseless and at the mercy of adult whims, for better or worse. It is difficult for parents who were wounded as children to resist the temptation to exercise their power. If they were not allowed to play freely as children, they will keep finding reasons to deprive their own children of this enjoyment, which is so crucial for development. Or they will pervert play by an overemphasis on achievement—in sports such as ice skating or in music lessons—and destroy the child's creativity by instilling a compulsion to excel.

Celan's experience as a child was that the weak have

no rights, but he was not allowed to *know* it about himself on the conscious level. Instead, he described in poetic language the situation of the camp inmate whose life is also impaired without any reasons having to be given. The guards are able to destroy the enjoyment and dignity of a defenseless person as a matter of course because they too have learned this lesson at such an early age. Thus, Celan's poetry *is* authentic, even though its highly personal dimension remained hidden from the poet himself and from most readers. If he had understood the source of his suffering, he would have found meaning in life and might have enjoyed it.

It helped Celan to articulate his suffering by displacing the experience of his childhood onto the situation of the camp inmate, but it did not save him from suicide. If his father had not been murdered in a camp in 1942, Paul Celan might have found his way to the feelings of his childhood; perhaps he could have confronted his father inwardly and thereby saved his own life. But a person whose father has been cruelly murdered will find it very difficult to call him into question, even if for the sake of clarifying their relationship. It is easier to search for a way out in mysticism, whereby the person can close his eyes and conceal the truth in eloquent symbolic images. Yet sometimes this approach becomes virtually intolerable too because the power of the quite prosaic truth, the truth of the "little self" so disdained by the mystics, can be inexorable. Particularly for people who at some point in their childhood experienced loving care, this truth won't allow itself to be silenced completely, even with the help of poetry, philosophy, or mystical experiences. It insists on being heard, like every child whose voice has not been completely destroyed.

The absence or presence of a helping witness in childhood determines whether a mistreated child will become a despot who turns his repressed feelings of helplessness against others or an artist who can tell about his or her suffering. I could cite an abundance of further examples, but I will mention only a few. I must leave it to the reader to verify my statements, to supplement my evidence with new material, or to refute my arguments, as the case may be.

It's a fact that Dostoyevsky's father forced his children to read the Bible and tormented them with his greed. I don't know whether he mistreated them physically, and I must base my assumptions on my knowledge of his son's novels. But we do know that after his wife's death, he "led the life of a wastrel, drunkard, and tyrant. He treated his serfs with such cruelty that in 1839 they murdered him most brutally."

In mid-nineteenth-century Russia, cruelty toward serfs was almost the rule. The elder Dostoyevsky must therefore have treated his serfs especially brutally or perfidiously to drive them to such a dangerous act of revenge. How was this father likely to have treated his own sons? Perhaps a good deal could be gleaned from *The Brothers Karamazov*. But this novel also shows how difficult it is for sons to acknowledge a father's wickedness without feeling

Chaim Soutine, Landscape Cagnes
1990 ARS N.Y./SPADEM

guilty and without punishing themselves. The serfs were able to free themselves from the domination of their master, but the children were not. Fyodor Dostoyevsky suffered from epilepsy; he searched for God, Whom he could not find. Why didn't he become a criminal filled with hatred? Because he found a loving person in his mother. Because of her he experienced love, and this was crucial for his later life. Can the explanation be that simple? Yes. But the way his life turned out hung by a thread; it could easily have been completely different.

In contrast, as a child Stalin never experienced a protective and unpossessive love. Descriptions of his childhood do not reveal anyone in his life who protected him from the excessive beatings his father gave him or compensated for them with love and a watchful presence. His mother, who was very religious, is portrayed as confused and self-absorbed.

> The family of Joseph Vissarionovich Djugashvili was unhappy in its own special way. The boy's father was a drunkard, a spendthrift, a man who possessed a violent temper, with no feeling for his wife or his son; he beat them unmercifully. He was a cobbler by trade, with a small shop in an obscure steet on the outskirts of Gori. The boy's mother was a quiet, withdrawn, deeply religious woman, beautiful in her youth, who found her chief pleasure in attending church services and in contributing out of her sparse earnings to the upkeep of the priests. She earned money by performing menial tasks in the houses of the rich, laundering, baking bread and running errands. She

was also an occasional seamstress, and one of the boy's childhood friends, who was not unsympathetic to him, remembered that she sometimes earned a living by cutting, sewing and laundering underwear. She was a proud woman and kept her sufferings to herself.

When Ekaterina Geladze married Vissarion Djugashvili in 1874, she was a girl of seventeen and her husband was twenty-two. The first three children are said to have died in childbirth, Joseph, born on December 21, 1879, being the only child to grow to maturity. Vissarion died when the boy was in his eleventh year, and Ekaterina survived her husband by nearly fifty years. She was a small, fragile, indomitable woman, who remained deeply religious throughout her life and always wore a black nunlike costume.

The family of Stalin might have come out of Gorky's play *The Lower Depths*. It was brutally unhappy. They lived in grinding poverty, constantly in debt. Sometimes the neighbors would have pity on the struggling seamstress and her undernourished son; and their pity may have done more harm to Joseph than the beatings he received from his father. Sometimes poverty drove Ekaterina close to madness, and we hear of her wandering through the streets with her hair disheveled, crying, praying, singing and muttering to herself. From a very early age the boy knew what it was to live alone in the world.

According to Iremashvili, who knew the family well and was constantly in and out of the house, the father beat the son vengefully, remorselessly, with a kind of brooding, deliberate passion, without pleasure and without any sense of guilt or wrongdoing, for no other purpose than to provide himself with some excitement in an otherwise empty and purposeless existence. The result was inevitable. The boy learned to hate. Most of all he hated his father, but gradually this hatred expanded until it included all other fathers, all other men.

"I never saw him crying," Iremashvili relates, and the statement has the ring of authenticity. The boy became hardened by his beatings, and became in the end terrifyingly indifferent to cruelty. His face and body were covered with bruises, but he was determined not to surrender. Somehow he would survive his father, but in order to survive it was necessary to become as brutal as his father. He was too puny to hit back, but he could provide himself with a brutal protective armor of indifference and scorn. "Those undeserved and fearful beatings," says Iremashvili, "made the boy as hard and heartless as his father." . . .

Church was a consolation, for no one beat him in church, no one scorned him or had pity on him. As a choirboy he walked in processions, sang hymns, wore brilliant vestments, and being close to the priests, he was closer to the source of the mystery. His earliest ambition was to be a priest; and his mother looked forward to the time when she would be blessed by her son.

His greatest consolation however was his mother, who worked herself to the bone to provide for him and who lived for him. . . . Her love for her son was an intense and possessive love. . . .

(It is obviously still possible for most biographers to designate as love both destructive attempts to possess one's child and total blindness to the child's situation.)

He was seven when he suffered an attack of smallpox, which left disfiguring scars that remained to the end of his life. It must have been a serious attack, for the scars were large and numerous, with the result that when he came to power thousands of photographs of him had to be carefully doctored.

An even more distressing affliction occurred when he was about ten. He only once spoke about it, and then only briefly when he was explaining why, when he was in exile in Siberia during World War I, he was not called up for military service. He told the story to Anna Alliluieva, his sister-in-law, who published it in her memoirs:

> The left arm of Stalin was badly bent at the elbow. The injury occurred during his childhood. An infection set in, and since there was no one to give it treatment, blood-poisoning followed. Stalin was close to death.
>
> "I don't know what saved me," he told us. "Either it was due to my healthy organism or to the ointments smeared on it by the village quack, but I got my health back again."
>
> The vestiges of that injury remain to the present day. . . .

As a result of the injury Stalin's left arm was some three inches shorter than the right, and he never had complete muscular control of his left hand. At various times he wore a brace to support the elbow; the outline of the brace can be seen in several photographs. A distinguished orthopedic surgeon has suggested on the basis of Alliluieva's account and a number of photographs that Stalin suffered "a compound fracture with resultant osteomyelitis and a subsequent hand deformity secondary to disturbance of growth of the arm, the hand deformity being produced by a Volkman's contracture subsequent to improper treatment of the fracture."

Such a diagnosis is, of course, largely speculative.

Chaim Soutine, Portrait of a Child
1990 ARS N.Y./SPADEM

The medical records of Stalin have never been published, and it is unlikely that they will be published for some years to come. What is certain is that the left arm was warped, lacked the strength of the right arm, and caused him pain and discomfort throughout his life. The awkward shoulder brace was a constant reminder that he suffered from an incurable deformity, and he had only to look at his left hand, which never opened properly, to remember that he was not like other men. He went to considerable trouble to conceal his deformity, which could only be successfully hidden when he was wearing a heavy greatcoat with unusually long sleeves. The crooked arm probably had a profound effect on his emerging character.

There is no clue as to how the injury occurred. It seems likely to have happened as a result of one of the ferocious beatings he received from his father.

Untreated fractures of the left arm are a frequently occurring phenomenon in battered children. The adult holds in his right hand the broomstick or clothes hanger used in a frontal attack on the child standing before him, and the child's left arm is exposed to the greatest danger.

Stalin's family was very poor, and his mother had to work. But Charlie Chaplin's mother was poor too. She even had to put her child in an orphanage, but she visited him there and gave him the assurance that he was loved, that he was valuable and important to someone. The experience of being loved can be sensed in all the Chaplin films. In spite of hunger, misery, and calamity, there is always room for feelings, for tears, for tenderness, for life.

For Stalin—who, like Hitler, was born after the death of several siblings—there was nothing but loneliness, the constant threat of beatings, the belief in his own ostensible worthlessness and guilt, and nowhere another human being to protect him from constant persecution and abuse, to tell or show him that he was not guilty. There was no one of influence in his life who could avert his fate, just as there was no mercy later for the millions of prisoners in the Gulag Archipelago. Without even being sentenced, they could be tormented, tortured, killed—or released— for no apparent cause. Everything was determined by the arbitrary whim of a tyrant who suspected enemy attacks from all sides because he had experienced perpetual threats at an early age and because there had been no witness to teach him that the whole world was not like his father: wicked, dangerous, unpredictable, frightening. When a child's boundless powerlessness never finds sheltering arms, it will be transformed into harshness and merci- lessness; when, in addition, it is spurred by a mother's ambition, it can result in a great career that introduces all the elements of the child's repressed misery into world history. Then millions of human beings are marched to Russian prisons or to Nazi gas chambers without knowing why, because once a little boy didn't know why he was being punished. How long are we going to tolerate these senseless marches now that we finally are in a position to discover their underlying causes?

Friedrich Nietzsche, 1861
Ullstein Bilderdienst

TWO

Friedrich Nietzsche:
The Struggle Against the Truth

A Mistreated Child, a Brilliant Mind, and Eleven Years of Darkness

Several years ago I wanted to demonstrate that the works of writers, poets, and painters tell the encoded story of childhood traumas no longer consciously remembered in adulthood. After having made this discovery in my own painting and in the writings of Franz Kafka, I was able to test it against other life histories. I wanted to share what I had found with biographers and psychoanalysts, but I soon learned that I was dealing with forbidden knowledge, by no means easy to share with "the experts."

And so I decided not to publish my study but to keep the knowledge I had gained to myself, devoting myself to other pursuits such as painting and confronting my own early childhood. Through these activities I gradually realized that my disappointment at the blindness of society and of the experts had something to do with my own blindness and that I really felt compelled to try to prove something to myself that a part of me refused to believe. Of course, I had long been aware of my parents' weaknesses, of the injury they had inflicted on me without knowing it, but my early idealization of my parents was still unresolved. I recognized it in my naive belief and confidence that the biographers of Hitler, Kafka, and Nietzsche must be capable of seeing and affirming what I had found.

That they were not capable of recognizing such forbidden knowledge finally became clear to me when I realized how strongly I was clinging to my childhood idealization of my parents. For a long time I couldn't stop hoping that my parents would someday be ready to share my questions with me, to stop evading them, react to them, and not be afraid to join me in seeing where they led. This never happened when I was a child, and I thought I had long since gotten over my deprivation. But my astonishment at the reactions of people whom I had expected to be more knowledgeable than I revealed that I still had not given up the image of clever and courageous parents who could be convinced by the facts. Once I became conscious of the connection, I no longer had any need to publish my study.

Now I have a different motivation for publishing. I would like to share the knowledge I have gained with people who can face the facts. They need not be experts but, rather, people who may be inspired by my work to read Nietzsche and to make a connection between their impressions of him and their own experience.

The need to share my findings with others was not my only motive in writing about Nietzsche. My work with the Nietzsche material had made me realize that society's ignorance about the injuries inflicted on children represents a great danger for humanity. Sentences from Nietzsche's writings could never have been misinterpreted in support of fascism and the annihilation of human beings if people had understood his words for what they were: the encoded language of the child who was forbidden to express his true feelings. Young men would never have been willing to march to war with his words in their pack if they had known that his ideology promoting the destruction of morality and traditional values such as charity and mercy stood for the raised fist of a child starved for truth who had suffered severely under the domination of hypocrisy. Since I myself had witnessed the way the deadly marching of the National Socialists in the thirties and forties was indirectly spurred on by Nietzsche's words, it now seemed to me worth the trouble to find and call attention to the genesis of these words, thoughts, and feelings.

Would Nietzsche's ideas have been useless to the Nazis if people had understood their source? I do not doubt it. But if society *had* understood, then the ideas of the Nazis would also have been unthinkable or at least would not have found the broad acceptance they did. The simple, commonplace facts of child abuse are not given a hearing; if they were, the human race would have greater understanding and wars could be prevented. Only if they are presented in a disguised, symbolic form can they arouse great interest and an emotional response. For the disguised story is, after all, familiar to most of us, but its symbolic language must guarantee that what has been repressed will not be brought to light and cause pain. Therefore, my thesis that Nietzsche's works reflect the unlived feelings, needs, and tragedy of his childhood will probably meet with great resistance. The thesis is correct nevertheless, and I will offer proof in the pages that follow. My proof can be understood, however, only by someone who is willing to temporarily abandon the adult perspective to gain insight into and take serious account of the situation of a child.

Which child are we talking about? The boy who learns in school to suppress his normal, human feelings and always act as if he didn't have any? The little boy who is trained day after day by his young mother, his grandmother, and his two aunts to be a "strong" man? The very little boy whose beloved father "loses his mind" and goes on living with the family for eleven months in an unstable condition? Or the even younger child who was punished most severely and locked in dark closets by the father whom he loved and was occasionally allowed to play with? It is not one or another but all these children rolled into one who had to bear so much without being allowed to express any feelings or, indeed, even to have any feelings. He was not supposed to cry, to scream, to be in a rage. He was only supposed to be well disciplined and to do brilliant work.

Friedrich Nietzsche survived this childhood; he survived the more than one hundred illnesses in one year of secondary school, the constant headaches, and the rheumatic ailments, which his biographers have assiduously listed without searching for their cause and which they finally attribute to a "weak constitution." At the age of twelve he kept a diary, the kind an adult might have kept, written in a well-adjusted, reasonable, well-behaved way. But in adolescence his once suppressed feelings burst forth, resulting in works that would deeply move other young people of later generations. And then at age forty, when he could no longer bear his loneliness and, since he was not able to see that the roots of his life history went back to his childhood, he lost his mind and everything became "clear": historians locate the cause of his tragic ending in a venereal disease he supposedly contracted as an adolescent. The outcome is in keeping with our moral standards: the just, though delayed, punishment, in the form of a fatal disease, for having visited a prostitute. This is similar to the present attitude toward AIDS. Everything seems to turn out for the best, and hypocritical morality is restored. But what those who raised and taught Nietzsche actually did to the boy did not happen so long ago that we can no longer find out about it. Young graduate students can uncover the story, read the letters from his sister and others, write dissertations about their findings, and reconstruct the situation that gave rise to his later works, such as *Beyond Good and Evil, The Antichrist*, and *Thus Spake Zarathustra*. But this can be done only by students who were not mistreated as children or who have worked through their mistreatment and therefore have open ears and eyes for the suffering of battered children. Their research is not likely to be greeted with enthusiasm by their professors. If they can persevere in their research nonetheless, they will produce evidence that the crimes committed against children have serious effects on all humanity. They will also be able to illustrate the unexpected ways in which these effects occur.

FAMILY LIFE

In my search for the facts about Nietzsche's early childhood I learned the following:

Both parents were the children of Protestant ministers and numbered several theologians among their forebears. Nietzsche's father was the youngest child from his own father's second marriage; when, at age thirty, he married a seventeen-year-old woman, he also took in both of his older, unmarried sisters and, later, his mother. Friedrich was born a year after the marriage, in 1844. When Friedrich was two, his sister was born and soon after that a brother, who died at the age of two shortly after the death of the father. According to reports, the father was a warm-hearted and feeling person who from the first loved his son very much and frequently had him by his side when he improvised at the piano. This important experience and the warmth the father may have shown his son probably played a role in enabling the boy to experience strong feelings in spite of his rigorous upbringing. Despite his affection, however, the father strictly forbade certain feelings and severely punished his son for expressing them. There are reports of temper tantrums, which stern measures soon put to an end.

> His father, when he had time, liked to spend it with his oldest child, once the boy had learned to talk a little. It didn't disturb him either when Friedrich came into the father's study and watched him "quietly and thoughtfully," as the mother writes, while he was working. But the child was completely spellbound when his father sat at the piano and "improvised." Already at the age of one, little Fritz, as everyone called him, would then sit up in his carriage, listen, quiet as a mouse, and not take his eyes off his father. Otherwise, however, he was not always a well-behaved child in those first years. If he didn't get his way, he threw himself to the floor and furiously kicked his little legs in the air. His father must have taken very energetic measures against this behavior, yet for a long time the boy was still stubborn and recalcitrant when he was denied something he wanted, although he no longer rebelled but withdrew silently into a quiet corner or to the privy, where he vented his anger by himself.

Whatever a biographer may mean by "venting" here, the feelings that had to be eliminated in the privy are unmistakably present in the philosopher's later writings. We mustn't forget that a grandmother and two young aunts also lived with the family. In addition to their charitable activities and their help with the household, they were mainly concerned with the upbringing of the firstborn child. When Friedrich was scarcely four, his father died after eleven months of suffering from a serious illness, probably the result of a brain tumor, which his son later referred to as "softening of the brain." The family perpetuated the story that the father's illness was caused by an accident, a version of events that somewhat lessened the shame that a brain disease may have caused them. The actual medical diagnosis is not completely clear to this day.

It is difficult for us as adults to imagine how a child of four feels when his beloved father, his closest attachment figure (which his mother at that time was not), suddenly becomes ill with a brain disease. At the very least Nietzsche must have been highly perplexed. His father's previously more or less predictable reactions were so no longer; the great, admired, and clever man had suddenly become "stupid." His family was perhaps embarrassed at the answers he gave to questions. Possibly the boy too was scornful, but he had to suppress his scorn because he loved his father. We can assume that this same father, who disappeared so soon as his son's companion, was proud of the child's intelligence. But as the father's illness progressed, the boy could no longer tell him things or ask him questions, no longer use him as a point of orientation or count on his response. Yet despite his condition, the father was still present.

Soon after the death of his father, Nietzsche's little brother died too, and now Friedrich was left as the only male in a household of women—his grandmother, two aunts, mother, and younger sister. This might have turned out well for him if one of these women had treated him with tenderness, warmth, and genuine concern. But they all tried to outdo one another in teaching him self-control and other Christian virtues. The originality of his imagination and the honesty of his questions were too much for their sense of morality, and so they attempted to silence the child's curiosity, which made them uncomfortable, by strict supervision and a stern upbringing.

What else can a child, so completely at the mercy of a regimen like this, do except adapt and suppress his genuine feelings with all his might? That is what Friedrich did, and he soon became a model child and a model pupil. One biographer describes a scene that clearly illustrates how extreme the boy's self-denial was. Caught in heavy rain on his way home from school, Nietzsche did not quicken his pace but continued to walk slowly with head erect. His explanation was that "upon leaving school one must go home in a calm and mannerly way. That's what the regulations require." We can imagine the training that must have preceded such behavior.

The boy observed the people around him and could not help but be critical; however, he was forced to keep such thoughts to himself and do all he could to suppress them, along with any other impious thoughts. In addition, he constantly heard the Christian virtues of neighborly love and compassion being preached all around him. Yet in his own daily experience no one took pity on him when he was beaten; no one saw that he was suffering. No one came to his aid, even though so many people around him were busy practicing the Christian virtues. What good are these virtues, the little boy must have kept asking himself. Am I not also the "neighbor" who deserves to be loved? But even questions such as these could have provoked more beatings. What choice did he have, then, but to keep his questions to himself and to feel even more alone with them than before because he could not share them with anyone?

But the questions did not go away. Later, much later, after Nietzsche finished his schooling and had nothing to fear from the authorities—in this case his professors—because he had become a professor himself, the questions and repressed feelings broke out of the prison where they had been locked up for twenty years. In the meantime, by finding an ersatz object they gained social legitimacy. Nietzsche did not direct his criticism at the real causes of his rage—his aunts, his grandmother, his mother—but at the values of his chosen field, philology. Still, this took courage, for they were values that had until then been held sacred by *all* philologists.

But Nietzsche also attacked values that once were dear to him although not respected by those around him —for example, the "truth," symbolized in the person of Socrates. In the same way that a person going through puberty must first reject everything he once loved in order to establish new values for himself, Nietzsche—who never revolted during puberty, who at the age of twelve made agreeable entries in his diary—now at twenty-five set out to attack the culture he had grown up with, to mock it, to make it seem absurd by standing it on its head. He did this not with the methods of a growing adolescent but with the highly developed intellect of a philologist and professor of philosophy.

It is all too understandable that his language became forceful and impressive. It was not empty talk that seized upon trite revolutionary slogans but a combination of original thoughts and intense feelings, rarely found in a philologist, that had a direct impact on the reader.

We are accustomed to thinking of Nietzsche as a representative of late Romanticism and to seeing the influence of Schopenhauer on his work. Which people influence us as adults is no accident, and Nietzsche's description of the euphoria he felt when he opened Schopenhauer's major opus, *The World as Will and Idea* (1819), and began reading indicates that he had good reason for discovering in Schopenhauer a world intimately related to his own. If he had been allowed to speak freely in his family as an adolescent, it is possible that he would not have needed Schopenhauer or, above all, the Germanic heroes, Richard Wagner, and the concept of the "blond beast." He would have found his own discriminating words with which to say: "I can't bear the chains that shackle me day after day; my creative powers are in danger of being destroyed. I need all my energies to rescue them and to assert myself in your midst. There is nothing I can confront you with that you would understand. I can't live in this narrow, untruthful world. And yet I can't leave you. I can't get along without you because I'm still a child and am dependent on you. That's why you have so much power although you are essentially weak. It takes heroic courage, superhuman qualities, and super-human strength to crush this world that is interfering with my life. I don't have that much strength; I am too weak and afraid of hurting you, but I despise the weakness in me and the weakness in you, which forces me to pity you. *I despise every form of weakness* that interferes with my life. You have surrounded me with restrictions; prisoner that I am of school and home, there is no free space for me except perhaps in music, but that is not enough for me. I must be able to use words. I must be able to shout them out. Your morality and your reason are a prison for me in which I am smothering to death, and this at the beginning of my life when I would have so much to say."

Words such as those got stuck in Nietzsche's throat and brain, and it is no wonder that he suffered continually from severe headaches, sore throats, and rheumatic ail-ments as a child and especially during his school days. What he was not allowed to say out loud remained active in his body in the form of constant tension. Later he could direct his criticism against abstract concepts such as cul-ture, Christianity, philistinism, and middle-class values without having to worry that someone might die as a result (all well-brought-up children are afraid that their angry words might kill those they love). Compared with this danger, criticism of society in the abstract is harmless for an adult, even if society's representatives are outraged by it. An adult is not facing them like a helpless, guilty child; an adult can use intellectual arguments to defend himself and even to make attacks—methods not usually available to a child and not available to Nietzsche as a child.

And yet Nietzsche's accurate observations concerning Western culture and Christian morality as well as the vehement indignation they aroused in him do not date from the period of his philosophical analysis but from his first years of life. It was then that he perceived the system and suffered under it, simultaneously as slave and devotee; it was then that he was chained to a morality he despised and was tormented by the people whose love he needed. Because of his brilliant intellect, the perceptions he stored up at an early age have helped many people see things they have never seen before. The experiences of one individual, despite their subjectivity, can have universal validity because the family and the child-rearing methods minutely observed at an early age represent society as a whole.

PUZZLEMENT

Along with its positive side, however, Nietzsche's manner of "mastering" his fate as a child had a devastating and disastrous effect because he used what had caused him the most trouble—his puzzlement—as a weapon against the world. In the same way that *he* became thoroughly puzzled—first by his father's terrible illness and later by the unbearable contradiction between the morality preached to him and the actual behavior of the attachment figures in his family and in school—he sometimes puzzles the reader, probably without knowing it. I had this feeling of puzzlement when I recently began reading Nietzsche again after three decades. Thirty years ago I would surely have disregarded my puzzlement because my only concern then was to understand his meaning. But now I let myself be guided by the feeling. As a result, I realized that other readers must have felt the same way, even if they did not use the word *puzzlement* and attributed their feelings to their own lack of education, intelligence, or depth. Blaming ourselves is exactly the reaction we learn as children. If the grown-ups (who are supposed to be more clever than we are) self-assuredly assert things that are inconsistent, contradictory, or absurd, how can children raised in an authoritarian way be expected to know that what they are hearing is not the ultimate wisdom? They will make every effort to accept it as such and will carefully conceal their doubts from themselves. This is the way many people read the writings of the great Nietzsche today. They blame themselves for their puzzlement and show Nietzsche the same reverence he must have shown his ill father as a child.

Although admitting my perplexity helped me recognize these connections, I do not consider my feeling to be simply a personal matter. I found a passage by Richard Blunck—who devoted himself to Nietzsche's life and work for forty years—that indirectly confirms my own impression. Since a large portion of the material Blunck had collected was destroyed in the war, he himself never published the major Nietzsche biography he had planned but left further work on it to Curt-Paul Janz. I found these words by Blunck in the introduction to Janz's first volume:

Friedrich Nietzsche and His Mother
Ullstein Bilderdienst

Those who come across a book of Nietzsche's for the first time, the way we did forty years ago, immediately sense that more is required to understand it than the intellect, that more is involved here than following someone's thinking from premise to conclusion and from concept to concept in order to arrive at "truth." They will feel that they have wandered instead into an immense field of force that is emitting shock waves of a far deeper nature than can be registered by intellect alone. They will be struck less by the opinions and insights expressed than by the person behind these opinions and insights. Readers will often react defensively to them if they have something to defend, but they will never again be entirely able to escape the man who expressed them. If readers pursue these ideas that confront, sometimes even assault, them in the form of commanding sentences, then they will soon have the feeling that they are in a labyrinth in whose intricate passageways they find not only immeasurable riches but also the threatening visage of a minotaur who demands human sacrifice. They will believe they are encountering the truest of truths, which go to the heart of things, only to have these truths cancel themselves out in the next book and to feel themselves thrust into a new passageway of the labyrinth. Still, if they have an alert mind and not merely a groping intellect, they will never lose the certainty that Nietzsche has brought them closer to life and its secrets than has any other thinker. Despite the contradictory character of his views and positions, a more profound and elevated intellectual force is communicated that is not confined to positions and truths but constantly both ignores and transcends them in the service of an authenticity that knows no law other than itself and the eternal flux of life with all its tranformations and creativity.

Such authenticity, however, does not consist in collecting knowledge and ordering things in a rational manner, little as it can do without these processes, but is a feature of the ethical personality, of the heart's courage, and the dauntless and indefatigable nature of the mind. It must be lived and suffered if it is to attain that intellectual force which Nietzsche's work demonstrates. And it is because his authenticity—in combination with a great receptivity to all aspects of the European intellectual tradition as well as a critical grasp of this tradition, in combination also with a profound understanding of human nature and a prophetic farsightedness and clarity of vision—is apparent to an extent unequalled in the history of Western thought that Nietzsche's life and work affect us so powerfully. Spurred on by this authenticity, he waged a single-minded, unwearying struggle against an age that was sinking deeper and deeper into hopeless dishonesty, a struggle against his own happiness, against fame, and even against his tender heart. This was an undertaking whose purity and necessity cannot be obscured or cancelled out, no matter how ambiguous or even dreadful its effects.

Because of his own upbringing, the author of these lines, who actually was very close to the truth, got caught in the labyrinth he refers to and was unable to track down its biographical origins; and if he *had* dared to do so, his life and work in the Third Reich would surely have been jeopardized. For Nietzsche was very much in vogue when Blunck was doing his work in pre–World War II Germany. His glorification of the "barbaric hero" was taken literally and was lived out with all its horrible consequences. But the very way the National Socialists adapted Nietzsche's ideas and formulations for their own purposes shows how dangerous it can be to view the last links in a biographical chain in isolation while remaining uninterested in and blind to the earliest links in the chain.

Today Nietzsche's biographers emphasize again and again a closer connection between his life and thought than biographers of other philosophers do. Yet Nietzsche's biographers rarely refer to his childhood, despite the fact that without understanding this crucial period a life remains an enigma. The two-thousand-page biography by Janz, which appeared in 1978, devotes less than ten pages to Nietzsche's childhood (not counting a genealogical history). Since the importance of childhood for later life is still a very controversial subject, biographers have done little investigation in this area. Nietzsche scholars search in his work for connections to the history of philosophy rather than to his life. His life, his illness, and his tragic ending, to say nothing of his work, have never been examined in the light of his childhood.

And yet today it seems to me a simple matter to recognize that what Nietzsche wrote was his hopeless attempt, which he didn't abandon until his breakdown, to free himself from his prison by expressing his unconscious but present hatred for those who raised and mistreated him. His hatred, and his fear of it, became all the more vehement the less he succeeded in becoming independent of its objects, his mother and sister. It is a known fact that his sister altered many of his letters for publication, that she intrigued untiringly to the detriment of his true interests and did not rest until his relationship with Lou Andreas Salomé was destroyed. Both mother and sister needed Friedrich's dependence on them until the very end. Since the perfectly raised child had learned at an early age not to defend himself but to struggle instead against his true feelings, the grown man was unable to find his way to real liberation. His writing kept alive the illusion of liberation because on a symbolic level he actually did take steps in the direction of truth and freedom. He took them in his life as well but only insofar as they did not involve the members of his family. After he became ill, for instance, he had the courage to give up his professorship in Basel to have more freedom to criticize the academic system. He was then free to write what he needed to say instead of having to conform to the demands of the university. But this was still an ersatz solution as long as he was unable to recognize his idealization of his parents, who were responsible for his suffering. For his true feelings (of anger, fear, contempt, helplessness, the wish to be free, destructive rage, and desperate dependence on his persecutors), originating in childhood, gave him no peace and kept demanding new ersatz objects.

HIS MOTHER

In several letters to Nietzsche's friends after the philosopher had completely lost his mental faculties, his mother describes the condition of the patient for whom she has sacrificed herself and whom she takes care of like a little child. In one letter she writes that her son uttered terrible screams although he had a cheerful expression on his face. We can't be sure how reliable this information is because mothers frequently interpret a look on a child's face in keeping with their own wishes. But if his mother's observation was correct, then the explanation may be that, in her presence, the very little child was allowed to scream loudly for the first time in his life and that he was enjoying the tolerance he had finally won from her. For we can scarcely conceive of someone screaming without a face racked with pain.

There are women who can be kinder to their children if the children are no longer capable of thinking (that is, of being critical), as the result of mental illness or a brain disease, for example. Although not yet dead, the children are helpless and totally dependent on the mother. If such a woman was brought up to fulfill her duty above all else, she will feel good and noble if she sacrifices herself for her child. If she had to suppress her own criticism as a child, it will make her angry the moment her son or daughter expresses criticism of her. She feels less threatened, on the other hand, by a handicapped child. In addition, her self-sacrifice is respected and admired by society. Thus, it is very likely that Nietzsche's mother—who was only eighteen when he was born and is described as cold, stupid, and disinterested even by sympathetic biographers—actually did sacrifice herself to look after her son in his last years when he no longer recognized his friends and could barely speak.

RICHARD WAGNER
(The Father: Seduction and Disappointment)

It would take a very careful reading of Nietzsche's letters to relate the individual episodes in his life to his childhood. In addition, the actual facts would have to be sifted from his sister's numerous falsifications. I can imagine that anyone who is not afraid of taking on the task of establishing the connections to his childhood would discover much that is new. One might look into the question, for instance, of whether Nietzsche's relationship with Richard Wagner, who was thirty years his senior, was not a repetition of the repressed tragic experience with his father, who had taken ill so suddenly. This conjecture seems justified by the fact that his initial admiration and enthusiasm for Wagner, beginning about 1868 and nurtured at Wagner's home in Bayreuth, so quickly turned into disappointment, rejection, and radical estrangement. Nietzsche's break with Wagner culminated in 1882 when Wagner wrote *Parsifal*, which in Nietzsche's eyes "betrayed" the old Germanic values for the sake of highly suspect Christian ones. Not until then did he become fully conscious of weaknesses in Richard Wagner, weaknesses he had previously overlooked in his idealization of the older man.

I have searched in vain in the extensive secondary literature about Nietzsche for information describing how the highly intelligent four-and-a-half-year-old child reacted to his father's fatal brain disease that lasted nearly a year. For lack of any indication in his youth, I turned to his later life and looked for clues there. I believe I found them in Nietzsche's relationship with Richard Wagner. However great the disappointment in Wagner's work may have been for the mature Nietzsche, it would never have provoked such an extreme degree of mockery and contempt (especially since Wagner hadn't done anything to alienate Nietzsche personally and was even very fond of him) if Wagner's personality and music hadn't reminded him of his father and of the misery of his early childhood.

From the mid-1870s, Wagner's entire work and the Bayreuth atmosphere, in which Nietzsche had previously felt at home, struck him as a gigantic lie. The one thing he could not deny was Wagner's dramatic gift, although he did not compliment Wagner with this admission, for he defined the psychology and morality of an actor in the following way: "One is an actor by virtue of being ahead of the rest of mankind in one insight: what is meant to have the effect of truth must not be true. . . . Wagner's music is never true. But *it is taken for true*; and thus it is in order." Wagner's music, according to Nietzsche, contained the pretense of sacred, noble, great, and good feelings, the hoax of pseudo ideals that have little to do with the authentic feelings of real people, such as Nietzsche found embodied in Bizet's *Carmen* (1875), with its ambivalence and its "killing for love." He saw *Carmen* several times with great enthusiasm, experiencing it as a liberation from the lie that had afflicted him not only since his younger years with Wagner in Bayreuth but even since his childhood. And now his attack against the fatherly friend he once admired, Richard Wagner, turned into a total one: he no longer saw anything good in him and hated him with all his heart like a deeply wounded child. His hatred was nourished by despair and grief over having let himself be deceived for so long, for admiring someone for so long whom he now considered contemptible. Why didn't he see through the weakness behind the facade sooner? How could he have been so mistaken?

Nietzsche saw himself as the victim of a seduction that he must now unmask by every means at his command. He found Wagner's admirers naive and could not grasp that they continued to go to Bayreuth, where they allowed themselves to be hypnotized by a lie, after he himself had seen through it. The pain this caused him kept showing through in the aspersions he cast on Wagner: Nietzsche would have liked to save the world from a great deception and bring the Wagnerians to their senses; he would have liked to lead them back to themselves and their own genuine experiences the way Zarathustra did by refusing to have any disciples.

Although Nietzsche's attacks derived their intensity from his repressed rage against his father and other attachment figures from childhood, they did not display any weakness in logic that would reveal their real roots. What he wrote about Wagner and substantiated with examples was so convincing (although probably not for Wagnerians) that it retains its claim to objectivity quite apart from the subjective, highly emotional background of his observations. I believe that Nietzsche's keen powers of observation had their beginnings in his relationship with his father, to whose music the little boy listened with rapt attention, admiration, and enthusiasm. But his father was not only a musician who played the piano but also a pedagogue who approved of certain feelings (such as his son's enthusiasm for his playing) but severely punished the display of others.

Perhaps the boy succeeded in accepting his father's two different sides and in overlooking the punishment as long as he was allowed to be with his father, to listen to his music making and let the music become part of him. But when his father fell ill and the child felt suddenly and completely abandoned by him, overwhelming feelings of disappointment, rage, and shame at being seduced and then forsaken would have had to break through—*if* the boy had not already learned that it was not permissible to show such feelings and if he had not been subsequently raised exclusively by women ("female Wagnerians") who condemned his feelings and kept them in the strictest rein. These feelings had to lie in wait for decades until they could be experienced toward another musician.

The sharpness and accuracy of Nietzsche's later observations about Wagner not only were unimpaired by his feelings but, on the contrary, seemed to be intensified by them. If it had not been made impossible for him to speak out, Nietzsche the child might have said: "I don't believe your music if you can also beat me and punish me for having genuine feelings. If your music is not a deception, if it really is expressing the truth, then I have every right to expect you to respect the feelings of your child. Otherwise there is something wrong, and the music I have absorbed through every pore is a lie. I want to shout it out to all the world in order to keep others—for example, my little brother and sister—from becoming the victims of your seduction. If your theology, your sermons, your words have been telling the truth, you would have to treat me very differently. You wouldn't be able to watch my suffering uncomprehendingly, for I am 'the neighbor' you're supposed to love. You wouldn't punish me for my tears, wouldn't make me bear my distress all alone without helping me, wouldn't forbid me to speak, if you were an honest and trustworthy man. After all that's been done to me, I think your ideas of goodness, neighborly love, and redemption are empty and false; everything I used to believe is nothing but theatrics; there is nothing real about it. What I experience is real, and what you have said must be able to be measured against my reality. But when the measurement is taken, your words prove to be pure playacting. You enjoy having a child who listens to you and admires you. It satisfies your needs. The others don't notice this and think you really have something to offer them. But *I* noticed. I guessed your state of neediness, but I wasn't allowed to say anything about it."

The boy wasn't allowed to say this to his father. But

as an adult he said it to Richard Wagner. He wrote it in no uncertain terms, and the world took what he wrote seriously. Neither Nietzsche nor "the world," unfortunately, wondered about its source. Thus both missed the important point.

NIETZSCHE THE WOMAN HATER

In contrast to the general validity of Nietzsche's censure of the Wagner phenomenon, of middle-class cultural values and Christian moral values, his ideas about "the nature of woman" often seem grotesquely distorted, but only if we are unaware of the actual women who gave rise to them. As a child, Nietzsche was surrounded by women intent on bringing him up correctly, and he had to use all his energies to endure this situation. He paid them back in later years, but only on a symbolic level, by attacking *all* women—except his mother and sister. The women who actually caused his suffering remained unassailable, at the cost of the loss of objectivity.

Nietzsche's misogyny becomes understandable, of course, if we consider how much distrust must have accumulated in someone who was whipped so frequently as a child. But this doesn't authorize him as an adult to write in his blind and irresponsible rage: "You are going to women? Do not forget the whip!" There is no doubt that Nietzsche was brought up according to the principles of "poisonous pedagogy" described extensively in my previous books. The documents I cite in *For Your Own Good* illustrate how children must be tricked, deceived, and manipulated to make them pious and good.

That is why Nietzsche was rarely able to show his discontent at his sister's manipulative and insincere behavior toward him, why he didn't allow himself to see her as she really was. If he ever did see the truth, he quickly retracted anything he may have said against her. Although he admitted on one occasion that he could not stand her voice, he immediately added that basically he had never really doubted her goodwill, her intentions, her love for him, or her trustworthiness. How could he, since he had only one sister and wanted to believe absolutely that she loved him and that her love was more than exploitation and a need to win recognition at any price. If he had been able to see *the way the women in his childhood really were*, then it would not have been necessary for him to generalize by making *all* women into witches and serpents and to hate them all.

F A S C I S M *(The Blond Beast)*

It is not my intention here to explain Nietzsche's life in terms of his childhood but rather to understand the function of his philosophy in his struggle against the pain stemming from his childhood. His formative experience consisted in *contempt for the weak and obedience toward those wielding power*. This seemingly innocuous combina-

Friedrich Nietzsche as an Infantryman in Naumburg, 1868
Ullstein Bilderdienst

tion, familiar to so many of us from childhood, is the nucleus of every fascist ideology. As a result of having been treated brutally in childhood, fascists of whatever stamp will blindly accept their leader and treat those weaker than themselves brutally. The fact that this behavior can be accompanied by a longing for the release of creative powers that the methods of "poisonous pedagogy" suppress in every child is to be seen very plainly in Nietzsche and others and also in certain statements by C. G. Jung. The human being's need to live and to be allowed to develop freely is coupled with the former persecutor's introjected voice. Just as the child's cries were once smothered by the principles of "poisonous pedagogy," so too the call to life is smothered by the brutality of fascism. The introjected system allies itself with the child's own wishes and leads to destructive ideologies that can have a fascination for anyone who experienced a cruel upbringing. Thus, it is not Nietzsche's writings that are dangerous but the child-rearing system of which he and his readers were the product. The Nazis were able to transform what seemed to be his *life-affirming philosophy* into a *death-affirming ideology* because it was never in its essence separate from death.

It is not by chance that *Thus Spake Zarathustra* became Nietzsche's most famous work, for his puzzled readers at least found in Zarathustra's way of speaking a frame of reference familiar to them since childhood: the rhetorical style of the preacher. How familiar, too, although clothed in novel words, was the struggle for life in the face of the deadening requirement to be obedient. Again and again Nietzsche circles around this dichotomy.

> I pursued the living; I walked the widest and the narrowest paths that I might know its nature. With a hundredfold mirror I still caught its glance *when its mouth was* closed, so that its eyes might speak to me. And its eyes spoke to me. [Italics mine]
>
> But wherever I *found the living*, there I heard also the *speech on obedience*. Whatever lives, obeys. [Italics mine]
>
> And this is the second point: he who cannot obey himself is commanded. That is the nature of the living.
>
> This, however, is the third point that I heard: that commanding is harder than obeying; and not only because he who commands must carry the burden of all who obey, and because this burden may easily crush him. An experiment and hazard appeared to me to be in all commanding; and whenever the living commands, it hazards itself. Indeed, even when it commands *itself*, it must still pay for its commanding. It must become the judge, the avenger, and the victim of its own law. How does this happen? I asked myself. What persuades the living to obey and command, and to practice obedience even when it commands? . . .
>
> And life itself confided this secret to me: "Behold," it said, "I am *that which must always overcome itself.* Indeed, you call it a will to procreate or a drive to an end, to something higher, farther, more manifold: but all this is one, and one secret.
>
> "Rather would I perish than forswear this; and verily, where there is perishing and a falling of leaves, behold, there life sacrifices itself—for power. That I must be struggle and a becoming and an end and an opposition to ends

—alas, whoever guesses what is my will should also guess on what *crooked* paths it must proceed.

"Whatever I create and however much I love it— soon I must oppose it and my love; thus my will wills it. And you too, lover of knowledge, are only a path and foot-print of my will; verily, my will to power walks also on the heels of your will to truth.

"Indeed, the truth was not hit by him who shot at it with the word of the 'will to existence': that will does not exist. For, what does not exist cannot will; but what is in existence, how could that still want existence? Only where there is life is there also will: not will to life but—thus I teach you—will to power.

"There is much that life esteems more highly than life itself; but out of the esteeming itself speaks the will to power."

Thus life once taught me; and with this I shall yet solve the riddle of your heart, you who are wisest.

Verily, I say unto you: good and evil that are not transitory, do not exist. Driven on by themselves, they must overcome themselves again and again. With your values and words of good and evil you do violence when you value; and this is your hidden love and the splendor and trembling and overflowing of your soul. But a more violent force and a new overcoming grow out of your values and break egg and eggshell.

And whoever must be a creator in good and evil, verily, he must first be an annihilator and break values. Thus the highest evil belongs to the highest goodness: but this is creative.

Let us speak of this, you who are wisest, even if it be bad. *Silence is worse; all truths that are kept silent become poisonous.* [Italics mine]

And may everything be broken that cannot brook our truths! There are yet many houses to be built!

Thus spoke Zarathustra.

How wicked and hard a child must feel who remains true to himself and does not betray what he perceives and sees. How difficult and at the same time how essential it is to be able to say no.

With the storm that is called "spirit" I blew over your wavy sea; I blew all clouds away; I even strangled the strangler that is called "sin."

O my soul, I gave you the right *to say No like the storm, and to say Yes as the clear sky says Yes*: now you are still as light whether you stand or *walk through storms of negation.* [Italics mine]

O my soul, I gave you back the freedom over the created and uncreated; and who knows, as you know, the voluptuous delight of what is yet to come?

O my soul, I taught you the contempt that does not come like the worm's gnawing, the great, *the loving contempt that loves most where it despises most.* [Italics mine]

O my soul, I taught you to persuade so well that you persuade the very ground—like the sun who persuades even the sea to his own height.

O my soul, I took from you all obeying, knee-bending, and "Lord"-saying; I myself gave you the name "cessation of need" and "destiny."

But the life the child seeks is fraught with danger, the loveliest fantasies dimmed by early experiences and threats.

My heels twitched, then my toes hearkened to understand you, and rose: for the dancer has his ear in his toes.

I leaped toward you, but you fled back from my leap, and the tongue of your fleeing, flying hair licked me in its sweep.

Away from you I leaped, and from your serpents' ire; and already you stood there, half turned, your eyes full of desire.

With crooked glances you teach me—crooked ways; on crooked ways my foot learns treachery. [Italics mine]

I fear you near, I love you far; your flight lures me, your seeking cures me: I suffer, but what would I not gladly suffer for you?

You, whose coldness fires, whose hatred seduces, whose flight binds, whose scorn inspires:

Who would not hate you, you great *binder, entwiner, temptress, seeker, and finder?* Who would not love you, you innocent, impatient, wind-swift, *child-eyed* sinner? [Italics mine]

Whereto are you luring me now, you never-tame extreme? And now you are fleeing from me again, you sweet wildcat and ingrate!

I dance after you, I follow wherever your traces linger. Where are you? Give me your hand! Or only one finger!

Here are caves and thickets; we shall get lost. Stop! Stand still! Don't you see owls and bats whirring past?

You owl! You bat! Intent to confound! Where are we? Such howling and yelping you have learned from a hound.

Your lovely little white teeth are gnashing at me; out of a curly little mane your evil eyes are flashing at me.

That is a dance up high and down low: I am the hunter; would you be my dog or my doe?

Alongside me now! And swift, you malicious leaping belle! Now up and over there! Alas, as I leaped I fell.

Oh, see me lying there, you prankster, suing for grace. I should like to walk with you in a lovelier place.

Love's paths through silent bushes, past many-hued plants. Or there along that lake: there goldfish swim and dance.

You are weary now? Over there are sunsets and sheep: when shepherds play on their flutes—is it not lovely to sleep?

You are so terribly weary? I'll carry you there; just let your arms sink. And if you are thirsty—I have got something, but your mouth does not want it to drink.

Oh, this damned nimble, supple snake and slippery witch! Where are you? In my face two red blotches from your hand itch.

I am verily weary of always being your sheepish shepherd. You witch, if *I* have so far sung to you, now you shall cry.

Keeping time with my whip, you shall dance and cry! Or have I forgotten the whip? Not I!

It is permissible to hate and whip the serpent and the witch but not the mother, grandmother, or aunts. In any case, feelings of anger, outrage, and mistrust are unmistakably present here. They may also be directed at "the mob," which has the same symbolic function as the serpent and the witch.

Is this today not the mob's? But the mob does not know what is great, what is small, what is straight and honest: it is innocently crooked, it always lies.

Have a good mistrust today, you higher men, you

stouthearted ones, you openhearted ones! And keep your reasons secret! For this today is the mob's.

What the mob once learned to believe without reasons—who could overthrow that with reasons?

And in the market place one convinces with gestures. But reasons make the mob mistrustful.

And if truth was victorious for once, then ask yourself with good mistrust: "What strong error fought for it?"

Over and over again Nietzsche attempts to find his way out of the mists of confusing moral principles and attain clarity. But his speculating continually obfuscates the truth.

Do not let yourselves be gulled and beguiled! Who, after all, is *your* neighbor? And even if you act "for the neighbor"—you still do not create for him.

Unlearn this "for," you creators! Your very virtue wants that you do nothing "for" and "in order" and "because." You shall plug up your ears against these false little words. "For the neighbor" is only the virtue of the little people: there one says "birds of a feather" and "one hand washes the other." They have neither the right nor the strength for *your* egoism. In your egoism, you creators, is the caution and providence of the pregnant. What no one has yet laid eyes on, the fruit: that your whole love shelters and saves and nourishes. Where your whole love is, with your child, there is also your whole virtue. Your work, your will, that is *your* "neighbor": do not let yourselves be gulled with false values!

The call to war has essentially only one symbolic meaning for Nietzsche: it represents nothing other than

declaring battle against the deadly coercion, lies, and cowardice that constricted his life so painfully as a child. But
Nietzsche doesn't say it clearly enough, he doesn't reveal
the source. That is why he opens the doors to a harmful
use of his words.

> A free life is still free for great souls. Verily, *whoever
> possesses little is possessed that much less*: praised be a little
> poverty! [Italics mine]
> Only where the state ends, there begins the human
> being who is not superfluous: there begins the song of
> necessity, the unique and inimitable tune.
> Where the state *ends*—look there, my brothers! Do
> you not see it, the rainbow and the bridges of the overman?
> Thus spoke Zarathustra.

And the man who was dependent all his life on his
mother and sister writes: "If you would go high, use your
own legs. Do not let yourselves be carried up; do not sit
on the backs and heads of others." In his own mind,
Nietzsche was not sitting on the backs of others, but in
his life he allowed the person closest to him to sit on his
back to the very end.

On January 14, 1880, he wrote to Malwida von Mey-
senbug: "For the terrible and almost unceasing martyrdom
of my life makes me thirst for the end, and judging by
several indications, the stroke that shall deliver me is near
enough at hand to allow me to hope." And in 1887 he said
these significant words to Paul Deussen: "I don't believe
I'm going to last much longer. I'm now near the age when

my father died, and I feel I'm going to succumb to the same affliction he had."

The medical diagnosis of the disease that befell Nietzsche at the age of forty-five was "progressive paralysis," and his biographers seem reassured when they "determine" that this later illness "had nothing at all to do" with the illnesses of his school days. And the *118 attacks* in one year (1879) were apparently sheer "coincidence," for in the opinion of many of his biographers, Nietzche was perfectly healthy until the appearance of his progressive paralysis.

"WHY I AM SO WISE"

Sometimes Nietzsche's words convey something that might be construed as delusions of grandeur and that the reader might easily find offensive. One author has referred to this as Nietzsche's "God complex," and there *are* passages in *Ecce Homo* (1888) and in the letters that actually point to such a complex. How are we to understand this "arrogance" on the part of a thinker as critical and self-critical as Nietzsche? Those who have read the diaries he kept from age twelve to fourteen will scarcely believe that those pages were written by the same person whose later writing they already know—not because the diaries are so childish but because they are so adult. In great part, they could have been written by his aunts, his grandmother, or his father—and in the same style. The writing is colorless and unassuming, as was expected of him. The feelings

expressed strike one as inauthentic, weak, sometimes theatrical, but for the most part false. We sense that what
the writer really feels must remain completely beneath the
surface without being revealed by a sentence or even a
single word.

But this boy, who at twelve wrote like an adult, was
also capable of other things. What could he do with his
sense of pride, with the certitude that he understood more
than those around him? If Nietzsche had expressed his
pride at that time, he would have been sinning against an
important Christian virtue, humility. He certainly would
have met with disapproval and indignation. The boy therefore was forced to suppress his healthy and understandable
feeling of joy at what he knew as well as his grief at being
alone with his knowledge; not until much later—in *Ecce
Homo*, for instance—was he able to express these feelings.
But then he did it in a way that people could not tolerate,
putting himself in the position of a "sinner," of someone
who violates society's norms—the norm of modesty, for
one. He was sure to reap the moral indignation of his
contemporaries and of posterity, an outcome he accepted
gladly, presumably even enjoyed, because he felt liberated
by his daring. A different kind of liberation, such as having
insights that could be shared with others, was unknown
to him. This man who was condemned to be alone with
his insights never learned that someone can speak the truth
without punishing himself for it and without giving others
grounds for dismissing what he says by applying the label
"delusions of grandeur."

But what strikes us as delusions of grandeur in

Nietzsche presumably has other roots than simply an inner compulsion to provoke others. Nietzsche was the firstborn child, and even after the birth of his sister he could not count on anyone sharing his experiences and perceptions with him, especially those connected with the change brought about in his father by illness. He therefore found himself alone with his discoveries and was deprived of the reassurance that it would be safe to share them with those close to him. If he had had older siblings, perhaps his perceptions would not have had such disastrous consequences for him. Perhaps he could at least have counted on an occasional understanding glance from an older brother or sister. As it was, however, he was always *alone* with his awareness, which in his case meant *abandoned* with his awareness, a situation that does not necessarily evoke feelings of pride but can also cause pain.

The many passages in which Nietzsche characterizes Christianity are a key to how he felt about his relatives. We need only substitute "my aunts" or "my family" for the word "Christianity" for his vehement attacks suddenly to make sense.

> In Christianity the instincts of the subjugated and oppressed come to the fore: here the lowest classes seek their salvation. The casuistry of sin, self-criticism, the inquisition of the conscience, are pursued as a *pastime*, as a remedy for boredom; the emotional reaction to one who has *power*, called "God," is constantly sustained (by means of prayer); and what is highest is considered unattainable, a gift, "grace." Public acts are precluded; the hiding-place, the darkened room, is Christian. The body is despised,

hygiene repudiated as sensuality; the church even opposes cleanliness (the first Christian measure after the expulsion of the Moors was the closing of the public baths, of which there were two hundred and seventy in Cordova alone). Christian too is a certain sense of cruelty against oneself and against others; hatred of all who think differently; the will to persecute. Gloomy and exciting conceptions predominate; the most highly desired states, designated with the highest names, are epileptoid; the diet is so chosen as to favor morbid phenomena and overstimulate the nerves. Christian too is mortal enmity against the lords of the earth, against the "noble"—along with a sly, secret rivalry (one leaves them the "body," one wants *only* the "soul"). Christian, finally, is the hatred of the *spirit*, of pride, courage, freedom, liberty of the spirit; Christian is the hatred of the *senses*, of joy in the senses, of joy itself.

It is not difficult to imagine how much Nietzsche suffered as a child because of his family's beliefs and assertions, because of their rejection of his bodily needs and his physical self, and because of their constant moral dictates, such as repentence, piety, neighborly love, chastity, loyalty, purity, and devotion. He regarded them—and rightly so—as empty concepts conflicting with everything that meant life for him, as for every child, and standing for "*hatred* of the natural (of reality!)." Nietzsche saw the Christian world as a fictitious one, as "the expression of a profound vexation at the sight of reality. *But this explains everything.* Who alone has good reason to lie his way out of reality? He who suffers from it. But to suffer from reality is to be a piece of reality that has come to grief."

Couldn't these words also be the child's speculations about his do-good maiden aunts, whose main concern in raising the boy was to destroy the vitality in him that had also been destroyed in them? If we see the principles of his own upbringing behind his description of Christianity's hypocritical morality, then we can easily recognize in the self-proclaimed representative of the "noble lords of the earth" the child who is still rooted in his feelings and is therefore strong, vital, and sincere but also in danger of having to sacrifice his vitality to pedagogical principles. When we read *The Antichrist* with this key in mind, passages that were previously perplexing now gain a clear meaning.

> If, for example, it makes men happy to believe that they have been redeemed from sin, it is not necessary, as a condition for this, that man is, in fact, sinful, but merely that he feels sinful. And if faith is quite generally needed above all, then reason, knowledge, and inquiry must be discredited: the way to truth becomes the *forbidden* way.
> Strong *hope* is a far more powerful stimulant of life than any single realization of happiness could ever be. Those who suffer must be sustained by a hope that can never be contradicted by any reality or be disposed of by any fulfillment—a hope for the beyond.

> So that it could say No to everything on earth that represents the ascending tendency of life, to that which has turned out well, to power, to beauty, to self-affirmation, the instinct of *ressentiment*, which had here become genius, had to invent *another* world from whose point of

view this affirmation of life appeared as evil, as the reprehensible as such.

Psychologically considered, "sins" become indispensable in any society organized by priests: they are the real handles of power. The priest *lives* on sins, it is essential for him that people "sin." Supreme principle: "God forgives those who repent"—in plain language: those who submit to the priest.

The tone becomes different when Nietzsche speaks about the man Jesus.

To repeat, I am against any attempt to introduce the fanatic into the Redeemer type: the word *impérieux*, which Renan uses, is alone enough to annul the type. The "glad tidings" are precisely that there are no longer any opposites; the kingdom of heaven belongs to the *children*; the faith which finds expression here is not a faith attained through struggle—it is there, it has been there from the beginning; it is, as it were, an infantilism that has receded into the spiritual. The case of puberty being retarded and not developing in the organism, as a consequence of degeneration, is well known, at least to physiologists. Such a faith is not angry, does not reproach, does not resist: it does not bring "the sword"—it simply does not foresee how it might one day separate. It does not prove itself either by miracle or by reward and promise, least of all "by scripture": at every moment it is its own miracle, its own reward, its own proof, its own "kingdom of God." Nor does this faith formulate itself: it *lives*, it resists all formulas.

His affirmation of the Redeemer does not, however, prevent him from expressing his disgust for the church and its priests.

> The concepts "beyond," "Last Judgment," "immortality of the soul," and "soul" itself are instruments of torture, systems of cruelties by virtue of which the priest became master, remained master.
>
> Everybody knows this, *and yet everything continues as before.*

From the beginning, he says, the priests used Jesus to attain power for themselves.

> In Paul the priest wanted power once again—he could use only concepts, doctrines, symbols with which one tyrannizes masses and forms herds. What was the one thing that Mohammed later borrowed from Christianity? Paul's invention, his means to priestly tyranny, to herd formation: the faith in immortality—*that is, the doctrine of the "judgment."*

> The great lie of personal immortality destroys all reason, everything natural in the instincts—whatever in the instincts is beneficent and life-promoting or guarantees a future now arouses mistrust. To live so, that there is not longer any *sense* in living, that now becomes the "sense" of life. . . . that little prigs and three-quarter-madmen may have the conceit that the laws of nature are constantly broken for their sakes—such an intensification of every kind of selfishness into the infinite, into the *impertinent,*

cannot be branded with too much contempt. And yet Christianity owes its triumph to this miserable flattery of personal vanity.

The priest knows only one great danger: that is science, the sound conception of cause and effect. . . . Man *shall not* look outside, he shall look into himself; he *shall not* look into things cleverly and cautiously, like a learner, he shall not look at all—he shall *suffer*. And he shall suffer in such a way that he has need of the priest at all times. . . . A *priestly* attempt! . . .

When the natural consequences of a deed are no longer "natural," but thought of an caused by the conceptual specters of superstition, by "God," by "spirits," by "souls," as if they were merely "moral" consequences, as reward, punishment, hint, means of education, then the presupposition of knowledge has been destroyed—

I have selected these quotations with various perspectives in mind. In addition to expressing clearly the adult Nietzsche's feelings about Christianity, they also convey to alert readers his unconscious feelings, repressed since childhood, toward his first attachment figures. These passages reveal as well the child-raising methods and principles Nietzsche must have been exposed to as a child without being able to call them by name: above all, contempt for everything vital, sensual, and creative; the struggle to replace the child's feeling of well-being with guilt feelings and repentence; the suppression of his ability to think for himself, of his critical capacities, of his need to understand connections (the intellectual disciplines), and of his need for freedom and spontaneity. Not only obedience and submissiveness were preached to him but also the so-called love of truth, which was pure hypocrisy, for the boy who was forbidden to say anything critical was also forced to lie repeatedly. It is this perversion of values that continually aroused Nietzsche's ire and that he tried to make tangible by his paradoxical formulations in the hope that he would no longer have to be alone with his anger.

THE GLORIFICATION OF EVIL
(*Vitality Is Evil*)

Nietzsche considered himself the advocate of evil in only one specific connection: where evil is seen as the opposite of what people *call* good. He writes:

> When the herd animal is irradiated by the glory of the purest virtue, the exceptional man must have been devaluated into evil. When mendaciousness at any price monopolizes the word "truth" for its perspective, the really truthful man is bound to be branded with the worst names.

And a few lines earlier he quotes Zarathustra:

> "False coasts and assurances the good have taught you; in the lies of the good you were hatched and huddled. Everything has been made fraudulent and has been twisted through and through by the good."
> "The good are unable to *create*; they are always the

beginning of the end; they crucify him who writes new values on new tablets; they sacrifice the future to *themselves*—they sacrifice all man's future."

"The good have always been the beginning of the end."

"And whatever harm those do who slander the world, the harm done by the good is the most harmful harm."

That these observations derive from Nietzsche's childhood experiences is corroborated by the following passage:

The condition of the existence of the good is the *lie*: put differently, not *wanting* to see at any price how reality is constituted fundamentally—namely, not in such a way as to elicit benevolent instincts at all times, and even less in such a way as to tolerate at all times the interference of those who are myopically good-natured.

This awareness leads to boundless loneliness, which was the fate of this man from the beginning. The more he came to understand his environment, the more isolated he felt because he couldn't communicate his insights and experiences to anyone. After he finally attempted to communicate them in *Thus Spake Zarathustra*, only to find that his hopes of being understood and of finding acceptance for his ideas had been in vain, he wrote these words in *Ecce Homo*:

Except for these ten-day works, the years during and above all *after* my *Zarathustra* were marked by distress without equal. One pays dearly for immortality: one has to die several times while still alive.

There is something I call the *rancune* of what is great: everything great—a work, a deed—is no sooner accomplished than it turns *against* the man who did it. By doing it, he has become *weak;* he no longer endures his deed, he can no longer face it. Something one was never permitted to will lies *behind* one, something in which the knot in the destiny of humanity is tied—and now one labors *under* it!— It almost crushes one.— The *rancune* of what is great.

Then there is the gruesome silence one hears all around one. Solitude has seven skins; nothing penetrates them any more. One comes to men, one greets friends— more desolation, no eye offers a greeting. At best, a kind of revolt. Such revolts I experienced, very different in degree but from almost everybody who was close to me. It seems nothing offends more deeply than suddenly letting others feel a distance; those *nobel* natures who do not know how to live without reverence are rare.

Thirdly, there is the absurd sensitivity of the skin to small stings, a kind of helplessness against everything small. This seems to me to be due to the tremendous squandering of all defensive energies which is a presupposition of every *creative* deed, every deed that issues from one's most authentic, inmost, nethermost regions. Our *small* defensive capacitites are thus, as it were, suspended; no energy is left for them.

I still dare to hint that one digests less well, does not like to move, is all too susceptible to feeling chills as well as mistrust—mistrust that is in many instances merely an etiological blunder. In such a state I once sensed the proximity of a herd of cows even before I saw it, merely because milder and more philanthropic thoughts came back to me: *they* had warmth.

Nietzsche's loneliness was caused by his inner plight, for only the very few were receptive to what he said, and perhaps he wasn't aware of even these few. Thus, he would rather be alone than together with people who did not understand him. In his solitude, he had new ideas and made new discoveries; since they were based on his most personal experiences, but at the same time concealed them, they were difficult to share with others, and they only deepened his loneliness and the gulf between him and those around him. It was a process that had already begun in childhood, a childhood consisting of his continually being the giver. The boy's *raison d'être* was to understand others, to be patient with them, to overlook their failings, and to validate their self-esteem but never to appease his own hunger to be understood. In "Night Song," Nietzsche describes the tragedy of his attempt to find a solution, the tragedy of the person who gives and who thirsts:

> Light am I; ah, that I were night! But this is my loneliness that I am girt with light. Ah, that I were dark and nocturnal! How I could suck at the breasts of light! And even you would I bless, you little sparkling stars and glowworms up there, and be overjoyed with your gifts of light.
> But I live in my own light; I drink back into myself the flames that break out of me. I do not know the happiness of those who receive; and I have often dreamed that even

stealing must be more blessed than receiving. This is my poverty, that my hand never rests from giving; this is my envy, that I see waiting eyes and the lit-up nights of longing. Oh, wretchedness of all givers! Oh, darkening of my sun! Oh, craving to crave! Oh, ravenous hunger in satiation!

They receive from me, but do I touch their souls? There is a cleft between giving and receiving; and the narrowest cleft is the last to be bridged. A hunger grows out of my beauty: I should like to hurt those for whom I shine; I should like to rob those to whom I give; thus do I hunger for malice. To withdraw my hand when the other hand already reaches out to it; to linger like the waterfall, which lingers even while it plunges: thus do I hunger for malice. Such revenge my fullness plots: such spite wells up out of my loneliness. My happiness in giving died in giving; my virtue tired of itself in its overflow.

This text speaks of the envy directed at those who are able to take, who received love as a child, who can feel secure in a group, who are not condemned to open up new worlds in their loneliness, bestowing those worlds on others and reaping hostility in return. But fate cannot be changed. Those who do not want to live without the truth must also endure the cold regions of loneliness. Nietzsche writes:

How much truth does a spirit *endure*, how much truth does it *dare*? More and more that became for me the real measure of value. Error (faith in the ideal) is not blindness, error is *cowardice*.

Every attainment, every step forward in knowledge,

follows from courage, from hardness against oneself, from cleanliness in relation to oneself.

I do not refute ideals, I merely put on gloves before them.

Nitimur in vetitum: in this sign my philosophy will triumph one day, for what one has forbidden so far as a matter of principle has always been—truth alone.

"For what one has forbidden so far as a matter of principle has always been—truth alone." These words are valid for the history of humankind as well as for Nietzsche's family. And because he was no longer willing or able to comply with this prohibition, he sought refuge in atheism. He did not want to parrot religious platitudes.

"God," "immortality of the soul," "redemption," "beyond"—without exception, concepts to which I never devoted any attention, or time; not even as a child. Perhaps I have never been child-like enough for them?

I do not by any means know atheism as a result; even less as an event: it is a matter of course with me, from instinct. I am too inquisitive, too *questionable*, too exuberant to stand for any gross answer. God is a gross answer, an indelicacy against us thinkers—at bottom merely a gross prohibition for us: you shall not think!

Every evening after saying his prayers and before going to sleep, the little boy tried to make himself remember not to think. This prohibition was directed against life, for the vitality of thoughts is destroyed if one is constantly checking and sorting them out to see if they are permitted or forbidden for the sake of adapting them to dogma.

This ultimate, most joyous, most wantonly extravagant Yes to life represents not only the highest insight but also the *deepest*, that which is most strictly confirmed and born out by truth and science. Nothing in existence may be subtracted, nothing is dispensable—those aspects of existence which Christians and other nihilists repudiate are actually on an infinitely higher level in the order of rank among values than that which the instinct of decadence could approve and call good. To comprehend this requires courage and, as a condition of that, an excess of strength: for precisely as far as courage may venture forward, precisely according to that measure of strength one approaches the truth. Knowledge, saying Yes to reality, is just as necessary for the strong as cowardice and the flight from reality—as the "ideal" is for the weak, who are inspired by weakness.

They are not free to know: the decadents *need* the lie—it is one of the conditions of their preservation.

Whoever does not merely comprehend the word "Dionysian" but comprehends *himself* in the word "Dionysian" needs no refutation of Plato or Christianity or Schopenhauer—he *smells the decay*.

For a physiologist such a juxtaposition of values simply leaves no doubt. When the least organ in an organism fails, however slightly, to enforce with complete assurance its self-preservation, its "egoism," restitution of its energies —the whole degenerates. The physiologist demands *excision* of the degenerating part; he denies all solidarity with what degenerates; he is worlds removed from pity for it. But the priest desires precisely the degeneration of the whole, of humanity: for that reason, he *conserves* what degenerates—at this price he rules.

When seriousness is deflected from the self-preservation and the enhancement of the strength of the body— *that is, of life*—when anemia is construed as an ideal, and contempt for the body as "salvation of the soul"—what else is this if not a *recipe* for decadence?

The loss of the center of gravity, resistance to the natural instincts—in one word, "selflessness"—that is what was hitherto called *morality.*— With the *Dawn* I first took up the fight against the morality that would unself man.

Nietzsche was of the opinion that the Renaissance was Western civilization's great opportunity to free itself from Christianity's life-denying moral system and that this opportunity was lost because of Luther.

Luther, this calamity of a monk, restored the church and, what is a thousand times worse, Christianity, at the very moment *when it was vanquished.*—Christianity, this denial of the will to life become religion!—Luther, an impossible monk who, on account of his own "impossibility," attacked the church and—consequently—restored it.— The Catholics would have good reason to celebrate Luther festivals, to write Luther plays.— Luther—and the "moral rebirth"!

The morality that would un-self man is the morality of decline *par excellence*—the fact, "I am declining," trans-

posed into the imperative, "all of you *ought* to decline"—
and not only into the imperative.— This only morality that
has been taught so far, that of un-selfing, reveals a will to
the end; fundamentally, it negates life.

This would still leave open the possibility that not
humanity is degenerating but only that parasitical type of
man—that of the *priest*—which has used morality to raise
itself mendaciously to the position of determining human
values—finding in Christian morality the means to come
to *power*.— Indeed, this is *my* insight: the teachers, the
leaders of humanity, theologians all of them, were also, all
of them, decadents: *hence* the revaluation of all values into
hostility to life, *hence* morality—

Definition of morality: Morality—the idiosyncrasy of
decadents, with the ulterior motive of revenging oneself
against life—successfully. I attach value to this definition.

Have I been understood?— I have not said one word
here that I did not say five years ago through the mouth
of Zarathustra.

The uncovering of Christian morality is an event
without parallel, a real catastrophe. He that is enlightened
about that, is a *force majeure*, a destiny—he breaks the
history of mankind in two. One lives before him, or one
lives after him.

The lightning bolt of truth struck precisely what was
highest so far: let whoever comprehends *what* has here been
destroyed see whether anything is left in his hands. Everything that has hitherto been called "truth" has been recognized as the most harmful, insidious, and subterranean
form of lie; the holy pretext of "improving" mankind, as
the ruse for sucking the blood of life itself. Morality as
vampirism.

Whoever uncovers morality also uncovers the disvalue

of all values that are and have been believed; he no longer see anything venerable in the most venerated types of man, even in those pronounced holy; he considers them the most calamitous type of abortion—calamitous because they exerted such fascination.

The concept of "God" invented as a counterconcept of life—everything harmful, poisonous, slanderous, the whole hostility unto death against life synthesized in this concept in a gruesome unity! The concept of the "beyond," the "true world" invented in order to devaluate the only world there is—in order to retain no goal, no reason, no task for our earthly reality! The concept of the "soul," the "spirit," finally even *"immortal* soul," invented in order to despise the body, to make it sick, "holy"; to oppose with a ghastly levity everything that deserves to be taken seriously in life, the questions of nourishment, abode, spiritual diet, treatment of the sick, cleanliness, and weather.

In place of health, the "salvation of the soul"—that is, a *folie circulaire* between penitential convulsions and hysteria about redemption. The concept of "sin" invented along with the torture instrument that belongs with it, the concept of "free will," in order to confuse the instincts, to make mistrust of the instincts second nature. In the concept of the "selfless," the "self-denier," the distinctive sign of decadence, feeling attracted by what is harmful, being unable to find any longer what profits one, self-destruction is turned into the sign of value itself, into "duty," into "holiness," into what is "divine" in man. Finally—this is what is most terrible of all—the concept of the *good* man signifies that one sides with all that is weak, sick, failure, suffering of itself—all that ought to perish: the principle of selection is crossed—an ideal is fabricated from the contradiction against the proud and well-turned-out human

being who says Yes, who is sure of the future, who guar-
antees the future—and he is now called *evil.*— And all
this was believed, *as morality!*— *Ecrasez l'infâme!*—

If we didn't already know that Nietzsche's forebears
on both sides were theologians for several generations back,
the following words would at least indicate that Nietzsche's
outburst is not simply a philosopher's mental gymnastics
but the bitter earnest produced by vivid, first-hand experiences.

It is necessary to say whom we consider our antithesis:
it is the theologians and whatever has theologians' blood
in its veins—and that includes our whole philosophy.
Whoever has seen this catastrophe at close range or,
better yet, been subjected to it and almost perished of it,
will no longer consider it a joking matter.

Not until he was an adult did Nietzsche read the
books by the theologians. But his hatred of "the lie" has
deeper roots and is connected with his hatred of the women
who passed his theological heritage on to him as a child.

May I here venture the surmise that I *know* women?
That is part of my Dionysian dowry. Who knows? Perhaps
I am the first psychologist of the eternally feminine. They
all love me—an old story—not counting *abortive* females,
the "emancipated" who lack the stuff for children.— For-
tunately, I am not willing to be torn to pieces: the perfect
woman tears to pieces when she loves.— I know these
charming maenads.— Ah, what a dangerous, creeping,

subterranean little beast of prey she is! And yet so agreeable!— A little woman who pursues her revenge would run over fate itself.—Woman is indescribably more evil than man; also cleverer: good nature is in a woman a form of degeneration.— In all so-called "beautiful souls" something is physiologically askew at bottom; I do not say everything, else I should become medi-cynical. The fight for equal rights is actually a symptom of a disease: every physician knows that.—Woman, the more she is a woman, resists rights in general hand and foot: after all, the state of nature, the eternal war between the sexes, gives her by far the first rank.

But the furious child doesn't stop with women; he also attacks their idol. For everything they did to him happened in the name of God.

The Christian conception of God—God as god of the sick, God as a spider, God as spirit—is one of the most corrupt conceptions of the divine ever attained on earth. It may even represent the low-water mark in the descending development of divine types. God degenerated into the *contradiction* of life, instead of being its transfiguration and eternal Yes! God as the declaration of war against life, against nature, against the will to live! God—the formula for every slander against "this world," for every lie about the "beyond"! God—the deification of nothingness, the will to nothingness pronounced holy!

Nietzsche was not permitted to vent his feelings—of rage, indignation, vindictiveness, mockery, and contempt, which were caused by concrete, tragic experiences—on those who made him suffer. In his intellectual prison he could attack only ideas or people in the abstract, such as, for example, "women."

Although it is not difficult for us to recognize which experiences incited his anger, *Nietzsche himself* was not conscious of its source. Thus, he is able to say: "When I wage war against Christianity I am entitled to this because I have never experienced misfortunes and frustrations from that quarter—the most serious Christians have always been well disposed toward me. I myself, an opponent of Christianity *de rigueur*, am far from blaming individuals for the calamity of millennia."

It is tragic that Nietzsche was unable to blame specific individuals for what he observed "in general." For the living roots of his insights, contrary to all appearances, remained concealed from his conscious self. Caught in the labyrinth of his thoughts, he was incapable of locating these roots. The only permissible way out was that he lose his mind.

PHILOSOPHY AS A PROTECTION FROM THE TRUTH

When I hear in Nietzsche's works, especially *The Antichrist*, the cry of the angry child who has never been heard, when I perceive the mute, despairing, but also colossal battle that this wounded, highly expressive child waged against the untruthfulness, insensitivity, confusion, stupidity, inconsistency, and weakness of those who raised him, I am by no means relativizing what Nietzsche has to say about Christianity but am simply pointing to its origins. We could ask ourselves the same question that we ask about poets: If Nietzsche had been allowed to experience *consciously* the suffering caused by the way he was brought up, would *The Antichrist* have turned out the way it did? Presumably, he would not have needed to write it in the form he did, as an outpouring of stored-up affect; he surely would have found a different form, appropriate for telling what he had discovered with the aid of his feelings. If it had not been written as an abstract analysis of Christianity but as a document about his own suffering, many readers would have rediscovered themselves in what they read. It would have been an indictment and testimony concerning conditions that people know from experience, but only subliminally. For most people do not have Nietzsche's ability to describe feelings of revulsion, contempt, and disgust with such sensitivity and to justify them so convincingly.

Presumably, the result would then not have been a philosophical work but an autobiographical account that would have opened readers' eyes to reality. Nor would it have been possible to use Nietzsche's writings for a destructive ideology if they had expressed directly all that had befallen him instead of disguising it in symbolic form (as an attack against Christianity in the abstract, for example).

But there was never an opportunity for Nietzsche to

write such a report, since its potential content—which, as it was, he could express only symbolically—was not accessible to his conscious mind, or in any case was not available to him in a direct form. Should our pedagogical system become more relaxed someday, however, should the commandment "Thou shalt not be aware of what was done to you as a child" lose its force, then our heretofore treasured "products of culture" will no doubt decline in number—from unnecessary, useless dissertations all the way to the most famous philosophical treatises. But their place would be taken by many honest reports about what *really* happened to their authors. These documents could give others the courage to see things as they actually are, to call a crime a crime, and to express what they themselves have gone through but have been unable, without any support, to put into words. Reports of this nature would doubtlessly be preferable to complicated speculative writing, for they would serve the crucial purpose of revealing, rather than concealing, the reality of universal human experience.

By establishing the connection between the content, intensity, and power of Nietzsche's thinking and his childhood experiences, I am by no means trying to call his genius into question. Nonetheless, I will probably be accused of this intent, for as a rule the significance of childhood experience is unfortunately minimized and dismissed as of no importance; what *is* seen as important, in this view, is to regard the abstract ideas of "great thinkers," of adults, as pure gold—without any admixture of childhood—and to admire and interpret those ideas at face value. Neither the secondary literature on Nietzsche nor the espousal of his writing by the fascists ever went beyond these limited boundaries.

From my perspective I would say that, on the contrary, most of Nietzsche's writings owe their persuasiveness specifically to his ability to express the experiences he stored up at a very early age. As in the case of Kafka and other great writers, the truth asserts itself so obviously that it is virtually impossible to deny it: the truth of a mistreated child who was not allowed to cry or defend himself. The sudden flashes of insight that can come from reading certain passages in Nietzsche are not the result of the author's power of suggestion but of the strength of experience (although repressed and unconscious) of someone who is telling about what he has suffered and perceived and whose perceptions relate to situations and conditions in which many other people have had to live—or still are living. Nietzsche has this to say about the sources a writer draws from:

> When I seek my ultimate formula for *Shakespeare*, I always find only this: he conceived of the type of Caesar. That sort of thing cannot be guessed: one either is it, or one is not. The great poet dips *only* from his own reality —up to the point where afterward he cannot endure his work any longer.
>
> When I have looked into my *Zarathustra*, I walk up and down in my room for half an hour, unable to master an unbearable fit of sobbing.

If Nietzsche had not been forced to learn as a child that one must master an "unbearable fit of sobbing," if he had simply been *allowed* to sob, then humanity would have been one philosopher poorer, but in return the life of a human being named Nietzsche would have been richer. And who knows what that *vital* Nietzsche would *then* have been able to give humanity?

THREE

The No Longer Avoidable Confrontation with Facts

1

When Isaac Arises from the Sacrificial Altar

I had been searching for an illustration for the jacket of the British edition of *Thou Shalt Not Be Aware*; I didn't want to leave the selection to chance but thought it important that I myself find an appropriate visual representation of the work's underlying theme. Two Rembrandt depictions of the sacrifice of Isaac—one in Leningrad, the other in Munich—came to mind. In both, the father's hand completely covers the son's face, obstructing his sight, his speech, even his breathing. The main concerns expressed in my book (victimization of the child, the Fourth Commandment admonishing us to honor our parents, and the blindness imposed on children by parents) seemed to find a central focus in Abraham's gesture. Although I was resolved to recommend this detail of Rembrandt's printings to my publisher for the cover, I went to an archive to look at other portrayals of Abraham and Isaac as well. I found thirty in all, done by very dissimilar artists, and with growing astonishment I looked through them one by one.

I had been struck by the fact that in both of the Rembrandt versions I already knew, Abraham is grasping his son's head with his left hand and raising a knife with his right; his eyes, however, are not resting on his son but are turned upward, as though he is asking God if he is carrying out His will correctly. At first I thought that this was Rembrandt's own interpretation and that there must be others, but I was unable to find any. In all the portrayals of this scene that I found, Abraham's face or entire torso is turned away from his son and directed upward. Only his hands are occupied with the sacrifice. As I looked at the pictures, I thought to myself, "The son, an adult at the peak of his manhood, is simply lying there, quietly waiting to be murdered by his father. In some of the versions he is calm and obedient; in only one is he in tears, but not in a single one is he rebellious." In none of the paintings can we detect any questioning in Isaac's eyes, questions such as "Father, why do you want to kill me, why is my life worth nothing to you? Why won't you look at me, why won't you explain what is happening? How can you do this to me? I love you, I trusted in you. Why won't you speak to me? What crime have I committed? What have I done to deserve this?"

Such questions can't even be formulated in Isaac's

mind. They can be asked only by someone who feels himself on equal footing with the person being questioned, only if a dialogue is possible, only if one can look the other in the eye. How can a person lying on a sacrificial altar with hands bound, about to be slaughtered, ask questions when his father's hand keeps him from seeing or speaking and hinders his breathing? Such a person has been turned into an *object*. He has been dehumanized by being made a sacrifice; he no longer has a right to ask questions and will scarcely even be able to articulate them to himself, for there is no room in him for anything besides fear.

As I sat in the archive looking at the pictures, I suddenly saw in them the symbolic representation of our present situation. Inexorably, weapons are being produced for the obvious purpose of destroying the next generation. Yet those who are profiting from the production of these weapons, while enhancing their prestige and power, somehow manage not to think of this ultimate result. Like Abraham, they do not see what their hands are doing, and they devote their entire attention to fulfilling expectations from "above," at the same time ignoring their feelings. They learned to deny their feelings as children; how should they be able to regain the ability to feel now that they are fathers? It's too late for that. Their souls have become rigid, they have learned to adapt. They have also forgotten how to ask questions and how to listen to them. All their efforts are now directed toward creating a situation—war—in which their sons too will be unable to see and hear.

In the face of mobilization for war—even a conventional one, a nonnuclear war—the questions of the younger generation are silenced. To doubt the wisdom of the state is regarded as treason. Any discussion or consideration of alternative possibilities is eliminated at a single stroke. Only practical questions remain: How do we win the war? How do we survive it? Once the point of asking these questions has been reached, the young forget that prosperous and prominent old men have been preparing for war for a long time. The younger generation will march, sing songs, kill and be killed, and they will be under the impression that they are carrying out an extremely important mission. The state will indeed regard highly what they are doing and will reward them with medals of honor, but their souls—the childlike, living, feeling part of their personality—will be condemned to the utmost passivity. They will resemble Isaac as he is always depicted in the sacrificial scene: hands tied, eyes bound, as if it were the most natural thing in the world to wait unquestioningly in this position to be slaughtered by one's father. (In my German translation of the Bible the verb used in this passage is *schlachten*, which refers to the butchering of animals.)

Neither does the father ask any questions. He submits to the divine command as a matter of course, the same way his son submits to him. He must—and wants to—prove that his obedience is stronger than what he calls his love for his child, and as he prepares to carry out the deed his questions vanish. He doesn't ask God for mercy or look for a way out, and if the angel didn't intervene at the last moment, Abraham would become the murderer of his son simply because God's voice demanded it of him. In the pictures I examined, there is no pain to be seen in Abraham's face, no hesitation, no searching, no questioning, no sign that he is conscious of the tragic nature of his situation. All the artists, even Rembrandt, portray him as God's obedient instrument, whose sole concern is to function properly.

It is astonishing at first glance that not one of the artists, each with his own distinct and independent personality, was tempted to give this dramatic scene an individual, personal stamp. Of course the dress, the colors, the surroundings, and the positions of the bodies vary, but the numerous depictions of the scene reveal a remarkably uniform psychological content. An obvious explanation is that all the artists were following the Old Testament text, but we are still justified in asking why. Why wasn't there room in the psyche of these artists for doubt? Why did they all take it for granted that the Bible passage could not be questioned? Why did all of these artists accept the story as valid? The only answer I can think of is that the situation involves a fundamental fact of our existence, with which many of us become familiar during the first years of life and which is so painful that knowledge of it can survive only in the depths of the unconscious. Our awareness of the child's victimization is so deeply rooted in us that we scarcely seem to have reacted at all to the monstrousness of the story of Abraham and Isaac. The moral expressed in the story has almost been accorded the legitimacy of natural law, yet if the result of this legitimacy is something as horrifying as the outbreak of nuclear war, then the moral

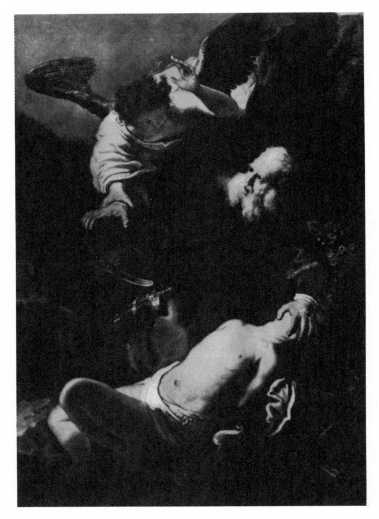

Rembrandt van Rijn, The Sacrifice of Isaac
Archiv für Kunst und Geschichte, Berlin

should not be passively accepted like a natural law but must be questioned. If we love life more than obedience and are not prepared to die in the name of obedience and our fathers' lack of critical judgment, then we can no longer wait like Isaac, with our eyes bound and our hands tied, for our fathers to carry out the will of their fathers.

How, then, can a condition that has endured for millennia be changed? Would it change if the young were to kill off the old so as not to have to go to war? Wouldn't that simply be a forerunner to the horrible war we are trying to prevent, and wouldn't the old situation then be reinforced, the difference being that Abraham's knife would now be in Isaac's hands and the old man would become the victim of the young man? Wouldn't the same cruelty be perpetuated?

But what would happen if Isaac, instead of reaching for the knife, were to use every ounce of his strength to free his hands so that he could remove Abraham's hand from his face? That would change his situation altogether. He would no longer lie there like a sacrificial lamb but would stand up; he would dare to use his eyes and see his father as he really is: uncertain and hesitant yet intent on carrying out a command he does not comprehend. Now Isaac's nose and mouth would be free too, and he could finally draw a deep breath and make use of his voice. He would be able to speak and ask questions, and Abraham, whose left hand could no longer keep his son from seeing and speaking, would have to enter into a dialogue with his son, at the end of which he might possibly encounter the young man he had once been himself, who was never allowed to ask questions.

And now that the scenario has changed and Isaac can no longer be counted on to be a victim, there will have to be a confrontation between the two, a confrontation that has no conventional precedent but that nevertheless, or perhaps for this very reason, offers a golden opportunity. Isaac will ask, "Father, why do you want to kill me?" and will be given the answer "It is God's will." "Who is God?" the son will ask. "The great and benevolent Father of us all, Whom we must obey," Abraham will answer. "Doesn't it grieve you," the son will want to know, "to have to carry out this command?" "It is not for me to take my feelings into account when God orders me to do something." "Then who are you," Isaac will ask, "if you carry out His orders without any feeling, and Who is this God, Who can demand such a thing of you?"

It may be that Abraham is too old, that it is too late for him to perceive the message of life his son is bringing him, that he will say, "Keep quiet! You understand nothing of all this." But it may be that he is open to Isaac's questions because they are his own questions as well, which he has had to suppress for decades. Even in the former case, however, the encounter is not doomed to failure as long as Isaac is unwilling to shut his eyes again but is determined to endure the sight of his father as he really is. If Isaac refuses to allow himself to be bound and blinded again for the sake of preserving the illusion of a strong and wise and benevolent father but instead finds the courage to look his fallible father in the eye and hear his "Keep quiet" without letting himself be silenced, the confrontation will continue. Then young people will not have to die in wars to preserve the image of their wise fathers. Once young men see what is actually happening, once they become aware that their fathers are steadfastly, unwaveringly, and unthinkingly developing a gigantic weapons system that they hope will not destroy them, although it may their children, then the children will refuse to lie down voluntarily like lambs on the sacrificial altar. But for this to be possible, the children first must be willing to stop obeying the commandment "Thou shalt not be aware."

The commandment itself provides the explanation of why it is so difficult to take that step to awareness. Yet the decision to take it is the first requirement for change. We can still avert our probable fate, provided we do not wait to be rescued by the angel who rewarded Abraham for his obedience. More and more people are refusing to go on playing Isaac's sacrificial role with all its consequences for the future. And perhaps there are also people who reject Abraham's role, who refuse to obey orders that strike them as absurd because they are directed against life. Their ability to ask questions and their refusal to accept senseless answers may signal the beginning of a long overdue reorientation that will help reinforce our Yes to life and No to death. The new Isaac—with his questions, with his awareness, with his refusal to let himself be killed—not only saves his own life but also saves his father from the fate of becoming the unthinking murderer of his child.

Monika Laimgruber, Drawing for Hans Christian Andersen's
The Emperor's New Clothes, *Artemis-Verlag © Monika
Laimgruber*

2

The Emperor's New Clothes

*I*n the preceding chapter, I chose the depictions in art of the sacrifice of Isaac to suggest that it is possible for grown children to have a creative confrontation with their parents. But I do not see the symbolic content of that scene as being limited to the relationship between father and son. Everything I said about Abraham's attitude is equally valid for mothers, and of course Isaac also symbolizes the daughter who can be hindered by both father and mother not only in her movements but also in her ability to see, speak, and breathe.

The assertion that men are solely responsible for conditions in today's world does just as little to expose and combat the presence of evil, destructive rage, violence, and perversion as does the demonization of women. Both sexes have always contributed to the genesis of the forces of evil. Mothers as well as fathers have considered it their duty to punish their children and have used their children to satisfy their own ambitions and other needs. Every aggressive reaction on the child's part to this abuse was suppressed, and this suppression laid the foundation for destructive behavior in adulthood. And yet there must always have been individual parents who were capable of giving love and who provided their children with a counterbalance for the cruelty they suffered. Above all, however, there must have been helping witnesses present—in the person of nannies, household staff, aunts, uncles, siblings, or grandparents—who did not feel responsible for raising the child and who were not camouflaging cruelty as love because they *had* experienced love in their own childhoods. If this were not the case, the human race would have died out long ago. On the other hand, if there had been more mothers and fathers capable of love, our world would be different today; it would be more humane. People would also have a clear understanding of what love is because they would have experienced it in childhood, and it would be inconceivable for biographers to call something an expression of maternal love that in its essence was a prison, concentration camp, refrigerator, or brainwashing institute. Yet according to most of today's biographers, Stalin and Hitler had "loving mothers."

When punishment is held up as proof of love, children

are filled with confusion, which bears bitter fruit later in life. If these children become involved in politics, they continue the work of destruction initiated with them in childhood, and they camouflage it by taking on the role of savior just as their parents did before them. Both Stalin and Hitler claimed that they wanted only to do good. Murder was simply the necessary means to good. This ideology was passed on to them by *both* parents. If this had not been so, if one parent had served as a helping witness and shielded the child from the other parent's brutality and coldness, the children would not have become criminals in later life.

Although it is men who make preparations for war, the confusion in their heads is the end product of child-rearing practices and ways of treating children that are attributable to men *and* women of past generations. The absolute power a mother has over her little child knows no limits, and yet no qualifications are required of her. It is therefore of the utmost urgency to examine more closely the effects of such unchecked power, to recognize parental power for what it is, and, through this awareness, to reduce its danger for the future.

While reflecting on these ideas, I was reminded of the fairy tale "The Emperor's New Clothes." Here a man, the emperor, symbolizes the seemingly mighty but actually helpless parents who are at the same time dangerous because of their total blindness and their great power over their children.

The Emperor's New Clothes

Many, many years ago there was an emperor who was so terribly fond of beautiful new clothes that he spent all his money on his attire. He did not care about his soldiers, or attending the theatre, or even going for a drive in the park, unless it was to show off his new clothes. He had an outfit for every hour of the day. And just as we say, "The king is in his council chamber," his subjects used to say, "The emperor is in his clothes closet."

In the large town where the emperor's palace was, life was gay and happy; and every day new visitors arrived. One day two swindlers came. They told everybody that they were weavers and that they could weave the most marvellous cloth. Not only were the colours and the patterns of their material extraordinarily beautiful, but the cloth had the strange quality of being invisible to anyone who was unfit for his office or unforgivably stupid.

"This is truly marvellous," thought the emperor. "Now if I had robes cut from that material, I should know which of my councillors was unfit for his office, and I would be able to pick out my clever subjects myself. They must weave some material for me!" And he gave the swindlers a lot of money so they could start working at once.

They set up a loom and acted as if they were weaving, but the loom was empty. The fine silk and gold threads they demanded from the emperor they never used, but hid them in their own knapsacks. Late into the night they would sit before their empty loom, pretending to weave.

"I would like to know how far they've come," thought the emperor; but his heart beat strangely when he remembered that those who were stupid or unfit for their office would not be able to see the material. Not that he was really worried that this would happen to him. Still, it might be better to send someone else the first time and see how he fared. Everybody in town had heard about the cloth's magic quality and most of them could hardly wait to find out how stupid or unworthy their neighbours were.

"I shall send my faithful prime minister to see the weavers," thought the emperor. "He will know how to judge the material, for he is both clever and fit for his office, if any man is."

The good-natured old man stepped into the room where the weavers were working and saw the empty loom. He closed his eyes, and opened them again. "God preserve me!" he thought. "I cannot see a thing!" But he didn't say it out loud.

The swindlers asked him to step a little closer so that he could admire the intricate patterns and marvellous colours of the material they were weaving. They both pointed to the empty loom, and the poor old prime minister opened his eyes as wide as he could; but it didn't help, he still couldn't see anything.

"Am I stupid?" he thought. "I can't believe it, but if it is so, it is best no one finds out about it. But maybe I am not fit for my office. No, that is worse, I'd better not admit that I can't see what they are weaving."

"Tell us what you think of it," demanded one of the swindlers.

"It is beautiful. It is very lovely," mumbled the old prime minister, adjusting his glasses. "What patterns! What colours! I shall tell the emperor that I am greatly pleased."

"And that pleases us," the weavers said; and now they described the patterns and told which shades of colour they had used. The prime minister listened attentively, so that he could repeat their words to the emperor; and that is exactly what he did.

The two swindlers demanded more money, and more silk and gold thread. They said they had to use it for their weaving, but their loom remained as empty as ever.

Soon the emperor sent another of his trusted councillors to see how the work was progressing. He looked and looked just as the prime minister had, but since there was nothing to be seen, he didn't see anything.

"Isn't it a marvellous piece of material?" asked one of the swindlers; and they both began to describe the beauty of their cloth again.

"I am not stupid," thought the emperor's councillor. "I must be unfit for my office. That is strange; but I'd better not admit it to anyone." And he started to praise the material, which he could not see, for the loveliness of its patterns and colours.

"I think it is the most charming piece of material I have ever seen," declared the councillor to the emperor.

Everyone in town was talking about the marvellous cloth that the swindlers were weaving.

At last the emperor himself decided to see it before it was removed from the loom. Attended by the most important people in the empire, among them the prime minister and the councillor who had been there before, the emperor entered the room where the weavers were weaving furiously on their empty loom.

"Isn't it *magnifique?*" asked the prime minister.

"Your Majesty, look at the colours and the patterns," said the councillor.

And the two old gentlemen pointed to the empty loom, believing that all the rest of the company could see the cloth.

"What!" thought the emperor. "I can't see a thing! Why, this is a disaster! Am I stupid? Am I unfit to be emperor? Oh, it is too horrible!" Aloud he said, "It is very lovely. It has my approval," while he nodded his head and looked at the empty loom.

All the councillors, ministers, and men of great importance who had come with him stared and stared; but they saw no more than the emperor had seen, and they said the same thing that he had said, "It is lovely." And they advised him to have clothes cut and sewn, so that he could wear them in the procession at the next great celebration.

"It is magnificent! Beautiful! Excellent!" All of their mouths agreed, though none of their eyes had seen anything. The two swindlers were decorated and given the title "Royal Knight of the Loom."

The night before the procession, the two swindlers didn't sleep at all. They had sixteen candles lighting up the room where they worked. Everyone could see how busy they were, getting the emperor's new clothes finished. They pretended to take the cloth from the loom; they cut the air with their big scissors, and sewed with needles without thread. At last they announced: "The emperor's clothes are ready!"

Together with his courtiers, the emperor came. The swindlers lifted their arms as if they were holding something in their hands, and said, "These are the trousers. This is the robe, and here is the train. They are all as light as if they were made of spider webs! It will be as if Your Majesty had almost nothing on, but that is their special virtue."

"Oh yes," breathed all the courtiers; but they saw nothing, for there was nothing to be seen.

"Will Your Imperial Majesty be so gracious as to take off your clothes?" asked the swindlers. "Over there by the big mirror, we shall help you put your new ones on."

The emperor did as he was told; and the swindlers acted as if they were dressing him in the clothes they should have made. Finally they tied around his waist the long train which two of his most noble courtiers were to carry.

The emperor stood in front of the mirror admiring the clothes he couldn't see.

"Oh, how they suit you! A perfect fit!" everyone exclaimed. "What colours! What patterns! The new clothes are magnificent!"

"The crimson canopy, under which Your Imperial Majesty is to walk, is waiting outside," said the imperial master of court ceremony.

"Well, I am dressed. Aren't my clothes becoming?" The emperor turned around once more in front of the mirror, pretending to study his finery.

The two gentlemen of the imperial bedchamber fumbled on the floor, trying to find the train which they were supposed to carry. They didn't dare admit that they didn't see anything, so they pretended to pick up the train and held their hands as if they were carrying it.

The emperor walked in the procession under his crimson canopy. And all the people of the town, who had lined the streets or were looking down from the windows, said that the emperor's new clothes were beautiful. "What a magnificent robe! And the train! How well the emperor's clothes suit him!"

None of them were willing to admit that they hadn't seen a thing; for if anyone did, then he was either stupid or unfit for the job he held. Never before had the emperor's clothes been such a success.

"But he doesn't have anything on!" cried a little child.

"Listen to the innocent one," said the proud father. And the people whispered among each other and repeated what the child had said.

"He doesn't have anything on. There's a little child who says that he has nothing on."

"He has nothing on!" shouted all the people at last.

The emperor shivered, for he was certain that they were right; but he thought, "I must bear it until the procession is over." And he walked even more proudly, and the two gentlemen of the imperial bedchamber went on carrying the train that wasn't there.

The belief that older people understand more about life because they supposedly have had more experience was instilled in us at such an early age that we continue to adhere to it even though we know better. Naturally, older craftsmen have more experience in their trades, and older scientists have more facts in their heads, but in both cases their knowledge has precious little to do with wisdom. Nevertheless, most people never give up hoping that they can learn something about life from their elders, whose advanced years must imply richer experience. Even people whose parents have long been dead will seek out parental substitutes such as priests, psychotherapists, gurus, philosophers, or writers, convinced that those who are older must know better, especially if they are famous. They wouldn't have gained recognition, the thinking goes, without some inherent justification for their fame—if the doctrines they proclaim, the values they represent, and the morality they preach didn't have significance for many others too.

And they actually do have significance. Even if the gurus and their disciples are not from the same culture, the repression of childhood experiences is common to all of them, for full awareness of early experiences is taboo in every culture, religion, and system of child-rearing. This situation was not noticed until after World War II, when the first scientifically substantiated reports about childhood appeared, calling into question many of the ideas that had been accepted as right and good for thousands of years. I am thinking here of René Spitz's discovery of hospitalism, John Bowlby's writings about infant abandonment and its consequences, Lloyd De Mause's new look at the history of childhood, Frederick Leboyer's revolutionary discovery that infants already have feelings at birth, and the corroboration provided by primal therapists that feelings repressed in childhood retain their potency and influence our body and mind, often for the rest of our life.

The fact that so many obstetricians still warn today against the dangers of gentle homebirth is attributable not only to their outdated training and the requirements of the hospital system but also to the stunting of their perceptive faculties. They lack the capacity to recognize that a newborn has feelings because such recognition has been blocked for them, possibly as early as the moment of their own birth or perhaps later when their own traumatic experiences are repressed. They examine the newborn infant, and even though they hear its heart-rending cries, they smile at the new mother and tell her that everything is just fine because now the baby's lungs have started to work. These physicians seem to be unaffected by the existing body of knowledge about the role of feelings in the human organism.

The above example of ignorant obstetricians attending childbirth makes clear why advanced age has nothing to do with the value of a person's experiences. Millions of women have given birth in hospitals in recent years under cruel and inhumane conditions, and no one seemed to notice that here a human creature of the tenderest age is being subjected to torture. All that was needed to change this pattern was for one obstetrician, Frederick Leboyer, to take the difficult path of discovering, with the aid of feelings, the memory of his own birth concealed in his psyche and his body. All that was needed was for him to relive his own repressed pain, and suddenly he was able to perceive for the first time what was self-evident: the cries of an infant in the delivery room are expressing pain that is altogether avoidable. To make this simple observation, he first had to overcome the resistance that each of us builds up as a child. We are entitled to this resistance, for we must protect ourselves as best we can from what is unbearable; but what happens when it makes us blind to the most obvious phenomena in our life?

Now computers are being used to help in the care of the newborn, and it has been determined that the child already begins to learn in the first hours of life. Scientists seem to be fascinated by this idea and are busily investigating various achievements of the newborn. But infants also experience feelings and hurt, even prenatally, that set the course for later life, yet these facts haven't attracted the attention of many scientists. It is true that the different functions of the newborn's body can be measured, its behavior observed, the correlates evaluated by the computer. However, as long as the adults involved have not gained access to their own childhood feelings, the infant's feelings, the cause of so many troubles in later life, go totally unnoticed.

What are we to think, then, of the wisdom of older people who had to learn as children that good behavior could be acquired only at the expense of genuine feelings and who were proud of having managed to accomplish this? Since they were not allowed to feel, they became incapable of perceiving vital facts and learning from them. What can these people have to tell us today? They attempt to pass on to the younger generation the same principles their parents once transmitted to them, firmly convinced that they are doing something useful and good. But these are the very principles that destroyed their ability to feel and perceive. Of what use are instructions and moral sermons if one's capacity for feeling and compassion has been lost? The most that will be achieved is to inculcate the absurdest of attitudes, which won't be perceived as such because they are shared by so many.

Thus, politicians can profess to be peace-loving Christians and at the same time advocate the production of weapons *five million times more powerful* than the Hiroshima bomb. These politicians can defend without a qualm the necessity for an absurd arms race because they learned long ago not to feel. It is therefore possible for those caught in this kind of mental system to plan multiple Hiroshima catastrophes and still to pray in church every Sunday for peace; what is more, they consider themselves entitled to bear the responsibility for the fate of the whole world because they are advanced in years, because they have experience with wars, because the last time, forty-five years ago, they took part in one. Yet what now awaits us hasn't the slightest to do with the way the world was forty-five years ago. The wisdom of our fathers, their experience with war and with the destruction of feelings since childhood, can be of little help to us today.

If anything can save us from catastrophe, it is not Abraham, the old man who raises his eyes to heaven and does not see what he is doing. It is his son, who we can only hope has *perhaps* not completely lost his ability to feel and who, owing to this ability, can also imagine the implications of preparing for nuclear war. If Isaac is capable of being horrified at his father's monstrous intent and of *feeling* outraged without repressing this feeling or acting it out, then he will be in a position to understand things that were kept from his father all his life. It is the ability to feel that enables us to establish the right connections, to notice what is going on around us, and to relinquish the illusion that age brings wisdom. Only this painful experience will open Isaac's eyes and make him a man of action instead of a victim. Someone who is not allowed to feel can't learn from experience. Again and again he will accept the so-called wisdom of his elders, which has proven to be unmistakably wrong in our generation—as, for example, "Spare the rod and spoil the child." All his life he will avoid crucial experiences because he must protect himself from pain, and this means ultimately from the truth. He must never doubt his father, must not confront him. Even when his hair has turned white, he will still be his father's obedient child.

Where does such obedience lead? It leads Abraham to the point of murdering his son for the sake of proving his devotion to God the Father, Who requires this act of him. And in our day it leads many old men to prepare for nuclear war with a clear conscience. They destroyed the feeling child in themselves long ago and in doing so learned to kill for the principles of their parents, in good conscience, without remorse and without being able to imagine the suffering of their victims. For a long time we were able to overlook their lack of imagination and their unawareness, thinking "for they know not what they do." But can we still afford to do this when we ourselves, like Isaac, are lying on the sacrificial altar and have not yet completely lost the capacity to imagine what nuclear war would mean? The Isaacs of today, the feeling young sons and daughters, have no alternative but to arise from the altar and confront the psychic reality of fathers preparing for war.

Isaac's actual superiority, if he were to refuse to be made the sacrificial lamb, would be based on his *awareness*, on the fact that *he finds out what his situation is* and clearly recognizes his own need: "I don't want to die for being obedient, and I don't want to kill others. I don't want to let myself be forced to kill by following absurd orders, no matter how cleverly they are packaged or accompanied by threats. I am ready *to look carefully*, to refuse to have my eyes bound any longer, and to find out who really has an interest in my being docile. There must be a way to prevent ourselves from repeating the war games of our fathers, and we now must search for it—without having any models because no models exist for this situation in which we are threatened with nuclear annihilation. We can and we must rely on our own experience and on our desire to create a world in which we can live without having to kill others. Since we want to be true to this desire and not to incomprehensible orders, we are willing to take a careful look around us. We are willing to look closely at the psychic landscape of those who label us naive pacifists. We are willing to examine the sources of their reasoning and to consider whether or not it can be valid for us today."

The cry of the child in Andersen's fairy tale—"But [the emperor] doesn't have anything on!"—awakens people from a mass hypnosis, restores their powers of perception, frees them from the confusion caused by the authorities, and mercilessly exposes the emptiness to which rulers as well as masses have fallen victim. All of this happens suddenly, sparked by the single exclamation of a child. Although these words are enormously liberating, we don't know what to do with our freedom. It is a great relief, to be sure, not to pretend to see the emperor's golden train when, despite our best efforts, we really don't see it—a relief not to have to think we're stupid for not seeing one. But since our fate lies in the emperor's hands, since we have to rely on his wisdom, perceptiveness, and sense of responsibility, our discovery at first fills us with fear. Who will protect us in times of danger? It is now obvious that this emperor can't do it. He appears to be so taken with self-admiration that it would be easy to talk him into doing something foolish. That much seems clear, but only to someone who is not dependent on this emperor. If our future does depend on him, however, *because he is the only one we have*, we would prefer *not* to know what he is really like but would rather believe he will protect us when we are in trouble. For this belief we are ready to sacrifice ourselves, to doubt our own perceptions.

Like children who endure psychic death to preserve the illusion of having an intelligent, foresighted father, soldiers go to war to die for the leader who misuses them. That has been the way of the world, until recently. Many can still remember it, and those who can't are still able to see in films the pageantry surrounding Hitler and the jubilant masses. But it needn't be this way. Indeed, it must not, for the methods of misleading people and destroying them have now taken on gigantic proportions. Therefore, we can no longer afford to deny our perceptions and evade the truth, even if it is painful, for only the truth can save us. It is frightening and painful not to have a strong father when we need his strength. Yet if holding fast to illusion should mean Isaac's death and our destruction today, then the first, imperative step toward turning things around is to relinquish the illusion. Even if this step is fraught with fear, is not even conceivable without fear.

For only a little child can uninhibitedly cry out, "But he doesn't have anything on!" and then only if that child cannot yet assess the consequences of these words. Moreover, the child in Andersen's fairy tale is taken seriously by the father and therefore feels secure. But for adults who never had such a father, the liberation of their senses also endangers or even destroys a vital hope: the hope of being protected. We are horrified at the sight of the deceived emperor without his clothes when we consider that he has the power to issue orders that determine our fate. Of course it would be more conducive to our momentary well-being to deny what we see and to go on believing that the affairs of state are in good hands. But this would be no solution for our future or the future of our children. The Isaac of today can't afford to close his eyes again once he has opened them. Now he knows that his father is not protecting him, and he is determined to protect himself. He is determined not to look away but to examine his situation.

Abraham's upward gaze and his childlike submissiveness are a symbol for numerous experiences Isaac had had earlier without being able to understand them. Likewise, the naive and vain emperor is transformed into a little child who wants to show his father his wonderful new clothes so that the father will finally notice the son. This child, this emperor, could have said, "Father, now that I appear in all my imperial splendor, surrounded by these throngs, you can't overlook me. Now at last you will admire and love me." And the politician who tries to make us believe he has our freedom at heart (even if we should be incinerated by a nuclear bomb), raises his eyes—like Abraham—to his father, who died long ago, and asks like a child: "Haven't I done splendidly? See how well I am representing your values? See how hard I am trying to keep the world the way you described it to me sixty years ago and to keep sacred the values you held dear? See how careful I am not to let anything change, just the way you always wanted? Now are you pleased with me? Now can you love me?" There are many varieties of politicians like this. Perhaps one had a father who always felt he was being persecuted. His son will say to him: "I won't rest until I have destroyed all your enemies. Now are you pleased with me?"

"But what does all that have to do with my fate?" Isaac asks himself. "I can well understand the dealings old men have with their fathers, but I don't want my life to be determined by my forefathers. For what I now have to lose is not real protection but only the illusion of it."

A great many politicians claim they are doing something for us, and we want to believe what they say because we are dependent on them and because the world has become so complicated that we need experts for everything: technical experts, computer experts, and above all safeguards, more and more safeguards so that the world won't fall victim to the bomb. But what is to be done if our fear of the danger that makes such vigilance necessary unceasingly produces new dangers for the simple reason that people who are blocked by their repressed past do not want to look to the future? "What I can try to do now," thinks Isaac, "is direct my father's eyes to me, away from his forebears and to me lying here on the sacrificial altar he has prepared for me. Perhaps that will bring him to his senses, perhaps it won't. But turning my eyes to that altar and to my father has brought *me* to my senses. I am not willing to die, not willing to march and sing war songs. I am not willing to forget that all this has always preceded a war. I have awakened from my millennia-long sleep."

APPENDIX

The Newly Recognized, Shattering Effects of Child Abuse

For some years now there has been proof that the devastating effects of the traumatization of children take their inevitable toll on society. This knowledge concerns every single one of us, and—if disseminated widely enough—should lead to fundamental changes in society, above all to a halt in the blind escalation of violence. The following points are intended to amplify my meaning:

1. All children are born to grow, to develop, to live, to love, and to articulate their needs and feelings for their self-protection.

2. For their development children need the respect and protection of adults who take them seriously, love them, and honestly help them to become oriented in the world.

3. When these vital needs are frustrated and children are instead abused for the sake of adults' needs by being exploited, beaten, punished, taken advantage of, manipulated, neglected, or deceived without the intervention of any witness, then their integrity will be lastingly impaired.

4. The normal reactions to such injury should be anger and pain; since children in this hurtful kind of environment, however, are forbidden to express their anger and since it would be unbearable to experience their pain all alone, they are compelled to suppress their feelings, repress all memory of the trauma, and idealize those guilty of the abuse. Later they will have *no memory of what was done to them.*

5. Disassociated from the original cause, their feelings of anger, helplessness, despair, longing, anxiety, and pain will find expression in destructive acts against others (criminal behavior, mass murder) or against themselves (drug addiction, alcoholism, prostitution, psychic disorders, suicide).

6. If these people become parents, they will then often direct acts of revenge for their mistreatment in childhood against their own children, whom they use as scapegoats. Child abuse is still sanctioned—indeed, held in high regard—in our society as long as it is defined as child-rearing. It is a tragic fact that parents beat their children in order to escape the emotions stemming from how they were treated by their own parents.

7. If mistreated children are not to become criminals or mentally ill, it is essential that *at least once in their life*

they come in contact with a person who knows without any doubt that the environment, not the helpless, battered child, is at fault. In this regard, knowledge or ignorance on the part of society can be instrumental in either saving or destroying a life. Here lies the great opportunity for relatives, social workers, therapists, teachers, doctors, psychiatrists, officials, and nurses *to support the child and to believe her or him.*

8. Till now, society has protected the adult and blamed the victim. It has been abetted in its blindness by theories, still in keeping with the pedagogical principles of our great-grandparents, according to which children are viewed as crafty creatures, dominated by wicked drives, who invent stories and attack their innocent parents or desire them sexually. In reality, children tend to blame themselves for their parents' cruelty and to absolve the parents, whom they invariably love, of all responsibility.

9. For some years now, it has been possible to prove, thanks to the use of new therapeutic methods, that repressed traumatic experiences in childhood are stored up in the body and, although remaining unconscious, exert their influence even in adulthood. In addition, electronic testing of the fetus has revealed a fact previously unknown to most adults: *a child responds to and learns both tenderness and cruelty from the very beginning.*

10. In the light of this new knowledge, even the most absurd behavior reveals its formerly hidden logic once the traumatic experiences of childhood no longer must remain shrouded in darkness.

11. Our sensitization to the cruelty with which children are treated, until now commonly denied, and to the consequences of such treatment will as a matter of course bring to an end the perpetuation of violence from generation to generation.

12. People whose integrity has not been damaged in childhood, who were protected, respected, and treated with honesty by their parents, will be—both in their youth and adulthood—intelligent, responsive, empathic, and highly sensitive. They will take pleasure in life and will not feel any need to kill or even hurt others or themselves. They will use their power to defend themselves but not to attack others. They will not be able to do otherwise than to respect and protect those weaker than themselves, including their children, because this is what they have learned from their own experience and because it is *this* knowledge (and not the experience of cruelty) that has been stored up inside them from the beginning. Such people will be incapable of understanding why earlier generations had to build up a gigantic war industry in order to feel at ease and safe in this world. Since it will not have to be their unconscious life-task to ward off intimidation experienced at a very early age, they will be able to deal with attempts at intimidation in their adult life more rationally and more creatively.

Notes

Notes

PART ONE

Chapter 1

7   "It appears that Picasso's reluctance": Palau i Fabre, *Picasso: The Early Years*, p. 32.

8   "One evening in mid-December 1884": Ibid., p. 29.

9   " 'My father thought it safer' ": Sabartés, *Picasso: An Intimate Portrait*, p. 6.

10   "not to say anything": Ibid., p. 11.

11   "Children's screams screams of women": Wiegand, *Pablo Picasso*, p. 105.

16   "Apparently, Picasso had such a difficult birth": Palau i Fabre, *Picasso: The Early Years*, p. 27.

17   "when taken to school Pablo always": Ibid., p. 31.

Chapter 2

23 "I do not remember much": H. Kollwitz, *The Diary and Letters of Kaethe Kollwitz*, p. 17.

25 "[My] stomach aches were a surrogate": Ibid., p. 17.

25 "On the whole I was quiet": Ibid., pp. 17–18.

25 "I needed to confide": Ibid., p. 23.

25 "There is a picture": Ibid., pp. 18–19.

26 "so that it would all lie behind me": Ibid., p. 20.

26 "I don't know just when I began": Ibid., p. 21.

27 This information held great significance: Miller, *For Your Own Good*, pp. 183–84.

29 Even if there are no dead siblings: Miller, *Prisoners of Childhood*, pp. 3–29.

34 "She often speaks": K. Kollwitz, *Ich sah die Welt mit liebevollen Blicken*, p. 34.

34 "Her awareness that her own child": Ibid., p. 36.

Chapter 3

38 "*My parents were*": Keaton, *My Wonderful World of Slapstick*, p. 14.

38 "A child born backstage": Tichy, *Buster Keaton*, p. 15.

39 "I appeared . . . before many different kinds": Kroszarski, *Hollywood Directors*, p. 145.

39 "In this knockabout act": Ibid., p. 151.

39 "One of the first things": Keaton, *My Wonderful World of Slapstick*, p. 13.

40 "If something tickled me": Blesh, *Keaton*, p. 40.

40 "*It is certain that Keaton's parents*": Ibid., p. 16.

Chapter 4

48 Then I thought of Kafka: Miller, *Thou Shalt Not Be Aware*, p. 242ff.

48 "Smilovitchi, the Lithuanian village": Forge, *Soutine*, p. 7.

51 I have often compared: Miller, *For Your Own Good*, p. 142ff.

52 A student has investigated: G. Bednarz, unpublished manuscript.

53–
54 The force of their message: Radström, *Hitlers Borndom*.

55 "Paul's father maintained": Chalfen, *Paul Celan*, pp. 36–38.

56 These were the witnesses: Miller, *Das verbannte Wissen*, chap. 2, sec. 2.

60 "led the life of a wastrel": Lawrin, *Fyodor M. Dostojevskij*, p. 9.

62 "The family of Joseph": Payne, *The Rise and Fall of Stalin*, p. 31.

63 "When Ekaterina Geladze married": Ibid., p. 32.

63 "The family of Stalin": Ibid., p. 33.

63 "According to Iremashvili": Ibid., p. 34.

64 "Church was a consolation": Ibid., p. 35.

64 "He was seven": Ibid., pp. 35–36.

PART TWO
Chapter 1

73 After having made this discovery: Miller, *Pictures of a Childhood*, p. 4.

73 and in the writings of Franz Kafka: Miller, *Thou Shalt Not Be Aware*, pp. 242–95.

79 "His father, when he had time": Janz, *Friedrich Nietzsche*, p. 48.

81 "upon leaving school": Ibid.

88 "Those who come across a book": Ibid., p. 10.

94 "One is an actor": Nietzsche, *Basic Writings of Nietzsche*, p. 629.

99 The documents I cite: Miller, *For Your Own Good*, p. 17ff.

101 The fact that this behavior: Miller, *Thou Shalt Not Be Aware*, pp. 87–88.

102 "I pursued the living": Nietzsche, *The Portable Nietzsche*, p. 226–228.

104 "With the storm": Ibid., p. 334.

105 "My heels twitched": Ibid., pp. 336–38.

106 "Is this today not the mob's?": Ibid., pp. 401–2.

107 "Do not let yourselves": Ibid., pp. 402–3.

108 "A free life is still free": Ibid., p. 163.

108 "If you would go high": Ibid., p. 402.

108 "For the terrible and almost": Nietzsche, *Werke*, vol. 4, p. 752.

108 "I don't believe I'm going to last": Deussen, *Erinnerungen an Friedrich Nietzsche*, p. 190.

111 "In Christianity the instincts": Nietzsche, *The Portable Nietzsche*, pp. 588–89.

112 "*hatred* of the natural": Ibid., p. 582.

112 "the expression of a profound vexation": Ibid., p. 582.

113 "If, for example, it makes men happy": Ibid., p. 591.

113 "So that it could say No": Ibid., p. 593.

114 "Psychologically considered": Ibid., p. 598.

114 "To repeat, I am against": Ibid., pp. 604–5.

115 "The concepts 'beyond' ": Ibid., pp. 611–12.

115 "In Paul the priest wanted power": Ibid., p. 618.

115 "The great lie of personal immortality": Ibid., pp. 618–19.

116 "The priest knows only": Ibid., pp. 629–30.

117 "When the herd animal": Nietzsche, *Basic Writings*, p. 786.

117 "False coasts and assurances": Ibid., pp. 785–86.

118 "The condition of the existence": Ibid., p. 785.

118 "Except for these ten-day works": Ibid., pp. 759–60.

120 "Light am I": Nietzsche, *The Portable Nietzsche*, pp. 217–18.

121 "How much truth does a spirit": Nietzsche, *Basic Writings*, pp. 674–75.

122 " 'God,' 'immortality of the soul' ": Ibid., p. 692–693.

123 "This ultimate, most joyous": Ibid., pp. 728–29.

123 "For a physiologist": Ibid., pp. 747–48.

124 "Luther, this calamity of a monk": Ibid., p. 776.

124 "The morality that would un-self": Ibid., pp. 789–91.

127 "It is necessary to say": Nietzsche, *The Portable Nietzsche*, p. 574.

127 "May I here venture": Nietzsche, *Basic Writings*, pp. 722–23.

128 "The Christian conception of God": Nietzsche, *The Portable Nietzsche*, pp. 585–86.

129 "When I wage war": Nietzsche, *Basic Writings*, p. 689.

130 Nor would it have been: Miller, *Das verbannte Wissen*, chap. 1, sec. 4; chap. 2, sec. 4.

132 As in the case of Kafka: Miller, *Thou Shalt Not Be Aware*, p. 307ff.

132 "When I seek my ultimate formula": Nietzsche, *Basic Writings*, p. 702.

PART THREE

Chapter 2

149 If this had not been so: Miller, *Das verbannte Wissen*, chap. 2, sec. 2.

150 "The Emperor's New Clothes": Andersen, *His Classic Fairy Tales*, pp. 119–124.

157 All that was needed: Leboyer, *Birth Without Violence*.

Appendix

167 Entire Appendix: From Miller, *For Your Own Good*.

Bibliography

ANDERSEN, HANS. *His Classic Fairy Tales*. Trans. Erik Haugaard. Illus. Michael Foreman. Garden City, N.Y.: Doubleday, 1978.

BLESH, RUDI. *Keaton*. New York: Macmillan, 1966.

CHALFEN, ISRAEL. *Paul Celan: Eine Biographie seiner Jugend*. Frankfurt a. M.: Insel, 1983.

DEUSSEN, PAUL. *Erinnerungen an Friedrich Nietzsche*. Leipzig: Brockhaus, 1901.

FORGE, ANDREW. *Soutine*. London: Spring Books, 1965.

JANZ, CURT-PAUL. *Friedrich Nietzsche*. 3 vols. Munich: Hanser, 1978.

KEATON, BUSTER, with CHARLES SAMUELS. *My Wonderful World of Slapstick*. Garden City, N.Y.: Doubleday, 1960.

KOLLWITZ, HANS, ed. *The Diary and Letters of Käthe Kollwitz.* Trans. Richard and Clara Winston. Chicago: Henry Regnery, 1955.

KOLLWITZ, KÄTHE. *Ich sah die Welt mit liebevollen Blicken.* Wiesbaden: Fourier, 1983.

KROSZARSKI, RICHARD. *Hollywood Directors 1914–1940.* New York: Oxford Univ. Press, 1976.

LAWRIN, JANKO. *Fyodor M. Dostojevskij.* Reinbek: Rowohlt, 1963.

LEBOYER, FREDERICK. *Birth Without Violence.* New York: Knopf, 1975.

MILLER, ALICE. *Prisoners of Childhood.* Trans. Ruth Ward. New York: Basic Books, 1981. (Paperback title: *The Drama of the Gifted Child.*)

———. *For Your Own Good: Hidden Cruelty in Child-Rearing and the Roots of Violence.* Trans. Hildegarde and Hunter Hannum. New York: Farrar Straus, 1983.

———. *Thou Shalt Not Be Aware: Society's Betrayal of the Child.* Trans. Hildegarde and Hunter Hannum. New York: Farrar Straus, 1984.

———. *Pictures of a Childhood: Sixty-six Watercolors and an Essay.* Trans. Hildegarde Hannum. New York: Farrar Straus, 1986.

———. *Das verbannte Wissen.* Frankfurt a. M.: Suhrkamp, 1988.

NIETZSCHE, FRIEDRICH. *Basic Writings of Nietzsche.* Translated and edited, with commentaries, by Walter Kaufmann. New York: Modern Library, 1968.

———. *The Portable Nietzsche.* Selected and translated, with an introduction, preface, and notes, by Walter Kaufmann. New York: Viking, 1954.

————. *Werke*. Ed. Karl Schlechta. 5 vols. Berlin and Vienna: Ullstein, 1972.

O'BRIAN, PATRICK. *Pablo Ruiz Picasso*. New York: Putnam's, 1976.

PALAU I FABRE, JOSEP. *Picasso: The Early Years: 1881–1907*. Trans. Kenneth Lyons. New York: Rizzoli, 1981.

PAYNE, ROBERT. *The Rise and Fall of Stalin*. New York: Simon & Schuster, 1965.

RADSTRÖM, NIKLAS. *Hitlers Borndom*. Stockholm: W & W, 1985.

SABARTÉS, JAIME. *Picasso: An Intimate Portrait*. Trans. Angel Flores. With eight Picasso reproductions. New York: Prentice-Hall, 1948.

TICHY, WOLFRAM. *Buster Keaton*. Reinbek: Rowohlt, 1983.

WIEGAND, WILFRIED. *Pablo Picasso*. Reinbek: Rowohlt, 1986.

Acknowledgments

Grateful acknowledgment is made to the following for permission to quote from previously published material:

Farrar, Straus & Giroux: Excerpt from *For Your Own Good* by Alice Miller. Copyright © 1983, 1984 by Alice Miller.

Doubleday: Excerpts from *His Classic Fairy Tales* by Hans Andersen, trans. Eric Haugaard. Copyright © 1978 by Doubleday, a division of Bantam Doubleday Dell Publishing Group, Inc.

Ediciones Poligrafa: Excerpts from *Picasso: The Early Years 1881–1907* by Palau i Fabre, trans. Kenneth Lyons. Copyright © 1981 by Rizzoli.

Verlag Gebr. Mann: Excerpts from *The Diary and Letters of Kaethe Kollwitz*, trans. Richard and Clara Winston. Copyright © 1955 by Henry Regnery, Chicago.

Carl Hanser Verlag: Excerpts from *Friedrich Nietzsche* by Curt-Paul Janz. Copyright © 1978 by Hanser.

Insel Verlag: Excerpts from *Paul Celan: Eine Biographie seiner Jugend* by Israel Chalfen. Copyright © 1983 by Insel.

The Literary Estate of Robert Payne: Excerpts from *The Rise and Fall of Stalin* by Robert Payne. Copyright © 1965 by Simon & Schuster.

Random House: Excerpts from *Basic Writings of Nietzsche*, translated and edited, with commentaries, by Walter Kaufmann. Copyright © 1966, 1967, 1968 by Random House, Inc. Reprinted by permission of the publisher.

Sterling Lord Literistic, Inc.: Excerpts from *My Wonderful World of Slapstick* by Buster Keaton. Reprinted by permission of Sterling Lord Literistic, Inc. Copyright © 1960 by Buster Keaton.

Viking Penguin: Excerpts from *The Portable Nietzsche*, trans. Walter Kaufmann. Copyright 1954 by the Viking Press, Inc. Copyright renewed © 1982 by Viking Penguin Inc. All rights reserved. Reprinted by permission of Viking Penguin, a division of Penguin Books USA, Inc.